The Song of COPPER CREEK

OTHER BOOKS AND AUDIO BOOKS

BY KRISTEN McKENDRY

Promise of Spring

The Ties That Bind

Garden Plot

The Worth of a Soul

Beyond the White River

Desperate Measures

Heart's Journey

The Governess

CHILDREN'S BOOK

The Holy Ghost Can Help

The Song of COPPER CREEK

a novel

KRISTEN
McKENDRY

Covenant Communications, Inc.

Cover image: *Thoughtful Young Woman* © ortra, *Midwestern Cornfield* © Willard, courtesy istockphoto.com.

Published by Covenant Communications, Inc.
American Fork, Utah

This is a work of fiction. The characters, names, incidents, places, and dialogue are either products of the author's imagination, and are not to be construed as real, or are used fictitiously.

Printed in the United States of America
First Printing: July 2017

23 22 21 20 19 18 17   10 9 8 7 6 5 4 3 2 1

ISBN-13: 978-1-52440-302-7

For the friends music has brought me

ACKNOWLEDGMENTS

THANK YOU TO MY EDITOR, Samantha Millburn, who knows just how much to fight with me and which points to challenge. I'm sorry for whining. My books come out stronger because of you. Thank you also to the rest of the team at Covenant for dressing up my books so nicely and sending them out into the world with their laces tied and faces polished.

Thank you to Lauren Cude of the Graduate Riding School for her patience and solid instruction in the fundamentals of riding and to Nick for being such a gentleman while teaching me to look terror in the eye.

Thank you to my long-lost friend Tracey Lee Smith, who taught me to card and spin. Thank you to Della Reid-Granberg and Wendi Neill for getting me started knitting and to Trish Scott for teaching me how to turn a heel. Thank you to Pentti Makela for the lovely gift of the loom, and thanks most especially to Jette Vandermeiden and Carole Neely for helping me get a good start on this new adventure. All of you have given generously of your time and attention and have enriched my life and broadened my horizon.

Thank you to my husband for all the cooking, cleaning, shopping, laundering, dog grooming, and child-shuttling you've done to free up my time to be able to write, wander in the garden thinking about writing, and be generally indolent.

Lastly, hugs to Rowyn and Eòghann, who remind me what it's all for.

AUTHOR'S NOTE

I HAVE TAKEN GREAT LIBERTIES with the town of Port Dover and its environs for this story. Readers who visit there will not find the Copper Creek Pioneer Village, the farm, or the LDS Church building. But they will find a pretty, energetic town of cheerful people on the edge of a vast lake that's well worth the journey to visit.

Sing your way home
at the close of the day.
Sing your way home;
drive the shadows away.
Smile every mile,
for wherever you roam
It will brighten your road,
It will lighten your load
If you sing your way home.

—traditional children's song

CHAPTER ONE

"I'VE FINALLY LOST MY MIND."

Grace sat gripping the steering wheel and peering through the drizzling rain at the muddy drive before her. She could just make out the white blur of the house fifty feet ahead, half hidden by trees. On the four-day drive it had taken her to get here, she had gone from determined anticipation to deep doubt and then dread. During the last half hour of bad roads and poor visibility, she had convinced herself this whole idea was a very bad mistake.

But she couldn't sit here with her wipers going forever. She had to do something, and going forward was as good as any other option. Taking a shaky breath, she pressed the gas pedal and lurched the Honda into the pitted drive. She cut the car's engine beside the house, and the wipers froze. She hadn't realized how annoying their squeaking movement had been until the relief of silence rose around her.

The door of the house opened, and a woman came out onto the porch, squinting through the rain toward Grace's car. The woman's confident stance and beckoning arm were reassuring. Grace climbed stiffly out of the car and hurried through the rain onto the porch.

"You must be Grace," the woman said with a broad smile. She was shorter than Grace by several inches, slim and wiry, and possessed of a head of wildly curly brown hair. Her smile brought out every weathered wrinkle. She wore a blue T-shirt under an open chambray shirt, the sleeves rolled up to the elbows, and jeans faded almost white with washing. She was as different from Grace's plump and grandmotherly mother as she could be, but there was something about her open expression and warm gaze that made Grace instantly feel like a child coming home.

"Laura Whelan," the woman said, holding out a hand.

Grace shook it and smiled back, the stretching of muscles unfamiliar. "Grace Whittaker. Thank you so much for having me," Grace began, but the woman waved it away.

"We're glad you're here. Do you want to bring your stuff in now or wait until the rain stops?"

"Will it?" Grace squinted up at the sky as Laura had done.

Laura gave a short laugh. "Eventually. Come on in and warm up. It's still a bit chilly."

The front door opened directly into the living room, a large space with wide-planked pine floors and comfortably heavy furniture.

"You can leave your shoes there." Laura indicated a mat to one side, and Grace obediently toed off her sneakers. Laura led her through the living room into the adjoining kitchen, a softly lit room of golden pine and blue-curtained windows. A wood stove was snugged into one corner, emitting a heat Grace could almost smell.

She went to it and held out her hands as if it were a campfire. "That's wonderful." She sighed. She must have been gripping the steering wheel harder than she'd realized. Her hands were cramped and chilled.

"Sit down at the table, and I'll get you some tea," Laura said.

"Oh. Thanks. Do you have anything herbal?" Grace asked and was relieved when Laura nodded. One less obstacle to have to deal with, at any rate.

"I have cinnamon, apple, or peppermint."

"Cinnamon, please."

Grace sat at the long table and rested her hands on the scarred and scrubbed surface. The wood had been rubbed and worn so much it felt like satin. You couldn't buy tables like this; you had to create them over years—decades—of use.

"I have to say I was expecting someone more . . . how do I say it? Robust? I mean, you look fit enough, but you're terribly thin," Laura said, looking apologetic. "Frankly, I'm hoping you will be able to handle the amount of work we're going to throw at you. I don't want to hurt you."

"Oh! I'm stronger than I look," Grace assured her, turning pink. "You can throw whatever you like at me."

"All right. We'll hope for the best, shall we? I mean, you're here now," Laura said practically, but Grace thought the remark lacked enthusiasm.

Laura filled a copper kettle at the deep stone sink. "I'm sorry the weather didn't cooperate today. It's usually a really pretty drive down here. You're not seeing it at its best. Of course, spring is never a pretty season, really. Too muddy and bare. Autumn is my favorite."

"Mine too," Grace said, accepting the ceramic mug and tea bag Laura handed her.

"Sugar?"

"Always."

Laura chuckled and set a sugar bowl and spoon before her. "It won't take long for the water to boil," she said. "The wood stove is always hot, so you don't have to wait for it."

A gust of wind threw raindrops against the windowpane that sounded like a handful of gravel hitting the glass. It was four o'clock, but the gloom made it seem more like evening.

"Martin is down at the greenhouse, but he'll be up soon, and we'll have an early supper," Laura told her. "Are you okay with beef stew?"

"Sounds perfect on a day like this," Grace assured her.

"Any allergies or dietary restrictions? Gluten okay?"

Grace fiddled with her mug. "Sure, I like everything. No allergies. But one thing—I don't drink regular tea, coffee, or alcohol." She shrugged one shoulder. "It's a religious thing."

Laura paused in her movement around the kitchen, looking at Grace with consternation. "But the herbal tea is okay?"

"It's just fine. Thank you."

Laura lifted the kettle from the stove and poured a steaming stream into Grace's mug. Grace poked the tea bag under the water and breathed in the scent of cinnamon. It reminded her of the Cinnabon she'd eaten for breakfast in the car that morning, and she realized she hadn't eaten anything since then. For the first time all day, she felt hungry.

The back door opened then, and a gray-haired man came in. He was scarcely taller than Laura and equally slim and wiry, but the defined muscles of his arms and his smooth-jawed face made him look twenty years younger than he probably was. He toed off his shoes, wiped his hands on his jeans, and came to shake Grace's hand as she rose from the table. His palm was calloused and rough against hers.

"So this is our WWOOFer," he greeted her. His voice was higher than she'd expected, with a gravelly rasp. While Laura's eyes were dark as chocolate, his were the startling blue of Icelandic poppies. His smile was kind, and she liked him instantly.

"I am," Grace said. "And you must be Martin."

"She's your what?" a deep voice asked.

Grace turned to see another man in the living room doorway. He was white-haired and probably well over seventy, but even though slightly stooped, he was more than six feet tall. He had an interesting face—craggy, intelligent, with a noble nose. He wore a brown cardigan over a button-down shirt and had on khaki pants. Grace thought he looked like an aging explorer returning from an African safari. All he needed was the hat. He shuffled forward, and Grace noticed for the first time the metal four-foot-tall cane he leaned on. Then she noticed one of his toes sticking out of his stocking, which spoiled the heroic explorer image.

"She's our WWOOFer," Laura replied, reaching on tiptoe for glasses from a high cupboard.

The first man turned a speculative blue eye on Grace.

"She doesn't look barking."

"It stands for World Wide Opportunities on Organic Farms," Martin said. Grace heard an accent in his voice that she hadn't noticed earlier. English? No. She decided that with a name like Martin Whelan, he was more likely Irish.

"It's that organization we belong to," Laura was explaining. "They match up established farmers with volunteers. You know, the same as that fellow we had staying with us last year. She gives us free labor on the farm for the summer. In exchange, we give her free room and board and teach her all we know about organic farming."

"And she wants to learn this why?"

Grace couldn't help grinning at his horrified expression. "It sounded fascinating," she said with a shrug. "I've always enjoyed gardening. This felt like the right step to take next."

"She *is* barking," the man said, but his grin matched hers, and he came over to shake her hand with a strong grip. "Toby McIntyre. Laura's—What is it? Second cousin? Third?"

"I try not to acknowledge any relationship whatsoever," Laura replied drily. She turned toward Grace. "He lives next door and does woodworking, leather, and blacksmith demonstrations for the tour groups."

"Last year's fellow was a student. You look older than that though," Toby said bluntly.

"Now, Toby, don't pry!" Laura said.

"I'm thirty-two," Grace replied, close to laughter.

"Well, that's all right, then. Some work still left in you."

"Toby!" Laura rolled her eyes.

"Yes, I think so," Grace agreed.

"Any trouble finding the place?" Martin asked.

"No, your instructions were very good. 'Straight up the highway, turn off when you see the billboard for the pioneer village, keep left, and go until the tarmac runs out.'" Grace smiled. "Couldn't miss it."

"Oh, good. We have a room over the garage for you," Laura said. "Well, technically it's the coach house, but we use it for a garage now, and there's the loft above. You have your own separate entrance and bath. We thought it would give you a bit of privacy, away from the lot of us, you know?"

"Thanks, that sounds terrific." Grace cupped her hands around her mug, letting the steam caress her face. She was smiling again, the muscles relaxing, feeling more normal.

"We can get a little noisy sometimes, you see," Laura added pleasantly. "We have our grandkids staying with us right now. They're good kids, mind, but they can get rowdy."

Grace's hand jerked, nearly upsetting her tea. She carefully set the mug down and moistened her lips before asking, "How old are they?"

"Declan's eight, and Lark is five. Declan's in school, of course, but Lark is only in half-day kindergarten. Until they get out in June. Then they're underfoot all the time."

Eight and five. *Oh, please, no.* Grace said nothing, not trusting her voice. More than a small part of the reason she had selected the Whelans from among the various choices had been that they were older, in their late fifties or early sixties. She'd assumed there would be no young children around. Well, there would be hordes of them going through the pioneer village on school trips, of course, and she was prepared for that, but she hadn't counted on living in close proximity to any. She should have asked, perhaps, but it would have been awkward, and they would have wanted to know why she'd asked. So she hadn't. And now here she was caught with no graceful way out. The whole purpose behind her starting on this entire adventure now lay shattered around her feet. Her hands were cold, and she cupped them around her mug again. She tried to focus on what the others were chatting about, but the woman's voice was just a low buzz in her ears. She could hear her own pulse throbbing.

A hand touching hers startled her and snapped her attention back. Laura was looking at her with concern.

"Are you all right, Grace? We sort of lost you there for a minute."

"Oh! I'm sorry. I'm fine. I—I think I'm just tired. It was a long drive."

"Of course. I'm sorry. I should have thought. How long did it take you?"

"Four days."

"Four! I hadn't realized Utah was so far away. Did you drive straight through or take your time to sightsee on the way?"

"Straight through."

"Then you must be exhausted! Would you like to go lie down for a while before supper? I can push it back awhile."

"Actually, that might be a good idea," Grace said, eagerly grasping the excuse to be by herself. She'd have a chance to collect herself before she had to face supper with the children. "Do you mind if I do? I could use a wash . . ."

"I'll show you where you'll sleep."

Grace retrieved her shoes and gave Toby and Martin a smile that took all her energy.

"It's nice to meet you all. Thank you for having me."

She followed Laura out the back kitchen door. The rain had lessened, but the wind had picked up, sending Laura's curls flying and chilling Grace's arms. They hurried across the side yard and up the wooden stairs attached to the side of the building next door. It was a former nineteenth-century coach house, and ordinarily Grace would have been keen on exploring it, but she wasn't in the mood to examine it closely now. All she could think about was finding a private place to collect herself.

Laura pushed open the door and let Grace enter first, then Laura entered, slamming the door against the wind and flipping on the overhead light. "It isn't much, but it's quiet," she said, running her fingers through her snarled hair in a futile attempt to tame it. "Extra blankets in the cupboard. There's the space heater. It has a timer in case you forget to turn it off when you leave."

Grace eyed the sullen-looking metal heater box in the center of the floor. "Does it get that cold in April? Back home people were already going out in shorts and sandals."

"Welcome to Canada." Laura laughed. "Wait until the weather lets up a bit, and then I'll help you bring up your luggage."

"Thanks, but I don't have all that much. I can carry it," Grace told her. She didn't let her mind linger too much on her own statement. It was a little hard to believe she had gone from a two-thousand-square-foot house full of belongings to two suitcases and a tiny self-storage unit about the size of a fridge in Salt Lake City. The bags in the trunk of her Honda represented almost all of her worldly possessions now. It had been rather unreal, going through the house and clearing things out, separating them into piles to either save, donate, or ditch. Most of it had gone to the donate pile. Most of it had hardly been used, after all.

"I'll leave you, then," Laura said, opening the door. "Come on over at about six, and we'll eat."

Grace thanked her and watched her go down the stairs before closing the door. She turned and faced the apartment she would occupy for the next five months. It was snug, the ceiling sloping from the center down to about four feet in height at the edges of the room. A single bed with a patchwork quilt was tucked into one corner, with a bedside table and lamp. This wasn't a showpiece quilt, meant to be admired from afar, but a comfortably worn and softened quilt, done in subtle shades of green and blue. Leaving her shoes by the door, Grace padded across the floor in her damp socks and ran her hand over the quilt appreciatively, admiring the work that had gone into it, the soothing feel of the soft cotton.

The room also held an armchair, a small wooden table with two chairs, and a row of cupboards to store her things. The adjacent bathroom consisted of a toilet, sink, and shower stall all fitted cleverly into a space the size of her old walk-in closet. The sink reminded her of the pink plastic toy kitchen Molly had gotten last Christmas. The bowl was barely big enough to wash out a pair of socks in.

She sank onto the bed. Her body ached from sitting for four days. Her heart ached. Well, it had done that for the past year and a half, so there was nothing new about that. But she felt a headache coming on in addition to it. She closed her eyes and willed herself into a brief and troubled sleep on the welcoming bed.

CHAPTER TWO

It took Grace next to no time at all to unpack when she woke. A few changes of clothing, her Sunday shoes and boots, a couple of books, her scriptures, and, tucked at the bottom of her suitcase in a plastic Ziploc baggie to protect them, two small squares of paper.

The first was a poem by Canadian poet Rashmi Pluscec, one Grace had carried with her and reread almost every day for the past year since she had discovered it. It was worn now, gray with handling, and the writing was starting to fade, but it captured perfectly the bleakness she couldn't shake.

The landscape of her mind lay barren—bruised
by a steady downpour of acid rain. a past that
was. a future that could have been: in memoriam

the tears had fallen, groping for the lights that had
been brutally snuffed out, leaving behind a void.
not blackness. not emptiness. just a nothingness . . .

Into that void, the flood of bitter questions had
finally settled, the tide of helplessness had now
receded. tired of running down her cheeks, down

memory lane, the teardrops paused to consider a
new identity. softened by the dreams, strengthened
by the hope, sparkling dewdrops shone through the

tragedy. In that twilight zone between "was" and "is,"
at the crossroads of existing and living, she took her
first steps. Perhaps homage would be paid to the lost

pieces of her heart yet . . . perhaps some day
the phoenix would rise from the ashes again.

Grace didn't need to see it to remember the words as she stuck it in the corner of the mirror frame. They were written on her heart, especially the one line—*A future that could have been . . .*

The second bit of paper was a photocopy of a photo. She hadn't wanted to risk bringing the original for fear something would happen to it; she had left it in the album in her storage locker back home, but the photocopy caught the three smiling young faces and waving hands clearly enough. She snugged it into the mirror frame above the poem, smoothed it briefly with her finger, and turned away.

When Grace reentered the warm and wonderful-smelling kitchen two hours after she'd left it, Laura was setting six bowls on the table. Toby was already seated, and Martin was washing his hands at the sink.

"Feel better?" he greeted her, drying his hands on a checkered towel.

"Yes, thanks. Just needed a lie-down."

As Laura placed the heavy pot of stew on the table beside a loaf of crusty bread, there was a thumping and rushing overhead. Feet thundered down a staircase, and two children burst into the kitchen. The words Grace had been about to add stopped in her throat.

She braced herself, her stomach instantly tensing as if to guard against a physical blow. But the children were dark haired and as petite as their grandmother, and though they had the usual energy and freshness of most children, they were not even remotely familiar. She let her breath out in relief and looked up to see Toby eyeing her curiously. Grace took the seat Laura indicated at the table and composed her face into polite amiability.

Laura made the introductions. The little girl slipped into a seat between Toby and Martin and sent Grace a shy smile, but the boy, openly curious, scrambled to sit next to the newcomer. He had the potential of Martin's good looks about him, though still in embryo. Declan and Lark, Grace reminded herself.

"Hi. You're going to stay with us?" Declan asked. "You know they're going to make you muck out the stalls."

Martin made a harumphing noise, but Grace nodded. "Yes, I hope so."

"Grace is from Utah," Laura announced, serving out the stew and bread with practiced efficiency.

Grace wondered if she should correct her. Technically she *lived* in Utah now. But she had spent her childhood here in Port Dover. The opportunity passed as Laura went on brightly. "Do you two know where that is?"

"It's in the States, isn't it?" Declan offered.

"Yes. It took her four days to drive here, and she came all by herself," Laura told him as if Grace had accomplished something brilliant. "She's going to live above the garage and help me and Granddad."

"Mucking out," Declan said again, and Lark giggled.

"That's the plan," Martin agreed, winking at Grace. "And starting seedlings in the greenhouse and getting the vegetable garden ready. And fixing fences and plowing and harvesting and bottling and everything. You see, Grace, even though this farm is part of the Copper Creek Pioneer Village Museum, it's still very much a working farm, and we rely on our produce for our living."

Grace smiled, picturing herself in overalls and a straw hat astride a tractor. It was a far cry from her usual self, demure in a linen dress, standing before a roomful of music students or on a stage in front of an expectant audience with not a hair out of place . . .

"And you can help me with the wool if you want to learn that," Laura added.

"Wool?" Grace's head came up. "You didn't mention you had sheep."

"I'm the one with the sheep," Toby said, buttering Lark's bread for her. Grace blinked at him and could instantly picture him in a long Australian coat, like the guy in *The Man from Snowy River*, striding over the misty hills with a shepherd's crook and a black-and-white dog. He looked up and caught her gazing at him, but instead of looking away as people usually do when eyes unexpectedly meet, they grinned at each other. She had the absurd feeling he could read her thoughts and was enjoying the image she'd conjured of him.

"Toby has a small herd of Jacob sheep. They provide the fleece, and I do the carding and spinning. I sell specialty yarn online and in the museum gift shop," Laura explained. "I call it Copper Creek Wool."

"I'd love to learn how to card and spin," Grace said, surprised to realize it was true. The spark of interest that had been steadily burning since she'd first heard of WWOOF was fanning into full flame. She pictured herself seated at a spinning wheel like someone in a fairy tale. She'd never suspected she was interested in such things.

"I can always use the help," Laura said lightly. "Tomorrow Martin's taking you down to the greenhouse to start working with him. He'll explain the plan to you and what we're trying to do here on the farm. And then on Sunday, I'll introduce you to the joy of carding."

From Lark and Declan's laughter, Grace surmised that perhaps carding was not the most joyful part of the process.

After the delicious meal, Grace helped Laura clean up while Martin played a game of Parcheesi at the table with the children. It seemed to involve a lot more noise and argument than she remembered it requiring. Toby reclined in an armchair with a newspaper and a pair of ridiculously thick black-framed reading glasses. When the kitchen was tidy, Grace turned toward the back door, assuming she was to go back to her room and leave the family to enjoy their evening together in peace. But Laura touched her elbow as she went toward the door.

"I'm popping popcorn if you'd like to stay and watch a movie with us. It's DVD night. No school tomorrow, so the kids can stay up late."

Grace could feel various emotions chase each other across her face before they finally settled into a smile. Laura gave her a curious look, and Grace forced herself to say brightly, "Thank you. I'd like that."

She shortly found herself snug on the couch between Laura and Declan. The movie itself was something animated and rather silly, on Lark's level. At one point, Declan collapsed against Grace in laughter, and she couldn't help flinching away from him. Declan didn't seem to notice, but when she looked up she found Toby watching her quietly from his armchair. Had he seen her abrupt avoidance of the contact?

Toby cleared his throat, and when one of the cartoon characters started to speak again, he inserted his own funny comment over the top of it. It wasn't anything brilliant, just an inane comment that had nothing to do with the scene. There was a pause, and then Declan snorted with laughter. So Toby did it again, inserting his own words into the characters' mouths.

Before long, the whole family was laughing. Toby turned out to have a knack for hilarious comments and impeccable timing. In the end, they turned off the movie's sound all together and let Toby provide the dialogue in a deep, gruff voice or high, squeaky one, depending on which character was on screen. He made up a fantastic plot line unrelated to the true story, and Lark lolled against her granddad in a fit of uncontrollable giggling. When once again Declan leaned laughingly against Grace's arm, she found she was able to nudge his shoulder with hers and genuinely laugh back.

When at last Grace made her way to her room, warmed by good food and good company, she climbed into her narrow bed and lay smiling up at the ceiling in the dark. There was something different about her already, she knew, just in the few hours she'd been here. The tension that always gripped her throat seemed to have eased. Her face didn't find smiling or laughing so unfamiliar anymore. She had joined in the evening whole-heartedly. Surrounded by these welcoming and accepting strangers, she had felt, for the first time in a year and a half, almost normal.

CHAPTER THREE

"THE MUSEUM TRIES TO RECREATE what life was like in a prosperous pioneer town in the early nineteenth century," Martin explained. "A bunch of Victorian-era buildings were brought from around Ontario and reconstructed here, and there are staff members and volunteers who demonstrate various skills to the tourists and school classes that come through. Some live on-site, and some live in town and just come out here to work. Our family lives on-site and manages the agricultural end of things."

"I think it's so unusual. What a neat opportunity," Grace said. She was following him along the dirt path to the greenhouse, having to hurry to keep up despite his smaller stature. The greenhouse she could see fifty yards ahead was not what she had expected. She had envisioned a structure like those that came in kits, with metal framing and plastic sheeting. But this building was a genuine, elegant Victorian, not even a replica. It had rosy brick walls about two feet high topped with an elaborate white wooden frame that held the glass panes, and it was much larger and longer than Grace had anticipated.

"As I told you last night," Martin went on, stopping at the door and fishing the key from his pocket, "even though the tourists see the farm as just another feature of the museum, it's a real working enterprise we rely on for our living. We try to use the old ways as much as possible, which, in fact, means raising the vegetables in an organic way. Nineteenth-century farmers didn't use the synthetic fertilizers and pesticides modern farmers do. To be organic, we went back to the original way of doing things . . . with a few improvements, of course. We're not entirely daft."

He unlocked the door, but before opening it, he gestured toward a wooden bench-like box beside them.

"Inside there you'll find some wooden shoes that will probably fit you. Leave your ordinary shoes out here and carry the clogs inside to put them on."

Wondering, Grace opened the lid of the box and found several pairs of white wooden clogs of various sizes. She toed off her tennis shoes and carried her selected pair of clogs inside. As soon as she entered, she was hit by a wave of warm, moist, delicious-smelling air. She took a deep, appreciative breath and smiled at Martin.

Martin had also exchanged his shoes, and now, as he closed the door behind them, he returned her smile. "It hits me that same way every time I come in here," he said, nodding.

"It's as if I can taste the water in the air."

"The only things we add to our crops are sunshine, water, compost, and good old-fashioned manure," he said. "We don't use synthetic inputs, petroleum products, or pesticides. That's why I make anyone who comes in here exchange shoes. They could track in bacteria or fungus that we couldn't fight so well without chemicals. We're more susceptible to disease here than a regular farm and have to be more careful."

The great glass room stretched away from them, filled with long, low wooden tables. There was a network of hoses and lights suspended above them. Some of the tables had trays of tiny potted plants on them, and others were bare. The floor was paved with more of the rosy brick, and with the sun streaming in, Grace thought it was like being in a bright, gentle oven.

Martin took a black plastic tray from a stack on one of the tables and handed it to Grace.

"I do make some modern allowances," he said sheepishly. "Plastic is just so much easier to wash up. The tourists aren't generally allowed inside here—we usually just shuffle them past so they can glance through the windows—so I figure no one will be likely to notice." He laughed and pointed toward a large oak barrel of what looked like soil to one side of the tables. "Fill the tray with starting medium and scoop the excess off so it's flat," he instructed. "Like this."

He took another tray from the stack, dipped it into the barrel to fill it with dirt, and swept his hand flat across the top, knocking the excess dirt back into the barrel. He gave it a light tap on the lip of the barrel to settle the soil in the tray. Looking closer, Grace could see little bits of a pearl-like substance mixed into the brown earth.

"It's a special mix that promotes seed growth," Martin explained. "Now, we plant only heirloom varieties. No modified genes or hybrids. Just time-tested seeds doing what nature intends them to do."

Grace scooped earth into her tray and leveled it off as she had seen him do, but she found it difficult to be as neat as he had been, and some of the dirt drifted to the floor.

"Sorry. I spilled some."

"No worries. There's no way to be tidy about it. We'll sweep up when we're done."

She placed it on the table beside the tray he had filled, then reached for another. It was rhythmic work, with no haste and no fuss. No deadlines. No phones ringing. Just the scent of good earth, the comfortable clicking of her clogs on the brick pavers, and a warm mugginess that curled the blonde hair escaping from her braid. Grace thought she could get used to this sort of job. What would her old employees back at the music school think if they saw her now, up to her elbows in dirt?

* * *

Martin, watching Grace surreptitiously as he worked beside her, was pleased with her economical movements and enthusiasm. He had admittedly experienced some uncertainty when he'd first met her. She was too delicate-looking for his liking, and he wasn't sure how she would hold up to strenuous labor. It was not so much her frame as the fragile look of her face. Laura had seemed to take a liking to her, so he'd said nothing about his own doubts, but Grace did seem eager enough to learn and willing to get her hands dirty, and he supposed that was enough to be getting on with.

He nodded approval. "I think you'll do okay here."

"Do you think? I hope so. I don't want you to regret having me here."

"Not a chance. And I hope you'll enjoy it here."

"I'm sure I will," Grace said. "I know there's a lot you can teach me."

"I'll be getting on with it, then," Martin replied cheerfully. "Now, then. The seeds we start indoors like this are the more tender plants that need longer growing seasons than we get here in Ontario," he explained as they worked their way slowly down the tables. "I've already started the peppers, tomatoes, and ground cherries. That's them over there." He gestured toward the sweep of delicate seedlings farther down the room. "These trays here will hold broccoli, cauliflower, kale, melons, and eggplant. It gives them all a head start. The cold-weather produce, like onions, peas, and lettuce, can be planted directly outdoors right now without being in the greenhouse first."

Grace levelled off another tray. "I should have thought to bring paper and a pen to take notes."

"You couldn't do that and work at the same time. I'll go slowly, and if you need me to repeat anything, just say so."

"Okay. I'll do my best to remember everything."

Martin paused, thinking that it felt good to have a willing, if captive, new audience. He liked talking about his work, but he suspected he had overdiscussed the topic of gardening with all the people he knew, including his patient wife. There was just something about this kind of work—the production of food, the sustaining of other people—that gave him joy, a bone-deep happiness, and he couldn't help discussing the source of that happiness with others.

"We'll plant the rest of the crops directly outdoors but not until early to mid-May," he said. His hands worked deftly as he talked, not missing a beat. "That will be the cucumbers, beans, chard, beets, carrots, squash, pumpkins, that sort of stuff. When it's warm enough outside, we'll crank open the greenhouse roof and let these babies pretend they're outdoors. And then when they're hardened off, we'll transplant them into the garden."

"I imagine that will involve a lot of crawling along the ground." Grace gave him an apprehensive glance.

"Your back is hurting in anticipation already?" Martin laughed. "Yes, true. There is some hard physical work to this job. It can't be helped."

"I knew there would be when I signed on," she assured him. "I'm sure I can manage. I know all these seedlings will produce a lot of food, but can you really make a living from it?"

"We can't if we compete against the big farmers, the agri-business crowd," Martin said. "But we don't try to. We don't supply stores. We supply garlic, gourmet greens, and vegetables to some high-priced restaurants in town, sell a bit to the museum patrons who come through, and sell the rest of the stuff through our CSA."

"What's that?"

He blinked at her, trying to tell if she was joking. When he saw that she was serious, he cleared his throat. "Community supported agriculture. The basic idea is that people help share the costs of the farm and the risks as well. They invest $300 at the beginning of the season, and in return, we give them a big basket of vegetables each week. They get whatever is ripe and ready. If it's a bad year and we lose some of the crop, we know we still have the money to keep going because of our investors, the members of our CSA."

"But then they've paid for something they don't receive," Grace pointed out.

Martin merely shrugged. "Farming is always a gamble. But if a lot of other people shoulder a small part of the risk, it doesn't harm anyone very much. If the farmer had to bear all the risk, he'd go out of business in a bad growing year. Call it guaranteed income."

"So you're protected against a bad growing year."

"That's the general idea."

"How many people do you supply with vegetables?"

"Two hundred," he told her, unable to keep a touch of pride from his voice. "And four restaurants."

"Two hundred people at three hundred dollars each? That isn't shabby. Do you have to deliver all those orders every week?"

"Luckily, no. Just to the restaurants. The CSA people come here to pick up their bins each week and drop off their empties. Fridays get busy around here. That's pick-up day."

Grace put her hands on her hips and surveyed the long tables waiting for trays. "It certainly seems like a reasonable arrangement. I'm surprised I haven't heard of it before. It certainly beats having to harvest vegetables you aren't sure you'll be able to sell at a farmer's market."

"That's the idea. It insures against the loss of unsold vegetables because they are all sold before the seeds are even planted." Martin was watching her with a quiet smile on his face.

She smiled back. "Pretty smart."

"Well, and Laura's wool brings in a bit too, mind," he said, his Irish accent coming further to the fore. He knew it grew stronger whenever he got sentimental, especially when talking about his wife or grandchildren, but it couldn't be helped. "She'll show you that end of things tomorrow."

"I'm looking forward to it," she said.

They worked steadily through the morning, speaking quietly only when necessary, as if they were working in a sort of cathedral. It had the same air about it, a hushed reverence, as if the vast glass room held something precious. And Grace supposed it did, really. The tiny seeds Martin carefully pressed into the trays were his livelihood and his passion. Grace could see the love he had for his work in the way he bent intently over each dark rectangle of earth, his movements efficient, his hands gentle, as careful as a monk's working on an illuminated manuscript. He showed her how to plant each type of seed, the depth and distance between each, and showed her how to rig up the slender, dangling watering hoses so each tray could either be dripped on from above or soaked from below, depending on individual needs.

The time passed quickly, and before Grace knew it, it was noon and Declan was in the doorway announcing lunch was ready. Grace watched the little boy run back toward the house ahead of them and, a bit nervously, decided to go ahead and ask Martin the question she'd been thinking about all morning. "How long are your grandchildren staying with you? I mean, is it permanent?"

He shrugged and brushed his hands together to dislodge the dirt encrusting them. "Seems to be the way it's headed," he said. "We enrolled them in school for this year, at least. We'll see about next year when it comes."

"Do you mind if I ask what happened to their parents?" Grace asked quietly. She kept her gaze on the horizon.

"Their mother's gone," Martin said briefly. "Our son works in Toronto and comes up every other weekend to see the kids." He glanced at her and added quickly, as if not wanting her to judge, "Mason is a good father, mind, just a very busy man. He wasn't one for the farm, never was. It was university and a career in the city for him. But after he lost Janet, he realized Toronto was no place to raise the kids on his own. He'd have to get a sitter and the like. And with him so busy, he'd never see them anyway, so he asked if we'd take them. It's best all around, I think, and they seem to like it here. Might get a farmer out of one of them yet."

Grace nodded. "I'm sure it's good for them to have you and Laura."

"It's good for us too. Keeps us young," Martin said with a chuckle. "Didn't plan on going to parent-teacher conferences and junior hockey practice in my sixties, but there it is. You never know what life is going to bring you."

"No," Grace agreed quietly. "You never do."

"You know, I'll be sixty-five soon."

"Are you going to retire?"

"No," Martin said, smiling. "You know the old saying: old farmers never die; they just work themselves into the ground."

CHAPTER FOUR

SATURDAY NIGHT WAS BATH NIGHT. Grace sat at the kitchen table picking stems out of a bowl of raisins for Laura and listening to the fight going on upstairs. Lark didn't seem to mind bathing, but Declan wasn't shy about voicing his opposition to the idea. She could hear his vehement "I don't feel like it" and "I don't want to—I'm not even that dirty" interspersed with Laura's low, firm murmurs. In the end, there was the sound of water gurgling down the pipes, and then Laura came downstairs. Some of her hair was steamed in streaks to her temples; the rest was in frizzy curls from the humidity.

She blew out her breath and dropped into the chair opposite Grace. "I'm too old for this," she muttered, running her sleeve across her face. But her smile was broad when she added, "I finally got him to cooperate by saying I'd throw him in the tub and scrub him myself if he didn't. That terrorized him enough to make him jump in the shower on his own."

"It's a fun age," Grace said, nodding. "I've finished your raisins."

"Oh, thanks. That's nice of you." Laura took the bowl and went to add the raisins to the bowl of batter on the counter. "This will be our breakfast. It's a coffee cake my mother used to make. She was Mennonite, and she could bake like nobody's business."

"How interesting!" Grace said, turning on her chair to lean her arms across the back so she could watch Laura work. "Were you raised Mennonite? That's sort of like Amish, isn't it?"

"Yes, it is. But I wasn't, no. My mother met my father at a cattle auction when they were both nineteen, and it was love at first sight for both of them. Of course her family was horrified. He was a Presbyterian from Nova Scotia. She ended up leaving the Mennonites and her family and running off with him." Laura scraped the batter into a greased glass pan and gave Grace a dreamy smile. "I thought that was so romantic when I was a girl."

"It is. But sad too. Did her family ever forgive her?"

"No, not really. Mom and Dad moved to Nova Scotia and didn't see her family again until she returned home for her mother's funeral years later, when we kids were in our teens. Her father wrote to tell her the news. I don't think he expected her to come for the funeral. There was some reconciliation at that time but not much. At least he spoke to her when she went." Laura put the pan in the oven and set the timer. "I never met him myself before he died. But I've met two of Mom's brothers. They're here in Ontario and still practicing."

"It's too bad they let the religion divide the family," Grace couldn't help saying. "Religion should unite families, draw them closer together, not force them apart."

Laura gave a laugh. "Well, I agree, but I have to tell you, I did my share of breaking up the family myself when I married Martin. The daughter of a staunch Presbyterian marrying the son of a rabid Irish Catholic? You'd have thought the world had ended. His father refused to attend the wedding because it was in a Protestant church. Stood outside on the church lawn with his arms folded and the wrath of God on his face. And my father—well, let's just say there was some weeping and wailing and waving of rifles before we got him settled down." She burst into hearty laughter, and Grace joined in.

"What are you two going on about?" Toby poked his head in the back door. "I can hear you clear out in the barn."

"Just telling Grace about when I married Martin," Laura replied, waving a hand at him.

"Ah, yes," Toby said, his craggy face relaxing into a broad grin. "You could hear your mum and dad raging all the way to our house in Picton. But I have to hand it to you; you stood by your guns on that one."

"And I turned out to be right, didn't I?" Laura added.

"You did indeed. Speaking of raging, are you aware that young Declan is hiding in the lilac bushes without a stitch on?"

Laura's face went blank. "What? He's in the shower upstairs."

"He's gone out the window. Saw him from the barn and came to tell you," Toby said.

Laura rolled her eyes toward the ceiling, where the shower was still peacefully running. "Wait till I catch the wee scamp," she muttered and headed out the front door. "At least the museum is closed for the night and there are no tourists to see him. You head him off 'round the back, Toby."

Toby left, giving Grace a wink as he departed. Grace was still giggling when Laura came back in the front door hauling the chastened-looking little boy by his arm. He held the cushion from the porch swing in front of him to preserve his dignity and shot Grace a pained look of humiliation as he was bustled up the stairs. Grace tactfully kept her eyes averted from his bare backside and tried to keep a straight face. After a few minutes, Lark came downstairs in her blue flannel pajamas carrying a stuffed toy; Grace couldn't tell if it was a cat or a skunk.

"Declan went outside wearing his *nothings*," the little girl crowed gleefully, forgetting her shyness in the excitement of the scandal. "Grandma caught him with his *nothings* on!"

"I guess he really didn't want that shower," Grace said, nodding.

Lark climbed onto a chair at the table and reached contentedly for the hot chocolate Laura had ready for her.

"He always hates to wash," she confided to Grace.

"I hear a lot of little boys do."

"It's no use trying to fool Grandma," Lark said sagely. "She always finds out. Do you have any brothers?"

Grace shook her head. "No, and no sisters either."

"That's too bad," Lark said. She finished her drink in one long pull and went to put the mug in the sink.

"Do you like having a big brother?" Grace asked.

Lark paused with one foot on the bottom stair and looked up at the ceiling with a thoughtful frown. "Most of the time it's all right," she finally decided. "Except when he's bossy."

Grace hid a smile. "Is he bossy often?"

Lark shook her head. "No," she said offhandedly. "Only after Dad comes. He's always grumpy for a few days after that." She went up the stairs.

* * *

Sunday morning brought perfect spring weather. The sunlight had a clearness to it that brought into relief every bud and twig on the maple outside Grace's window. The air was exactly body temperature, so when she stepped out onto the wooden stairs from her room over the coach house, the only way she felt the air at all was that it whispered lightly against her arms. There was the smell of hyacinth heavy around the kitchen door, where fat stocks of purple and pink blossomed, and the faintest green haze showed over the fields beyond the barn. Birds were chiming in the trees. In the distance, on a rise of land, she could see the other buildings of the pioneer village glistening enticingly in the sunlight. She would be sure to explore those later.

When Grace entered the kitchen, Laura was just setting a platter of buttermilk pancakes on the table. The smell was divine.

"The kids have already eaten and are away to the greenhouse with Martin," she told Grace. "So it's just you and me."

"Oh, I'm sorry if you waited for your breakfast because of me," Grace said, sitting at the table opposite the older woman.

"Not at all. I like to eat last when I'm making pancakes. That way I don't have to keep jumping up to flip them all the time. I can just sit." Laura poured a stream of amber syrup over her plateful and handed the jug to Grace. "Locally made syrup. How are you finding your room? Warm enough?"

"It's perfect, thank you." Grace helped herself to rich butter and syrup and thought a brief blessing in her head, too shy to bow her head or close her eyes in front of her employer. The two women dug into the pancakes, and for a while, there was only the sound of clinking cutlery.

"This is delicious," Grace told her as they both started on second servings. It certainly beat her usual breakfast of a piece of toast snatched on the way out the door and eaten in the car on the way to the music school.

"Today the museum is closed, and I don't have anything I have to do. I'll show you how I deal with Toby's wool," Laura said. "I have a fleece I've already washed and half carded. We can finish the carding today, and if there's time, we can get to some spinning."

"I'm excited to learn."

When they'd finished eating, Grace helped clean up and then pulled out her iPhone.

"I'd like to look up my local church congregation for next week," she explained. "I'd like to attend on Sundays if it isn't too far away. If—if that's all right with you, I mean."

"Of course. Sundays are yours to do what you like. You can go today if you want," Laura said.

"It's probably too late this morning. I'll give myself a few days to settle in and go next week," Grace said.

As she thumbed for the information, Laura leaned companionably on her elbows. "What church is it?"

"It will be listed under The Church of Jesus Christ of Latter-day Saints."

Laura nodded. "Mormon. I thought you might be when I heard you were from Utah."

"You've heard of us?"

"Just Larry King's wife and those nice Osmonds. Oh, and Mitt Romney. I remember that. Martin's a big one for American politics. He paid more attention to them than he did our own elections."

Grace found the listing and was pleased to find that the Port Dover chapel was only five kilometers from the museum. She noted and saved the address and number; she would call later to find out the meeting times. Returning her phone to her pocket, she followed Laura into the back room where she worked her wool.

The room itself instantly conveyed a feeling of comfort and welcome. The floor was of scarred pine planking, and there was a deep-seated window looking over the yard and the greenhouse. A white ceramic sink stood below a slowly dripping tap in one corner. Deep wooden shelves lined two of the walls, most of them stuffed with skeins of thick brown, cream, or gray yarn. In one corner stood a square wooden frame with thick pegs jutting from it every few inches, reminding Grace of the little plastic loom she had used as a child to make hot pads with stretchy loops of fabric. A table in the center of the room held a laptop computer, and a smaller table to one side held a strange gadget—a sort of box with a cylinder on it that turned by way of a hand crank at one end, like a hurdy-gurdy. The room smelled of lanolin and—admittedly—wet sheep.

Laura nodded with satisfaction. "There. You have it."

"Have what?"

"When you came into the room just now, you got this dreamy little smile on your face. It's the same smile I feel on my own face whenever I come into this room, and I'm glad to see it affects you the same way. Maybe we're kindred spirits of a kind, after all." Laura went to a cupboard and pulled out a fat pillow, which turned out to be a pillow case stuffed with washed wool. It was kinked and curly and a mix of colors, from rich black and brown to creamy tan and white. Laura told Grace to sit at the table beside the hurdy-gurdy and placed the pillowcase at her feet. Then she placed a clean cloth over Grace's lap to protect her jeans. She watched with an approving smile as Grace ran her hand softly over the motley-colored fibers in the bag, taking in their feel and smell.

"First you take a handful of wool and tease apart the individual locks, then you card them. That means combing them. You want all the little individual hairs to end up laid out the same direction, not tangled up like they are now."

"Why is that?"

"You couldn't form proper yarn from the fibers if they all lay in different directions. And the individual hairs aren't strong, see, but if they're laid side by side facing one direction and then tightly twisted around each other, they become very strong. It's a little bit amazing to me how strong a few hairs become when they stand together." She laughed. "Like a community, you know? Or a family."

"I see." Grace thought this was a beautiful sentiment, but it made her heart give a lurch. It was too soon after the loss of her own family to contemplate it. She coughed to push away the sorrow before it could rise in her throat. "I'm looking forward to learning how to do this. I've never seen it done before."

Laura demonstrated how she separated the fibers and mixed short with long to create a stronger yarn. Then she began slowly turning the handle on the instrument on the table. The drum revolved in slow motion, the bristly little spikes on the drum's surface snagging the fibers Laura held close to them. It reminded Grace a little of a music box she had once taken apart. The little prongs on the music box's cylinder had plucked the thin metal bars to make music. But in this case, the little bristles on the cylinder caught the wool fibers in Laura's hand as the drum turned, drawing them out of her hand. The wool was combed along the bristles as the drum turned until after awhile the whole surface of the cylinder was a fine mat of combed wool that looked like quilt batting. Laura demonstrated how to loosen it and do it all again to comb it a second time. Then she removed the mat and rolled it into a fat, loose sausage. She placed the rolled sausage of wool in a basket.

"And that's all there is to carding," she told Grace. "It's sort of like using a dog brush, only instead of moving the brush over the dog, you sort of move the dog over the brush."

"I get it."

"Once you have the fleece turned entirely into those rolls, we'll be ready to start spinning. But be sure to turn it slowly so you're not stretching the fibers, or they'll just kink up."

So Grace began carding and soon got the hang of it. The wool fibers were soapy feeling and softened the skin of her hands. Laura left her to it, pulled out mailing envelopes and boxes, and started processing Internet orders. From what Grace could see, most orders were for four or five skeins, though some customers ordered more. No one ordered less. She wondered what Laura charged per skein but felt it impolite to ask. The turning carder made a soft, rhythmic whisper of music, almost hypnotic, and it seemed little time at all had passed before the bag of wool was empty and the basket was piled with rolls of fluffy wool, like some enormous gray-brown sheep curled in the corner. Grace couldn't believe it when her watch told her three hours had passed.

Laura took down a whisk broom and gathered up the bits of dirt and cocklebur that had been released by the carder. "That's a very good start," she said, nodding at the basket. "You've done a fast, neat job of it. We'll stop for lunch, and then I'll show you the spinning."

Through the window, they could see Martin returning to the house with the children, who bounced and jumped around him in high animation, splashing mud with their red rubber boots. Grace could hear their happy chatter. Her lungs felt suddenly constricted, but she forced herself to smile and wave at them when Laura did. The squeeze in her chest loosened a little, and she drew a deep breath. She couldn't keep having these sorts of reactions, she told herself firmly. She had to find a way to stop them. She wasn't going to get through life without bumping into a child, and she'd better learn to deal with it.

Laura and Grace met Martin and the children in the kitchen, and Laura started making sandwiches for lunch. Grace sat at the table to peel carrot sticks, and Declan, recovered from his embarrassment over the shower-escaping incident, chatted cheerfully at her without letting her get a word in edgewise. Lark had decided to drop the last of her shyness and sat on Grace's other side, nodding and agreeing with everything Declan said like a tiny backup singer. She even volunteered to recite a poem she had learned in kindergarten that week.

"I'd love to hear it," Grace told her sincerely. But when Lark recited it, Grace was astonished to realize the little girl was speaking French. She didn't understand a word of it, but she clapped and exclaimed in amazement with the others at the table and afterward asked Laura about it.

"The kids go to the French immersion school in Port Dover," Laura explained. "Not all people who live this far out of town have the opportunity because there's no bus for the French school, but Mason thought they should have the experience, so we drive them. He went to French school too, you know, growing up, and he uses it a lot in his job."

"What does he do?"

"He's an immigration lawyer. He lives in Toronto and comes down on weekends when he can, usually a couple of times a month."

"Yes, Martin told me that." Grace had to bite her lips together to keep from blurting what she was thinking. How could a man be so busy that he saw his children only twice a month? Didn't he realize what he was missing? If she had a chance to be with her children again, she wouldn't waste a single precious minute of it . . .

And yet she had. She had immersed herself in her work too, dropping the kids at day care and rushing to join the sweep of traffic flowing into the city, spending all day at the music school, returning ten hours later to children whose day she had entirely missed. Whole weekends spent rehearsing for performances. Late evenings at the recital hall. It had always seemed there would be time enough in the future. Time to catch up with each other. Time to mother. And then, in the end, there had been no time at all.

No, it was no good thinking along those lines. It would have her sniffling into the wool basket if she wasn't careful, and the last thing she wanted was to let her new employer—and new friend—catch her weeping. Grace straightened her shoulders and followed Laura back to the wool room.

CHAPTER FIVE

There was a lovely maple spinning wheel in the corner that Grace was itching to get her hands on, but Laura told her she was first going to teach her to use the drop spindle, a funny-looking disk with a stick poking through its center. The basic idea was to set the thing spinning, letting it twist the wool fibers, and then wrap the twisted wool strand onto the stick or spindle to keep it from unwinding. This called for a coordination Grace struggled to acquire. Roll the spindle off the thigh, let it hang and spin, then capture it between the knees and coax the twist up the sausage of fluffy wool. Laura's smooth, rhythmic demonstration made it seem simple, but there was a trick to keeping the object spinning in one direction and capturing it before it unwound itself. The romantic fairy-tale image swiftly faded. Try as Grace might, she couldn't keep the wool from forming lumpy little bulges along the strand and kinking up on itself. Within fifteen minutes, her arms were aching and she thought she was developing carpal tunnel syndrome.

Laura just laughed. "It takes practice, is all," she assured Grace.

"But you make it look like it should be easy."

"I've been doing it for thirty years or more," Laura reminded her. "Go easy on yourself."

Grace managed a small laugh. "Yes, well, that's something I'm not so good at."

Laura reached for another roll of wool roving to merge with the one on the spindle. "You'll get it."

"But in the meantime, I'm wasting all your lovely wool," Grace said sadly. "No one could knit with the kinked stuff I'm producing."

"We're not done with it yet," Laura said. "Once it's been wetted and stretched to hold its shape, it will be fine for making something bulky, like a rug." She laughed, but it was a kindly sound. Then she added, "And remember, the sheep, bless their hearts, will no doubt grow more."

By the time evening fell, Grace's efforts had improved to the point that she could actually sit back and enjoy the rhythm and feel of it. Her yarn still wasn't as slender and uniform as Laura's, but it wasn't such a terrible embarrassment as before. It was a delight to watch the fluffy, formless wool turn instantly, obediently, into recognizable yarn. She had filled the drop spindle four times, and Laura had shown her how to remove it, wet it, and wind it tightly on the pegged frame to stretch it. Once it had been stretched and dried, Laura explained, the yarn wouldn't be in danger of unwinding itself and could be tied into skeins. Because the wool was naturally multicolored, there was no need to dye it. It could be sold right away to specialty knitters and hobbyists across North America.

When they stopped for a supper of soup and salad, Grace shyly showed the others the best results of her efforts, feeling foolishly proud at their compliments.

"You're very kind. I know it's nowhere near as good as Laura's," she said but couldn't help grinning. She was euphoric. It was a small thing, but somehow it felt good to produce something with her hands, to be able to say "I did this." It seemed like it had been ages since she'd felt the energy to do much of anything. Now she was invigorated with her first taste of accomplishment.

"I feel like a proud parent," Laura declared. "You have potential."

"Do I?" Grace asked, delighted.

"You learn quickly, and you show some pluck when faced with a challenge. This whole thing might work out all right after all."

"I'm glad," Grace told her sincerely. "I really want it to."

After supper, the children went off with Laura to do last-minute homework before school on Monday, and Martin settled with a notebook and calculator to go over finances. That left Grace and Toby to entertain themselves.

Toby slapped the arms of his chair and stood up, reaching for his cane. "Come out for a walk with me," he suggested. "It's not too chilly out."

"More like 'come out for a hobble,'" Martin murmured, tapping his teeth with his pencil.

"Your turn is coming," Toby replied with icy dignity.

Grace followed Toby out onto the back porch and down the steps. They crossed the yard to the rail fence, and she expected him to go through the gate leading into the vegetable gardens beyond. But instead, he leaned his arms on the top rail and put one foot on the bottom.

"That's as far as I go," he said and shot her a wry smile. "I used to be a runner in my younger days. Ran half marathons in college. Now I consider it an accomplishment if I make it as far as the gate."

Grace rather thought he was exaggerating—after all, the man obviously had the stamina to raise sheep and operate a blacksmith forge—but she smiled and leaned against the fence beside him, looking out over the fields lit lavender by the fading sun. The temperature had dropped to a pleasant coolness on her face, and a light breeze hummed through the telephone wires overhead. She could still taste the cinnamon from tonight's apple pie. She thought about the yarn that had started off so badly in her hands that afternoon and that was now at least recognizable as she improved. Beside her, Toby was quiet, watching her as if expecting her to say something.

"It must be difficult to grow older," she finally said, not knowing what else to say.

"It's better than the alternative," he replied. "That wasn't the point I was making though."

"You were making a point? I thought you were making conversation."

He chewed on his thoughts for a moment and then said, "Some times in your life are for running marathons. And some times are for hobbling to the gate without falling over. That's what I meant. Both are admirable, equally valid accomplishments, depending on the circumstances. The trick is to know which time you're in and not expect things to be otherwise."

"Not beat yourself up for hobbling sometimes, you mean?"

He shifted his gaze to the fields now gone dark. The light had gone in a blink, like the flip of a switch.

"You strike me as someone who is used to running marathons," he said quietly.

Grace was silent a moment and then kept her voice carefully toneless as she replied, "And now I'm not."

"When my brother Ian got back from Korea after the war, he never spoke about his experiences, but you could see them in his face. You knew instinctively that he'd gone to the brink and back again." Toby slid his gaze toward her. "You have some of the same look about you."

Grace felt a moment of defensiveness, of anger that he would presume to know anything about her. But it faded quickly. She didn't have the energy to get upset or turn it into an argument. And really, how could she argue? He was right on the mark. She remained silent, picking at the splintery rail with her thumbnail.

"Welcome as you are, I can't help wondering why you're here," Toby continued.

"To learn about—"

"Yeah, I know, to learn about organic farming. But that isn't really the answer, is it?"

Grace shrugged. "I'm buying myself some time and space to sort some stuff out in my head," she said.

"I thought as much." Toby hesitated, then said gently, "The first time you saw Lark and Declan, you looked like someone had flung a cobra into your lap. Not so much today. Now you look . . . reconciled to their presence."

"I like them," Grace protested. "They're great kids."

"Of course you like them. And they are terrific kids. But when you're around them, at the table, you're not relaxed, and you're not happy." He leaned slightly toward her and nudged her shoulder with his arm. "I'm an amazing specimen of a man, and you wouldn't know it to look at me, but I'm over eighty," he said, perfectly straight-faced. "I don't have time to beat around the bush. When I want to know something, I ask. And I'm asking. What war have you gone through that's turned such a pretty face so sad?"

Grace couldn't help chuckling. "And they say the Irish have honeyed tongues."

Toby looked at her thoughtfully, studying her brief smile like a birdwatcher waiting for the return of a barely glimpsed flash of color in the bushes. "That's better," he said.

Grace couldn't meet his steady, serious gaze. She returned to picking at the fence rail. The evening had grown completely black around them. The stars were out. Across the yard, the glow of the kitchen window looked like a Hallmark welcome-home card.

"You have some experience with children," Toby observed, making it a statement and not a question. "There's still a mark on your finger from a wedding ring. I'm thinking there's where the story lies."

Grace breathed in deeply, letting the cool air steady her. Carefully, keeping her eyes from his, she answered. "I had a family. My husband, Greg, and three children—Sam, Mark, and Molly." He said nothing, didn't react at all, and gaining courage, Grace went on. "The boys were a little older than Declan, and Molly was a little younger than Lark." It felt odd, and a relief, to taste their names on her tongue again.

"The similarity threw you," Toby said.

"I hadn't known there would be any children here, that's all. In their photo online, Laura and Martin looked like they were in their fifties or sixties . . . I just wasn't prepared."

"What happened?"

Grace pinched her lips together a moment. "I'm not sure I'm ready to talk about it."

"How long ago was it?"

"Eighteen months."

He tucked in his chin, looking solemnly down at her along the bridge of his prominent nose. "Eighteen months, and I take it you haven't been able to talk about it with anyone?"

She gave a half shrug. "I had a therapist for a while. It—it sort of helped. I could talk to her."

He spread his hand on his broad chest. "But not to me, your very best friend in the world whom you've known for over two whole days?"

Grace laughed aloud in spite of herself. She leaned slightly to return his nudge. "Not even you. But I will when I can."

He nodded, satisfied. "I'll be here."

As they turned to go back to the house, Grace touched his sleeve with her fingertips. He glanced down at her. "Thanks," she said.

They walked slowly back across the yard, Toby's cane swinging in a quiet rhythm. A breeze painted Grace's face, and she tipped her head back to breathe in the scent of lilacs. The stars were out in full force now, more than she'd ever seen before. They were more visible here because there were fewer lights in the countryside to interfere with them. She glanced over at Toby and saw he had his head tipped back too, gazing up with an approving expression on his face.

"What about you?" she asked softly. "Were you ever married?"

"Me? No, no," Toby said, shaking his leonine head.

"Why not? Never found the girl of your dreams?"

"Found plenty of them. But marrying one of them would have required that I talk to them."

"What, are you saying you're shy?" Grace laughed. "I don't believe that for a minute."

"I was a gawky sheepherder with muck on my boots and three dollars to my name." Toby sighed. "Now talking to females doesn't intimidate me so much. I have nothing to lose."

Grace linked her hand through his arm. "Well, I think the women of Canada missed out on a swell opportunity."

His hearty laughter carried them into the house.

* * *

On Monday morning before the museum opened, Laura announced she was taking Grace on a tour of Copper Creek Pioneer Village.

"It's a quirky, interesting place to live in," she told her. "Life in a museum may not be for everyone—it took some getting used to, being in a fishbowl for every passing school kid or tourist to see—but I found it suited me. It was just the right balance of social interaction and isolation, where I was free to hone skills in things that interested me and then share them with other people. Not everyone can say that."

Toby's combination blacksmith forge and carpentry shop and the settler's log cabin where he lived stood a hundred feet from the Whelans' house, on the opposite side from the barn, coach house, and greenhouse. They passed it, walking along a winding gravel road that ran from the farm to the other part of the museum grounds. Grace saw a pair of faded blue overalls flapping on a line behind the forge and wondered if they were there for authenticity or if Toby actually wore them. Somehow she couldn't picture him in them.

Laura told her about everything as they walked. The museum grounds covered fifty acres and included a modern brick visitors' center and gift shop near the main gated entrance, a stately brick Victorian house where the curator and his wife lived on-site, and an old post office cum general store. A sawmill had been reconstructed on a wide, quiet river that went through a front corner of the property and gave Copper Creek Pioneer Village its name. There was a teahouse that served authentic Victorian high teas, a bakery and smokehouse, a schoolhouse, an 1840s physician's office where an herbalist demonstrated the making of essential oils, and a sugar shack where they made maple syrup each spring.

"That's my favorite thing about spring," Laura added. "That's where they made the syrup you had on your pancakes."

"When you said it was made locally, you meant it!" Grace remarked.

They walked on. Grace saw that there was a model of an outhouse behind the old schoolhouse, with a sign alerting tourists not to take the realism of their experience too far and that modern facilities were available at the visitors' center. She saw that essentially an entire town had been reconstructed here on the edge of Port Dover. All of the buildings were linked together by the narrow gravel road that wandered through the grounds. Flowerbeds of early spring bulbs added splashes of yellow, pink, and blue, and ropes suspended between posts kept schoolchildren on the designated paths. Tall willows and maples were scattered across the site, looking ancient and permanent, perhaps planted in the nineteenth century themselves. Their leaves moved gently in the cool breeze, and Grace could smell lilacs.

As they walked, their shoes crunching the gravel, Laura explained the function of each building and who worked there, giving museum patrons demonstrations of old pioneer handicrafts.

"I'll have to introduce you to our herbalist who works in the physician's office," she said. "Her name is—and I'm not making it up—Rainbow Warner. Her parents were hippies, no doubt. Like that Zappa fellow who gave his children the weird names. She's an interesting character, all filmy skirts and crystal earrings." She paused, pondering. "I wonder if people turn out odd because of their names. I mean, how could you lead a normal life with a name like Rainbow? I knew a girl named Honeycomb in high school, and the poor child never was quite right in the head."

"It's probably not the name," Grace said. "It's more likely being raised by people who would name their child Honeycomb."

"You're probably right." Laura laughed and resumed the tour.

"I give carding and spinning demonstrations three times a day," she said. "I have a little demo room set up in the visitors' center so people don't have to traipse through our living quarters. Our farmhouse is a museum building, of course, but they consider it our private residence."

"Do you have to dress in nineteenth-century costume when you're doing a demo?" Grace asked, trying not to giggle at the thought.

Laura rolled her eyes. "Yes, heaven help me. That's the only part of this gig I don't enjoy. Oh, I don't mind the swishy skirts and all that. But I have a profound appreciation of what our pioneer ancestors went through, having to function while wearing yards of fabric. You can't kneel or crawl around or even sit on the ground and then get up again without difficulty. I had no idea how much I sat on the floor until I had to start wearing those skirts. There is no way to keep the hem from getting muddy or dusty, and they had to do all their washing by hand, don't forget."

"That alone makes me glad I didn't live back then."

"I made it very clear when we first came here fifteen years ago that I wouldn't wear hoops or a corset. And so far, no one has forced me to. I have a few pioneer-style dresses, much more practical than what the fashionable ladies were wearing in Victorian England, let me tell you."

Grace had a sudden thought. "I don't have to dress in costume, do I?"

Laura laughed at her expression. "No. You'll be off in the fields or the greenhouse, for the most part, and the tours will miss you, by and large. You can wear whatever you want. You're not an official museum volunteer or staff member anyway. You're our employee, not the museum's."

"That's a relief," Grace said. "I thought maybe I'd missed something in the fine print."

They wandered toward the general store and went in. Grace immediately noticed the delicious smell of old wood and lemon oil; it reminded her of being in a library or an antique bookshop. The building was small, with windows across the front and a polished wood counter running across the back wall. The smooth patina of the wood had a golden glow that begged to be touched. Deep shelves took up all available wall space, loaded with bolts of cotton fabric, antique tins, glass jars of colorful stick candy, and printed flour sacks.

"This looks so authentic," Grace marveled, trailing her fingers along a shelf as she examined its contents. "It's fascinating. I feel like I just walked into the set of *Little House on the Prairie*."

"Something like," Laura said, looking pleased at Grace's rapt interest. She turned to the woman who stood smiling behind the counter. "Good morning, Sarah."

"Hi, Laura. You're out and about early today." The woman looked to be about thirty and wore a blue, long-sleeved dress with an apron over it that looked like it had been made from one of the flour sacks. Her chocolate hair was swept up in a puffy Gibson Girl bun, and Grace wondered how she kept it in place. Her own hair never stayed where she put it for more than ten minutes.

"Sarah, this is Grace Whittaker. She's helping us on the farm for the summer," Laura said. "This is Sarah Carson-Flake, one of the historical interpreters."

"Welcome to Copper Creek," Sarah said, shaking Grace's hand.

"This would be such a fun place to work," Grace commented.

Sarah nodded brightly, her dark eyes lighting up. "It is. I really get into the whole living-in-the-1800s role. I've been here eight years, and I can't think of a day I didn't love it."

"Sarah likes the crowds of kids more than I do," Laura confessed.

"I'm a former kindergarten teacher," Sarah told Grace. "I get such a kick out of watching the poor frazzled teachers try to control the herd. I load the kids up on sugar candy and imagine the sticky fingerprints on the school-bus windows and the noisy sugar high they'll be on all the way home." She flashed a grin and held out a wide-mouthed glass jar. "Want a piece?"

Grace looked at Laura, who laughed and fished out a stick the color of amber. "Butterscotch is the best, but the blueberry ones are pretty good too."

Grace took a blueberry one. "Thank you."

"Anytime," Sarah told her, replacing the jar on the shelf.

"Do you live here on-site?"

"No, I live in Port Dover," Sarah replied.

"In a fifth-floor condo with granite kitchen counters, a Jacuzzi bathtub, and surround sound," Laura added out of the side of her mouth. "So much for living in the 1800s!"

They said good-bye and continued on their tour, sucking on their candy sticks. Grace couldn't remember feeling so contented in ages. But as they rounded the schoolhouse and headed back toward the visitors' center, the peacefulness of the morning was shattered by the gabble and thunder of a group of students stampeding through the front gate.

"The museum's open." Laura sighed, moving them both to the side of the road to let the group pass.

The kids were probably high school students, the boys all gangly elbows, the girls high-pitched and chattering. They weren't wearing school uniforms, yet there was a similarity in their styles and dress, the unspoken code of teenage-hood. The boys' jeans were low and baggy, the girls' jeans as tight as scuba gear, and most of the boys wore baseball hats turned just enough off-center to make Grace's fingers itch to straighten them. Each student carried a notebook and pencil and wore a yellow paper bracelet as proof of their museum admittance.

As the group tramped by, one head rose above the others, and Grace decided it must be their teacher's. It wasn't his greater height—he was about six foot four or five—or his tweed jacket that set him apart so much as the grim look on his face, the look of a warrior leading his troops into battle. Grace recognized that expression—it had been on her own face plenty of times when she'd been a teacher. It struck Grace as funny, and she began to laugh.

She hadn't meant to laugh aloud, but the teacher heard her. His head turned in curiosity, and their eyes met. He had longish brown hair and a rather beaky nose and looked to be in his midforties. At first sight, he wasn't classically handsome, but his face was interesting. Then he grinned at her, and she readjusted her opinion. He was definitely handsome.

"Grade-ten history class," he called apologetically. He made sweeping movements with his arms above the children's heads as if doing the breast stroke through the crowd. Because he was only visible from the shoulders up, he really did look as if he were swimming.

"Enjoy your visit to the museum!" Laura called back.

As he swam past, he turned backward and pretended to do the back stroke so he could wave good-bye, and the students foamed and eddied around him and flowed into the schoolhouse in a noisy rush. The door closed mercifully behind them. Laura and Grace chuckled as they went on their way.

"I could never be a teacher." Laura sighed, shaking her head. "That would take a particular kind of courage I just don't have."

Grace was about to reply, "I was a music teacher," but something stopped her. She didn't want to bring that up. She didn't want to let her old life intrude on this cheerful morning. It was all in the past, and mentioning it now would only lead to questions from Laura and answers she couldn't give. So she only shrugged and nodded and popped the rest of her blueberry candy into her mouth.

CHAPTER SIX

THAT AFTERNOON, GRACE AND MARTIN finished planting the seeds in the greenhouse. Martin could tell Grace knew her way around now and had acquired the knack of handling the tiny seeds without dropping them in the wrong spots or covering them with too much dirt. He kept up a running commentary on the various vegetables' needs and traits, and he felt Grace soaking up the information like the soil soaked up water.

"You know," Martin told her after awhile, "it's been a long time since I've had anyone pay such close attention to what I'm saying."

Grace laughed. "Really? I find it all so fascinating."

"Laura does her best, mind, but her head is so full of everything she has to do, and after thirty-seven years of marriage, I admit there is really nothing I have to say that she doesn't already know anyway." Martin chuckled. "Our last WWOOFer was amiable enough and a hard worker, but I had the distinct impression all information funneled into his head just long enough to be acted on and then funneled right out again."

"Well, I hope I can retain everything you're teaching me. I feel like I should be writing all this down."

"It's not as if I have anything to say that's profoundly important," Martin said, embarrassed.

"You're teaching me how to grow food to feed people. What's more important and beautiful than nourishing people?" Grace replied.

Martin felt a little bubble of happiness rise in his chest, and he knew a goofy grin had spread across his face. "You understand," he said.

She paused and looked at him. "Understand what?"

"The joy that's to be found in caring for other people. In caring for the earth. In *caring* in general." He spread his hands. "What it means to me."

He wished he could express himself more clearly, but Grace seemed to grasp what he was saying because she smiled back at him warmly.

"It means something to me too," she said. "I think I'm going to be truly happy here, Martin."

He studied her face a moment, noticing the fragility had lessened at some point. Her face looked somehow softer.

"The farm is starting to work its magic on you," he said, pleased.

There was a brief time that day, though, when he noticed all that change. It was when Declan came to tell them supper was ready. He saw Grace watch the little boy run back to the house, and her face grew still and sad. Then, for a little while after that, her attention seemed to drift and there was something in her eyes that made him feel she was suddenly far away. She only murmured vaguely when he said something to her. But it didn't last long. Eventually she seemed to snap back to attention like a person waking from a daydream, and then she was fully engaged in their work again, as if nothing had happened. He shrugged it off, thinking perhaps she was tired.

* * *

On Tuesday, Martin announced it was dry enough to plow the fields and prepare them for planting. Grace figured she could learn to drive a tractor easily enough, but she was caught off guard when Martin led two huge draft horses out of the barn. He walked between them, a hand on each lead rope, seemingly unaware of the danger he was in from being crushed between the two massive forms.

Astounded, Grace watched him back them up and hitch them to an old-fashioned steel plow. He didn't hesitate to reach under and around them, fastening their harnesses while they stood like a pair of placid black mountains. Their bodies glistened like polished onyx, and she could hear the whoosh of their breath through their flaring nostrils. Martin turned and caught her gaping at him.

"What?" he asked innocently, a smile twitching up the corners of his mouth.

"Don't you use a tractor?" Grace asked. "You plow with *horses*?"

"It's all part of the pioneer ambiance, you know," he said, shrugging. "And I told you we don't use petroleum products here if we can help it."

"But I thought that meant, you know, for fertilizer or something," Grace said. "I don't know how to—I can't do this!"

"Sure you can. These old mares know what to do. You just guide them along, and they'll do it," Martin said cheerfully. "Come on, I'll show you."

Grace didn't know how to tell him it wasn't her lack of knowledge that worried her. She was terrified of these huge animals. Their shaggy white feet looked like they could squash her tennis shoes into jelly, and her head barely reached their broad backs. How on earth had the pioneers used horses?

Martin threw some of the confusion of leather straps over his shoulder, caught up others in his hands, gripped the plow handles, and made a chirping sound of encouragement. The horses pricked their ears forward and began to walk, vibrating the ground with their great, deliberate feet. The plow followed obediently behind them as if it weighed nothing. Without seeming to do so, Martin guided them down to the field behind the greenhouse and settled the plow into the soft earth. The horses lowered their heads and got to work.

And it was just that simple. Grace watched in fascination as the earth curled over in dark, rich waves from the blade of the plow and turned upside down. A long, straight furrow wound its way out behind Martin like a rope being stretched out from the back of a ship. Martin made it look so easy. The horses plodded amiably along, nodding their heads in unison. There was a pleasant sucking sound as the damp earth lifted and curled. Grace walked a good distance behind, observing with interest the treasures turned up by the blade—worms, small stones, a darker layer of clay beneath the loam. The soil looked like chocolate cake, and she had a sudden silly urge to kneel down and taste it. Instead, she lifted a handful to sniff. It smelled of secrets—moisture, living things—she couldn't identify. Didn't some cultures eat earth? She understood the idea a little.

When they reached the far side of the field, Martin chirped again and pulled the horses around in a loop to face back the other way. By the time they reached the place where they'd started, a cloud of seagulls was forming and swirling overhead.

"See? Nothing to it," Martin called to Grace. "Come take a turn."

She shook her head violently. "I'll be killed."

"These old Shires won't hurt a fly," he assured her. "I've had them for almost fifteen years, and they haven't killed anyone yet."

"I'll just watch from here," Grace said.

"I won't leave you alone with them," Martin said, gesturing insistently. "Come earn your keep."

When he put it that way, she couldn't very well refuse. She *was* here to work and learn, after all. He was her employer. Grace crept closer on trembling legs. She had ridden horses before, of course, but those had been worn-out, sleepy individuals at a riding stable with barely enough energy to swat at flies with their tails. They'd also not been much taller than Grace herself. They hadn't been *elephants*.

Martin reached out and placed Grace's hands on the handles of the plow, keeping his over hers in a firm grip. It was awkward but reassuring. Before she was ready, he chirped to the horses and they were off, moving at a surprising speed. The jolt and jitter of the plow handles caught her off guard. It wasn't as smooth and easy as he'd made it look. Grace stumbled over the uneven ground, catching her foot on a rock, jogging to keep up, and dodging the great clods of muck the horses' hooves tossed up behind them.

When they reached the far side, Martin let her step away while he turned the horses and got them facing the right way again. Then he stepped back and motioned for her to take his place. But this time, he placed the heavy reins over her shoulder instead of his own.

"What, *alone*?" Grace squealed. "I can't. I'm not strong enough. They'll run away with me. The plow will tip over."

"You'll be grand," he replied stoutly. "And I'll walk by their heads."

One of the horses turned its big head and stared inquiringly at her to see what the holdup was. Grace was left with no choice but to take the handles again. Martin reached out, gave the straps on her shoulder a twitch, and chirped. They were off again.

The plow blade wobbled, and the dirt turned over in strange chunks instead of a graceful curl. The rhythm of it was lost on her. Martin walked along for a while with one hand on a bridle and didn't look back. Halfway across the field, he stepped away from the horse and stood to one side.

"What are you doing? Don't let go!" Grace cried.

"You're all right," he replied. "I'm just observing."

Grace tried to stand straighter and look competent, but she knew she was fooling no one. She *wasn't* all right. She was botching the whole thing.

As they neared the other side of the field, Grace began to panic. She felt as if she were being dragged behind a train. She was too small, too weak to do this.

"How do I stop them? I can't turn them!" she called.

"You're all right," he repeated. "They'll stop when they run out of ground."

And they did. And then Martin was there, taking the handles to turn them around again.

Gulping air, Grace looked at the wobbly, crooked line she had just spun out behind her. Her arms and legs felt quivery. "I messed it up," she said. "I've ruined your nice striped pattern."

Martin laughed. "This is just step one," he said. "By the time we're done, all those dirt clods will be broken up tiny and you won't even see the stripes anyway." He gestured for her to take her place again.

Doubtfully, Grace gave it another try. Her second furrow was as wobbly as the first, a good five inches from the previous furrow in places and even nonexistent in places where the plow had hit a rock with a clang and jumped out of the ground. But Martin showed her how to get the blade to bite into the earth again, and her third furrow was better than the first two. The next was even straighter.

"Don't look down at the ground," he said from behind her. "Lift your chin up. Look ahead. If you aim for a landmark on the opposite side of the field, you'll go straighter."

"If these horses have been doing this for fifteen years, you'd think they'd know how to walk a straight line by now without me," Grace called back.

"Aren't you glad you don't have to do this in a corset and long skirts?" he said peacefully.

"Oh! Goodness, yes."

Her fifth furrow wandered too far from the fourth, but by the time she reached the midway point of the field, she had caught some of the rhythm of it and felt herself gaining confidence. She decided to let go of her fear, forget self-consciousness, and just plow. She was of sturdy Mormon pioneer stock, after all. Maybe some of their blood ran in her veins and she could call on it to help her. She looked back at the mess curling out behind her. Or maybe not.

By the time Martin called for them to halt, Grace's arms and legs felt boneless with fatigue, mud was smeared over her face and arms and caked her shoes, and she felt as if she'd been hit with a truck. Her back ached, and she had a stitch in her side and blisters on both palms. But there was the field torn up like a battlefield and more or less ready for the next step.

"Ta-da! You did it," Martin cheered, relieving her of the reins.

"It was better when you walked beside the horses' heads," she told him. "You should have stayed there."

"You did a fine job without me," he said.

"But it looks awful," she said. "It looks like a drunken man plowed it."

"But it's done. It doesn't have to be gorgeous. It's all mud in the end. The plants don't care how beautiful it is."

"But how will you weed if it's crooked? Won't you have to drive the horses between the rows?"

Martin chuckled and reached over to wipe a clinging clump of muck from her cheek. "Like I said, we're not done yet. Don't judge a field until it's finished. We'll straighten it out on the second pass."

"Second pass?" She'd forgotten about this in her stress. "You mean we have to do the whole field over again?"

Martin couldn't help laughing heartily at her horrified expression. "Yep, but with a different implement called a harrow. To break up the clods. I can't put a tiny seedling into that great trench, now can I?" He slapped the horses lightly with the reins. "Let's go give them a drink and a rest, and then we'll start again."

When at last they stopped for lunch, Grace could hardly make it back to the house. Laura looked up in alarm from the sink, took in Grace's haggard expression and muddy condition, and faced Martin with her hands on her hips. "Tell me you didn't make her plow with the horses! What were you thinking?"

Martin shrugged and came over to the sink to wash up.

"She did it."

"She's not strong enough."

"No, I'm not," Grace agreed miserably.

"But you did it," Martin told her gently.

"I was terrible at it. I botched the whole thing."

"But you did it."

"I've never done anything so hard."

"But you did it," he repeated, smiling.

She paused, then smiled back. "Yes, I did."

That night she stood before the mirror in her little room and eyed herself critically. She had gotten the dirt out of her hair and rubbed lotion into her sun-baked skin, but nothing could hide the lines of exhaustion on her face. She leaned closer in the dim light. There was something else in her face she hadn't seen before . . . at least not in a long while. She tried to put a name to it. Confidence? No, that wasn't what she felt. But the set of her jaw did give her a determined look. And maybe there was a little less panic in her eyes than usual.

She leaned forward to whisper to herself. "You did it. You did a lousy job of it, no matter how nice Martin was about it, but you did it. And tomorrow you'll do better."

For the first time in a long time, she felt eager for tomorrow to come. As she turned to reach for her toothbrush, she caught sight of the scrap of paper in the mirror frame. Her eyes skipped over the sorrowful first few lines and drifted down to the center of the poem, where the words seemed to stand out from the paper.

The flood of bitter questions had
finally settled . . . tired of running down her cheeks, down
memory lane, the teardrops paused to consider a
new identity . . .

CHAPTER SEVEN

THAT WEEK WAS TORTURE FOR Grace. She couldn't remember ever being so exhausted. Her back and arms ached, her palms stung, and she felt she was never clean. She even found muddy grit between her teeth at the end of the day. She cringed whenever a stream of museum visitors walked by, hoping they wouldn't judge her plowing demonstration too harshly.

"I'm afraid I'm not giving them a very good impression of how nineteenth-century farmers harrowed," she told Martin one afternoon when a particularly noisy crowd of school kids filed past the field, gawking while their teachers pointed.

"You're doing fine," Martin assured her kindly. "Besides, half those kids have never seen a horse outside of a video game. They wouldn't know if you were plowing a field or riding a zamboni. Just try to ignore them."

Steadily the fields went from green to deep brown, the earth dried and crumbled into rich softness, and by the end of the week, Martin declared the fields were ready for planting.

He had tried to teach Grace to harness and care for the horses, but she wasn't going anywhere near them, no matter how much her employer persisted. She still had a deep, abiding fear of them.

Laura took her side, defending Grace's position, saying, "After all, Martin, she wasn't raised to be used to them like you were!" So in the end Martin conceded the battle, and he did the harnessing and unhitching.

On Saturday morning when Grace came into the kitchen, a stranger was sitting at the kitchen table, eating breakfast. Grace's hand automatically went to her hair hanging down her back, still wet from the shower. She'd forgotten Mason Whelan was coming this weekend. As he stood to greet her, she was painfully aware of her ratty jeans and faded sweatshirt.

Somehow she had expected the children's father to be as dark as they were and as short and wiry as Martin and Laura. But the man who pulled himself out of the chair was a hulking bear of a man, at least six foot three, with brilliant blue eyes with laugh lines crinkling the corners. His bright-gold hair flopped over his forehead like a boy's, and he had a bushy trimmed mustache and beard like a lumberjack's, slightly darker than the hair on his head. His broad shoulders looked capable of carrying a cow across them. She had pictured him taciturn, maybe even grim to the point of silence from missing his wife and children, but she could catch a hint of Declan's mischief in his crooked smile as he held out a friendly hand. Grace had a hard time picturing this fellow stuffed into a suit, sitting behind a desk in a shiny downtown office.

"I'm Mason, Laura and Martin's son," he explained, and his voice was a big bass to match his size.

"Grace Whittaker," she answered. His hand was soft, a city dweller's hand, and her own felt rough within his grasp. The thought amused her. As their hands drew apart, though, he hit one of her blisters, and she couldn't help wincing.

He took her wrist in his hand and turned her palm over to look at it. "I see my folks have been keeping you busy," he said ruefully. "You should put some Polysporin on that."

"It's fine."

"You don't want it to get infected. You should have told my dad."

Grace withdrew her hand and tucked it into the pocket of her sweatshirt. "Is Laura around?"

The look on her face made it clear she wasn't going to discuss her injuries further, and he let the topic drop.

"She's dressing," Mason said. He nodded toward his cup on the table. "I've just made coffee if you want some."

"No, thank you." Grace reached into the refrigerator for the pitcher of orange juice. She was pouring herself some when there was a banging overhead and the thumping of small feet on the stairs. Like a missile, Lark burst into the room and ran straight into Mason's arms.

Mason caught her with a laugh and swung her around. "Good morning, my girl," he greeted her, rubbing his beard against her cheek.

Lark squealed and planted a fat kiss on his forehead. "Hi, Daddy. Did you bring me something?"

"As a matter of fact, I did." Mason set her down and reached into a briefcase that squatted beneath the chair where he'd been sitting. Extracting a comic book, he gave it to Lark, who danced with pleasure.

"Breakfast first," Laura intoned, coming into the kitchen. She greeted Mason with a squeeze. It was amusing to think such a small woman had given birth to this hairy giant. "Good morning, dear. Good morning, Grace. I see you've met Mason."

"And I've seen what Dad's done to your guest in the space of a couple of weeks," Mason replied. He seized Grace's wrist and pulled her hand from her pocket before she knew what he was about. She cringed with embarrassment as he displayed her angry, red palms to Laura.

"Oh my goodness! Why didn't you say something, Grace?" Laura cried. "I have some salve that should work on that. You should have told me."

"It's not anything," Grace assured her, flashing an irritated glance at Mason. "I'll toughen up and get some calluses, and then I'll be fine. I'm just not used to the work yet."

"Weren't you wearing gloves?"

"Yes, but they didn't seem to help much."

"No sense hurting yourself," Laura said. "I have some good, heavy leather gloves you can use next time. They might work better. I should have thought. *Martin* should have thought."

"Martin should have thought what?" Martin asked, coming into the room, still pulling on his jacket.

They went over the whole thing again for his benefit, then applied the salve Rainbow Warner had whipped up that would heal anything from abrasions to burns. They gave her bandages, and Grace settled at the table with her breakfast, feeling very self-conscious about all the attention. She wasn't used to people fussing over her, and it made her uncomfortable.

"What are we going to do today, Daddy?" Lark asked, climbing into Mason's lap as soon as he'd resumed his chair.

"Well, it depends what Grandma and Granddad have planned," he told her.

"Just some quick errands into town this morning," Laura said, waving a hand. "And my wool demonstrations, as usual."

"You need my help with anything?"

"Well, if you're offering, it's time to take the storm windows down," Martin said, reaching for the plate of toast Laura set on the table.

"Martin! He's not going to spend his only time with us taking down storm windows!" Laura scolded.

"He asked."

"I'm happy to do it," Mason said.

"No. I won't hear of it," Laura said. "We can do that later this week."

"And I can help," Grace said.

"Thanks. Are you sure? Then I guess that means our day is free to do whatever you'd like," Mason told Lark. "What do you suggest?"

Lark pushed her dark head under her father's chin and pressed against him in an armless hug since her hands were busy with his toast. "I need some new library books," she said. "And ice cream."

"Ice cream, is it?" His chuckle was a deep rumble. "Well, maybe so, on the way back from the library. And if you'd like, we could go mini golfing in Port Dover. Does that sound fun?"

Grace wanted to laugh. There was nothing "mini" about this man, and the idea of him hunched over a tiny golf club was ludicrous.

Lark nodded. "And more ice cream after that."

"We'll see." Mason looked around the kitchen. "Where's Declan?"

The room fell silent. Laura and Martin exchanged looks. But before one of them could speak, Lark said casually, "He's out in the barn."

"What's he doing out there? Someone go let him know he's missing breakfast," Laura said.

"I'll tell him." Lark squirmed off Mason's lap and headed for the door.

"I didn't even hear him go out," Laura said. "But I slept in a bit this morning. Anyone for fried eggs? Grace?"

"Yes, please. Let me help."

As the two women got to work fixing the eggs, Martin and Mason sat nursing their coffee cups at the table. Mason leaned back with his long legs stretched under the opposite chair, but Martin leaned forward on his elbows.

"How are you?" Martin asked. "Everything going okay?"

"You ask me that every time I come, Dad. It's not as if my life has tumbled into ruins since my last visit."

"Just asking, son."

"I know. I appreciate your concern. But everything's going fine, Dad," Mason said, glancing at Grace and shifting in his chair. "Everything's good."

By the time the eggs were firming in the pan, Lark was back from the barn. "He's not hungry," she reported, climbing into her own seat and reaching for her glass.

"Isn't he coming?"

"No."

"Did you tell him your father is here?" Laura asked.

"Yep. He doesn't want to come in."

Grace watched a dull pink color climb Mason's neck to his ears. He scooted his chair back from the table. "I'll go get him."

"No, let me," Martin said. He went to the door, pulled on his boots, and went out. There was a short silence around the table. No one wanted to comment on the fact that Declan didn't want to see his father.

"I want mint chocolate chip ice cream," Lark informed Mason. "In a cone, not a cup."

"All right," he said quietly.

The others finished their eggs and toast, but Martin had still not returned from the barn. The mood of the group had shifted, somehow tense, and Grace sensed Mason was uncomfortable having her there and aware of the disquiet in the room. She excused herself on the pretense of having to do some laundry and went back to her room. When she emerged an hour later, Mason and both children were gone, Martin was in the greenhouse, and Laura was bent over her spinning wheel.

Laura looked up when Grace paused in the doorway of the wool room. "Come in, dear. I just wanted to get this batch done this morning. It's an order for a woman out in Calgary."

"Can I help?"

"There's more wool to card, if you like."

Grace took the bag of raw wool from the cupboard, sat, and began teasing out a handful of fibers. The wool felt warm to her touch and soapy on her fingers, but it snagged a bit on her Band-Aids.

"You didn't tell me your son was Grizzly Adams," Grace said lightly, not looking up.

"That's a good description of him. Believe me, nobody's more surprised about how he turned out than Martin or me. Of course, look how tall Toby is. So I guess it runs somewhere in the family."

For a little while, the two women worked in a silence broken only by the soft pulse of the spinning wheel's pedal.

Finally, Laura took a deep breath. "Declan has taken this whole situation hard," she said as if Grace had asked a question. "Lark seems to have adapted more easily. But Declan . . . sort of blames his father for all this."

Grace nodded, not sure what to say.

"He's three years older than Lark," Laura added. "He liked living in Toronto. He misses his friends. And he isn't as able to let go of his mother. Not that he should, really. But he has to be able to move on . . . You know what I mean?"

"Yes."

"At some point, Lark was able to make the shift and accept her new circumstances. Declan still resists it all."

"How long has it been?" Grace asked quietly.

"Just last May," Laura said. "Almost a year. I guess some people just take a little longer to grieve."

Grace bit her lower lip, concentrating fiercely on the wool in her fingers. Not even a year yet! That was no time at all. It was still fresh as yesterday. Her heart went out to Declan. How could they expect a little boy to get over his loss that quickly? His world had been shattered. Grace's own loss had happened eighteen months ago now, and it was still as raw and painful as if it had just happened. She scowled and thrust her hands deep into the bag of wool, grasping great handfuls of it and just squeezing it, focusing on the pain in her palms, taking her emotion out in the hidden depths of the bag so it wouldn't show on her face. People who hadn't gone through grief couldn't possibly understand what it was like for those who suffered through it. They were in no position to judge how much time a person needed to reach the point where they could begin to breathe again.

She looked over at the older woman's face. She was frowning slightly as she concentrated at her wheel. There were hard lines around her mouth and forehead that Grace hadn't noticed before. She felt a sudden deep sense of shame. She couldn't judge Laura any more than Laura could judge Declan. Surely this woman had been close to her daughter-in-law. She was intimate with grief and loss. Grace wasn't the only one.

Mason and the children returned from town in time for supper. Lark sported a green ribbon pinned to her chest for some accomplishment at mini-golf, an armful of new library books, and a ring of melted chocolate around her triumphant smile. She ran noisily into the kitchen to show her grandmother what she had collected. Declan was more subdued, following his sister into the house with a sullen expression. He carried an empty paper ice cream cup, which he wordlessly placed on the counter.

Grace had to duck her head to hide her smile. Blaming his father or not, the boy had not turned his nose up at ice cream.

When Mason kissed his mother on the cheek, she ducked and told him to shave. Mason chuckled and went to wash his hands at the kitchen sink. When the children had left the room, Laura asked him how the day had gone.

Mason shrugged. "Not what I'd call a success, but it is what it is."

"Lark is happy."

"Yes, there's always that. At least Lark is always happy." Mason glanced out the window.

"I've planned supper for late because I figured you'd be full up on ice cream."

"That's fine. Is Dad outside?"

"In the barn, seeing to the animals."

"I'll go help him." Mason went out the back door, and Laura watched him from the window as he walked toward the barn, his hands in his pockets, his head lowered in thought. She shook her head but said nothing.

* * *

It was with some trepidation that Grace attended church the next Sunday. She had located the chapel situated near the edge of Port Dover in a copse of maple trees, half a mile from Lake Ontario. She was a little late arriving, having gotten stuck behind a slow-moving tractor for half the drive, and when she got there, the parking lot was nearly full.

As soon as Grace stepped inside, a wave of familiarity washed over her, catching her off guard with such intensity that she had to physically stop and catch her breath before she could continue. She dropped into an empty seat near the back and returned the smile of the matronly woman next to her, feeling as if her face were someone else's.

It hadn't changed. She hadn't expected to remember it. She'd been barely twelve when her family had moved to Utah, and much of Port Dover was no longer familiar to her. The chapel itself had been built only a couple of years before she'd left town, and she hadn't even remembered where it was located, for pity's sake. But the building was incredibly the same; she remembered it all. The generic silk flower arrangements entrenched beside the podium. The blue industrial carpet. The smell of cleaner and chalk. Good grief, it even looked like the same organist, a wizened old woman with a permanent hump, her dark-rimmed glasses perched right on the end of her nose as she craned to see the hymnbook before her. Grace even fancied she recognized the woman's pink sweater. Had the poor lady been sitting here playing for *twenty-two years*?

And then the chilling thought: If the place hadn't changed, if the people were the same, would any of them recognize *her*? What if someone remembered her family? Asked about them?

But no, surely not. She wasn't the pig-tailed, scrawny twelve-year-old she'd been when she'd left. No one would be able to see that happy, energetic girl in her somber face now. She glanced around fearfully, afraid to make eye contact but searching for a familiar face. A woman two rows ahead—she looked about Grace's age. Had they known each other then? She didn't think so. What about the bishop, who was standing now and striding to the pulpit? Of course not. Bishop Gray would be about seventy by now. This man was a stranger to her.

Grace wondered for the hundredth time what had brought her back to Port Dover after all this time. Was she in fact *hoping* someone would recognize her? Take her hands and look into her face and say, "Yes, you are still Grace. You have come back to yourself." Was that what she was trying to find? She shook her head grimly. It would take more than a feeling of familiarity to give her roots again, to restore her foundation.

Grace was relieved when the meeting began and all attention turned toward the front. The organ trembled into "On This Day of Joy and Gladness"—the organist had a preference for heavy vibrato—and Grace followed along in her hymnbook but didn't sing. She didn't think she could find her voice if she tried. But she didn't want to try.

It was obvious why she could no longer bring herself to sing, of course. She had gone over and over it with her therapist after the accident. She had been onstage rehearsing when the call had come from the police. She hadn't been in the car with her family because she'd been singing somewhere else, and the guilt and grief of that moment had stifled her voice. Grace understood all this intellectually. But understanding didn't make any difference. Music was not the same beautiful thing for her now. As she tried to find her fit in her new reality, she knew music could no longer be center stage. She wasn't even sure if she wanted it to wait in the wings. Perhaps it was best to root it out completely, start afresh, and bring nothing of her old self into her new life. The idea was both comforting and frightening at the same time.

The meetings progressed as they did in LDS churches everywhere, with the same routine, the same music, and the same themes Grace had enjoyed in Utah. Even most of the artwork on the walls was the same as in her old ward in Salt Lake. She was comforted by the predictability of it all. As the morning passed, Grace relaxed and enjoyed herself and even brought herself to speak to some of the other women in Relief Society. They were naturally curious about where she was from and were astounded to learn why she was in the area.

"Let me get this straight. You're an itinerant farmhand," one of them said slowly, shaking her head. She had short-cropped blonde hair, a slightly pudgy frame, and a friendly smile. She had introduced herself as Annie Fisher. Grace couldn't help laughing.

"Well, not exactly itinerant. It's a program to provide free instruction and housing to one person while providing free labor to the other."

"It's a great idea," another woman spoke up. "I think it sounds fun."

"I think it sounds dreadful," someone else said. "Who would want to spend all day hoeing weeds in the hot sun?"

Grace thought about the perfect stillness and cozy diffused light of the greenhouse, the tender, delicate seedlings beginning to surface in the trays, the smell of the rich warm earth, and she smiled.

"It's not all working outdoors either," she added. "I help spin wool too."

"Oh! I know now where you're staying," Sister Fisher cried. "The farm out by the river, in the pioneer village. My son works there, in the museum. I don't know the woman's name, but I buy her hand-spun yarn from the gift shop all the time. It's wonderful stuff."

"Laura Whelan," Grace said, pleased. "That's her name."

"I won't forget it," the woman said. "And maybe I'll see you out there once in a while." She held out a hand to shake Grace's formally. "I'm glad you'll be with us for the summer, Grace."

Only for the summer. A strange feeling crept over her. Grace knew when the summer ended she wasn't going to want to leave. The Whelans weren't her family, she told herself firmly as she drove back to the farm after church. She couldn't use them as a substitute, and she couldn't use their home as a hideaway. She had to move on when the time came.

CHAPTER EIGHT

MASON LEFT SUNDAY EVENING FOR the long drive back to Toronto. Lark was irritable the next morning as Laura hurried her through breakfast and got her ready for school.

"I wish Daddy could stay longer," she whined. "I wish he could stay all week."

"He has to get back to his job," Laura explained, threading the little girl's arms through her pink backpack straps.

"Yeah, he has to get back to his real life," Declan said, hoisting his own backpack over one shoulder. He glanced at Grace where she stood washing dishes at the sink, and she kept her eyes on her hands and pretended she wasn't overhearing.

Laura shot Declan a look. "You know he would stay if he could."

"Why does he have to work? Why can't he live here with us and work on the farm with you and Granddad?" Lark asked.

Lark's wistful tone made Laura's smile falter, and she sighed. "We've been over that. Your daddy isn't a farmer. He's a lawyer. He has to live in a place where people need a lawyer."

"I want him to meet my teacher," Lark said.

"Maybe one day he can. Maybe he could come for your spring festival."

"It's on a weekday," Declan said sourly. "A Friday. He wouldn't come."

"We can ask him," Lark said, brightening. "Grandma can call and ask."

"Let me know what date it is, and I'll do that," Laura said. "Now hurry up. Granddad's waiting in the car to take you."

Lark scampered for the door, but Declan stopped to look back over his shoulder at Grace. "You could come too," he said. "To our school festival. If you want."

"I'd like that very much," Grace said, surprised he'd think to invite her.

He followed Lark out, and Laura shook her head as she helped clear away the wreckage of breakfast.

"At least," she said, "when Mason comes on the weekend, he is able to give them his undivided attention. He couldn't do that if they lived with him in the city."

"I suppose," Grace said doubtfully. When she saw the troubled look on Laura's face, she wiped off her hands and went to touch Laura's arm. "I'm sure it will all work out in the end," she said more strongly. "And in the meantime, the children have a loving home here with you."

"Yes." Laura sighed. "I suppose that counts for something."

That evening Grace volunteered to cook the family supper to give Laura a break. Laura accepted with unabashed alacrity and announced she was going to go visit a friend for the evening whom she hadn't seen for a while. Grace was chopping onions when Declan wandered into the kitchen and leaned his elbows on the counter to watch.

"Whatcha making?" he asked.

"Pasta. Carbonara, to be exact."

"What's that?"

"It's like fancy bacon and eggs. Do you want to help?"

"I don't know how to cook."

"If I can drive a plow horse, you can make a salad," Grace reasoned. "Wash your hands, and bring a chair over."

Declan looked doubtful but obeyed. When he was perched beside her, Grace set a glass bowl before him and set him to tearing up lettuce. She placed a large pot of water on the stove to boil and hunted through the cupboards.

"What are you looking for?" Declan asked.

"The salt."

"Above the stove."

"Thanks." Grace sprinkled some in the water and pulled bacon and eggs from the fridge. She began to fry three bacon strips in a pan. The sizzle reminded her of the hushed rustling of an audience waiting for the curtain to go up.

"Three pieces isn't enough for all of us," Declan pronounced gloomily.

"It is when it's carbonara," Grace said. "It's more of a flavoring, really."

Declan brushed his hands together. "Finished with the lettuce," he said. He had turned it into confetti instead of bite-sized pieces, but Grace didn't remark on it.

"Then you can put in some of these chopped onions. And you can cut up some of this celery."

His dark eyes grew wide. "With a knife?"

"Yes, that's what a person usually uses to cut things up." She laughed.

She found him a cutting board and a knife that wasn't too sharp and showed him how to split the celery stalks up the middle before dicing them. He started this task with more interest than he'd shown the lettuce. He worked carefully, making the pieces all exactly the same width.

"Well done," Grace praised him, adding spaghetti to the boiling water. "Throw those in the bowl, and then you can cut up this pepper. But be careful not to touch your eyes or face while your hands have pepper juice on them or it will sting. Let's see, what else can we put in the salad?"

"Shredded carrots. I like when Grandma puts carrots in it."

"Okay."

Declan opened and gutted the red pepper with gusto. Just as he was dicing it up, Lark came into the kitchen looking for a drink of water. Her mouth fell open when she saw her brother at the counter. "Grandma never lets us use knives!" she cried.

Grace eyeballed Declan. "You didn't tell me that."

He shrugged. "You didn't ask. But I did all right, didn't I?"

"Yes you did. You did a fine job. And I was here to make sure you were safe. But I guess we'd better ask your grandma before we do it again."

"But can I keep helping?"

Grace was about to say no to be on the safe side, but something in his eager face made her swallow back her original reply. "Just this once," she said reluctantly. "Do you want to help, Lark?"

"I'm watching cartoons," she said and went out.

Grace expected Declan to go with her, but instead he wiped his hands on his shirt and peeled the carrots. Grace lifted the bacon out of the pan and minced it into tiny pieces. Then she cooked the rest of the chopped onion in the bacon grease. After that, it was just a matter of whisking up a couple of eggs with parmesan and parsley—Declan proved experienced at cracking eggs—and then waiting for the pasta to finish cooking.

Declan peered into the boiling pot and nodded in satisfaction. "When this is done, you add all the other stuff to it, right?"

"Yes. After you drain the water off the pasta first, of course."

"This is going to be good."

"It will be delicious. Carbonara is always the star of any meal, and your salad will be the perfect accompaniment. This will be ready in just a minute. Why don't you go let your granddad know it's time to come in?"

Declan pushed his chair back into place at the table and started for the door, then looked back at her with a grin. "Thanks, Grace."

"For what? Letting you use a knife behind your grandma's back? I'm going to be in trouble."

"No, you won't," Declan said confidently. "Grandma only gets mad over the *big* stuff."

"Ah. You speak from experience, I take it." Grace shook her head. "What's the biggest thing she's ever gotten mad about?"

He grinned again. "Oh, the biggest thing is still coming," he said impishly. "I just haven't thought it up yet."

* * *

The row of seven-year-old faces appeared rather unimpressed as they looked at the basket of fluffy brown wool and the spinning wheel.

"In Rumpelstiltskin, the miller's daughter spun the straw into gold," one of them observed.

"Yes, that's pretty amazing," Laura agreed. "But I don't have any straw here to demonstrate with today, so we'll just make do with wool."

"Don't the sheep get cold if you take their fur off?" another of the children asked. *No doubt a budding activist ready to call the Humane Society*, Grace thought. She tried not to smile as she waited to see how Laura handled that one.

Laura tugged at the collar of her high-necked, uncomfortable-looking dress, but her smile was peaceful and showed no hint of impatience as she faced her young audience in the demonstration room at the visitors' center.

"We only take it off during warm weather," she explained. "They like it because then they don't get too hot in the summer. You wouldn't want to wear your coat all summer, would you? Well, the sheep are the same. They grow it back again before winter. And it's not called fur; it's—"

"My dad wears the same coat all summer," one of the children piped up. "*And* all winter. It's his old high school football jersey, and he *never* takes it off. My mom says it's because he hasn't done anything great since high school and he likes to remember—"

"My mom got a new red coat last winter, and my dad said if she got one more, she could have a different one to wear every week." This came from a cherubic redheaded girl with a Barbie backpack.

"Does it hurt the sheep when you take off their fur?" another child asked, face creased with concern. This set off a volley of comments from her classmates.

"They ought to have zippers so you can take it off without cutting them."

"You don't cut them, stupid. You cut their hair. It doesn't hurt."

"My mom cut my hair, and I could hear it *screaming*."

"Do you get red yarn from red sheep?"

"If you get a striped sheep, does the yarn turn out striped too?"

Grace, who had come along to observe and knew she shouldn't get involved, felt sorely tempted to get the demonstration back on track with a sharp word or two. She glanced at the group's schoolteacher, a painfully thin girl who looked as if she were fresh out of high school. She was idly fingering some of the finished balls of yarn and not paying the least attention to her class.

But Laura was unfazed. She was a veteran of this sort of thing, and Grace watched as the older woman gently drew the group back to the task at hand. She invited the most unruly of the children to come forward and turn the handle of the carder for her while she demonstrated its use, and she got the most vocal child to count the number of turns aloud. She got the grumpiest of the bunch to help hold the wool while Laura showed how it was spun, and when the activity at last was over, she removed the little length of kinked yarn and handed it to a small girl who had remained silent at the back of the group. The girl's hair was greasy and hung in two frayed braids that looked days old, and her clothes were ill-fitting and worn compared to her classmates'. But when Laura gave her the bit of yarn from the spindle, the child's face broke into a beautiful, beaming smile, and her dark eyes danced. She happily led her classmates out of the room as the group moved on to the next demonstration, followed wanly by their teacher.

Afterward, walking back to the house with Laura with the wool basket over her arm, Grace complimented the way Laura had calmed the group.

Laura shrugged. "They're just energetic and excited to be on a field trip," she said. "And I like it when they ask questions, even silly ones. That's better than the kids who don't ask any at all. Those just stare like you're a frog in a tank, and you don't know if anything you're saying is sinking in."

"I'm a bit alarmed at how little they seem to know about sheep."

"They don't know much about anything at that age," Laura said. "It's more alarming when they're asking if sheep have zippers at age fourteen." She laughed. "Really, kids don't have much of an idea about where anything in their lives comes from—who made it, how it got there, what's in it. That's why what we do here at the pioneer village is so important. Kids need to know the old ways, the basics, where their food and clothing come from. They might become inspired to produce something useful themselves. At the very least, they'll know who to thank."

"That's an interesting thought."

"Do you know, a twelve-year-old once asked Martin if he planted a poppy seed, would it grow a new bagel."

That weekend, Mason wasn't visiting, and Martin and Laura decided to take the children on a rare getaway to visit some distant relatives in Mount Forest. As Laura put it, now that Grace was here, they were freed up to escape the farm a little more from time to time, and they were going to take advantage of it while they could before the CSA season began. Laura cancelled her three Saturday wool demonstrations, and Martin wrote out a page and a half of instructions in his careful hand for Grace so she would know how to care for the horses and hens while they were gone. It was so detailed and gave the numbers of so many emergency contacts that any qualms she might have had dissipated.

"So long as I don't have to actually *touch* them, I'll be fine," she quipped as Martin loaded their overnight bags into the car.

"You have our cell number," Laura told her. "I really appreciate this. Are you going to be okay out here all alone, do you think?"

"Toby's within shouting distance," Grace assured her. "And I'm used to living on my own. I'll be fine."

She watched them pull away in the car, waving from the front door, and then she pulled on her boots and went out to the barn. She walked down the wide aisle until she reached the stalls where the horses were munching their breakfast in their great hollow jaws. The noise was loud in the still air, as if they were rattling gravel around in buckets instead of chewing grain. Both raised their massive heads and blew their nostrils at her when she appeared. They sounded like chuffing steam engines.

Staying well back from their half doors, Grace eyed them determinedly. They looked back mildly with liquid brown eyes.

"I'll make a deal with you girls," she said. "You behave and don't get out of your paddock, and I'll do what I have to do to take care of you. Truce, okay?"

One of them shook out her mane and let out an ear-piercing whinny. The other turned away, looking bored. Grace knew Martin sometimes gave them sugar lumps as treats. She took two from the canister on the tack bench and set them on the tops of the doors. She was too chicken to feed them from her hand. The horses didn't care. They nipped up the sugar with their velvety lips and regarded her calmly, accepting the truce. Grace fled back to the house, relieved.

It was strange to have the usually noisy house to herself. She spent Saturday carding wool, watching TV, and reading. A couple of times, a group of museum patrons wandered by the locked greenhouse, and Grace thought with affection of the tiny seedlings they would be able to see through the windows. They were beginning to really come on now, creating a hazy green mist over the long wooden tables. Grace stood in the kitchen window and watched as a young father hoisted his toddler onto his shoulders so he could get a better look. The little boy clapped his hands and laughed as if he was witnessing a miracle . . . and Grace supposed he was. It *was* a miracle that you could put a tiny seed into the earth and it would know what to do. It would flourish and produce fruit and give you back seeds a hundredfold.

Grace made herself a simple salad for lunch, but then the quiet started to lie heavily on her, so she fetched a sun hat and went for a walk. The air smelled of sunshine, if such a thing was possible, and she breathed it in deeply, smiling to herself. It was a smell, a taste, she could get very used to.

Without planning it, she found herself on the winding little road to the museum village. It was possible, walking past the restored Victorian buildings, to think she was actually in the nineteenth century. A breeze caught the wooden sign over the post office and set it swinging gently. Her shoes made a pleasant crunchy beat on the gravel. All was quiet and peaceful, and she felt herself taking deep, restoring breaths of the fresh air as she walked.

Life seemed simpler back then, Grace thought, picturing herself rocking in the rocking chair on the curator's house's wide white porch. They did the work before them each day, ate all their meals together, gathered around the table, and relied on their hands and the skills of their close neighbors to see them through every situation. No electronics summoning their attention every five minutes, no television telling them what they should and shouldn't want, no high-stress treks to work on a congested freeway. And this—the utter, deep silence. No cars, no lawn mowers, not even any airplanes. The only sounds Grace could hear were the trees murmuring in the breeze and her own feet on the ground.

There weren't many tourists about, and she thought she'd stop in to see Sarah at the general store, but when she arrived, she found an unfamiliar teenage boy standing behind the counter. He wore denim overalls that looked fresh from the department store over a long-sleeved white shirt, with a straw hat on his head. He had a spattering of freckles on his cheeks and nose. All he needed was a straw of wheat dangling from the corner of his mouth to look picture perfect. The thought amused her, so she was smiling when the boy looked up. He brightened and reflected her grin back at her.

"Good morning! Welcome to the general store," he said, winding up for his spiel.

But Grace waved a hand. "Not a tourist," she told him. "I live here."

He laughed. "Thanks for stopping me. If I have to say it one more time today, I'll throw myself on a pitchfork. You live here?"

"I'm a farmhand. I live with the Whelans," Grace said.

"Oh! The people with the big horses, right?"

"That's right."

"I love the horses. I watch them sometimes working out in the field. I've never met them. The Whelans, I mean. *Or* the horses," he added wistfully.

"You should come by. They're nice people. I'm sure Martin would let you meet the horses up close if you want."

"You think? I'd like that. Are they as scary up close as they seem from far away?"

"More so." Grace laughed. She stuck out her hand. "Grace Whittaker."

"Caleb Fisher."

"Fisher. Oh, are you Annie Fisher's son?"

"Yes. You know my mom?"

"I met her at church. I'm LDS too. She mentioned she had a son working here at the museum."

"That's me. Every other Saturday afternoon and occasional fill-ins when Sarah can't make it in." He shrugged. "It doesn't pay much, but it's fun."

"Except for having to recite your lines a thousand times a day," Grace said.

"Yeah, well . . ."

"And being bombarded with schoolchildren."

"Actually, not many come on Saturdays. The school groups come through during the week, but I don't mind kids anyhow. There are eight of us at home." He paused. "Seven, now. My oldest brother's on a mission in Brazil. I know it sounds funny when there's still seven kids at home, but the place seems kind of empty without him, you know?" He reached for the jar of candy sticks. "Want one? Sarah always gives them out to visitors."

"No, thanks. I just had a healthy salad, and I'm feeling righteous," Grace said. "I'm just out for a walk."

"Go down by the mill where the river cuts across the field," Caleb suggested. "That's the prettiest place to walk."

"I'll do that. Thank you." Grace said her good-byes and turned toward the door but nearly collided with a woman just entering. "Oh, excuse me!" Grace said without looking at the other person. "I'm sorry—"

"Grace Whittaker, isn't it?"

Grace looked up, surprised to see Annie Fisher grinning at her. It was an exact replica of Caleb's smile, and she could instantly see the family resemblance. Annie looked different—lighter—in jeans and a blouse instead of her flowered Sunday dress.

"Sister Fisher! We were just talking about—I just met your son."

"Yes, that's one of mine," Annie said. She handed a paper bag across the counter to Caleb. "You forgot your lunch. I thought I'd bring it so you wouldn't have to spend your hard-earned cash on a donut at the gift shop. I was coming to get some yarn anyway."

"Thanks, Mom. You're the best."

"Aren't I though?" Annie laughed.

She and Grace stepped out into the sunshine together.

"I'm out for a walk, and Caleb suggested I go down to the river," Grace said.

"Yes, that's the best place for walking. Would you like some company? I'd enjoy a walk myself."

"Sure," Grace said. "But didn't you want to go to the gift shop for yarn?"

"Oh, I have bags of it already," Annie said. "I just told Caleb I had to come anyway so he wouldn't know I drove all this way out here just so I could mother him. I mean, he's a working man now, after all. I didn't want to look *too* pathetic!" She strode briskly along the road, swinging her arms, and Grace fell in step beside her. The mill, a tall stone structure, lay some distance away, and trees grew in a line nearby the river, Grace assumed.

"He told me you have a son on a mission."

"Isaac, yes."

"And you have a lot of other children."

"Yes, I do. Eight in all. Hence my need for a peaceful walk by a river with an adult," Annie Fisher replied, shooting her a grin. "How about you? Any kids?"

"I did have three. They died in an accident," Grace replied and then paused, surprised at herself.

Annie stopped short, looking at her, shocked. "Oh dear." When Grace didn't move, Annie added, "Are you all right? I guess that's a stupid question. Of course you aren't all right."

"Yes, I'm okay. I've just never been able to say it that simply before," Grace told her. "Usually it stabs like a knife when I say it or think it. But it didn't that time. It's just a statement—I had three children, and they died in a car accident." She shook her head. "It still sounds a little unreal to me, but . . . but—"

"But it didn't knock you to the ground when you said it aloud?" Annie said gently. She put her arm around Grace's shoulders as they resumed walking along the road, and it felt completely natural to Grace.

"Something like that," Grace said.

Annie nodded. "And maybe you think it should have."

"Yes," Grace admitted. "It should strike me dead just to say it. But . . . it didn't. It hasn't."

"Good," Annie said after a thoughtful pause. "I wouldn't want you struck dead just yet, not when I've just met you. Maybe later, though, after I've gotten to know you."

It struck Grace as such an absurd thing to say that she began to laugh, and before she knew it, they were just two women laughing together as they walked along the river in the shade of the trees.

CHAPTER NINE

GRACE FIXED HERSELF LEFTOVER MEATLOAF for supper, then took care of the animals' food and water and made sure the hens were securely fastened in their coop. She reread Martin's instructions twice to make sure she had done all she was supposed to. She spent the evening reading in the hushed silence, and it was with a deep sense of satisfaction that she went to bed that night.

Grace woke with a start in the dark night, tense with the instant knowledge that some sudden sound had awakened her. She didn't know if she had dreamt it or actually heard it. She sat up in bed, clutching her blanket to her chest, and listened. Nothing. She reached for her lamp and realized her hand was shaking. She had that nauseous feeling that came with being awakened from a deep sleep too swiftly. If she had been dreaming, she couldn't recall it, but she knew what it would have been about anyway. Her nightmares were always the same.

The golden pool of lamplight calmed her somewhat, and she climbed out of bed and went to her door. Opening it slightly, she poked her head out and felt the cool night air pour over her. She couldn't see anything unusual, and all appeared to be quiet. The sky was black, that blackness a city dweller never got used to, and the only sound was the distant murmur of the river at the edge of the property. She could smell damp earth and, faintly, a steadying whiff of horse.

Grace closed the door again and stood looking around her little room. She wouldn't be able to get back to sleep now. The digital clock read three. Too late to sleep, and too early to get up. Grace put on her shoes and pulled her sweater over her pajamas. Shivering with both cold and nervousness, she went out once more, hurried down the stairs, and let herself into the Whelans' house. She found the light switch in the kitchen and snapped it on, jolting the room into brilliant familiarity. She locked the door again behind her and put the kettle on, thinking to make some herbal tea. She thought about carrying it back to her room over the garage and decided she would just settle herself here in the house for the rest of the night. She would find a blanket and curl up on the couch. Maybe she should run back, though, and get her scriptures to read while she drank her mint tea. That sounded cozy and comforting.

Grace left the kettle warming and strode to the back door. She threw it open and stopped short with a scream.

Toby screamed right back at her. Then they both gasped and laughed and gripped their throats with their hands.

"Good grief, you scared me, woman!" he growled. "What are you doing bursting out of the house like that?"

"What are you doing lurking on the back step at three in the morning?" she countered. "I think I'm having a heart attack."

"I saw the light on and came to make sure everything was okay," he said defensively. "If anyone's having the heart attack, it's me. I'm the octogenarian."

"I'm fine. I don't need you to check up on me."

"Well, I didn't know that until I got here, did I?"

"What were you doing awake at this hour anyway?" Grace had pulled him inside and shut the door behind him and was getting out a second mug.

"I'm old. I never sleep," Toby said peevishly. He dropped onto the couch where she'd been planning to curl up. She felt a twinge of irritation and pushed it away. Truth be told, she was glad for the company. She handed him a mug of mint tea and carried her own to the armchair by the woodstove.

"Yes, well, as you can see, I'm fine," she said. "Just a nightmare, I guess. I thought I'd read for a while."

"Don't let me stop you. I'll drink my mug and get out of your way."

Grace ran her fingers through her hair, mussing it further. "I don't know why I'm snapping at you. I'm sorry."

"It's the adrenaline. It causes a fight-or-flight response." His lips twitched. "At least it's good to see you're a fighter."

"You too." She grinned. "Let me start this conversation over again. Thank you for coming to check on me, Toby. It was kind of you."

"Yes, it was," he replied, and then his features too relaxed into a grin.

"Even if it was a false alarm, it's nice to know I'm not alone."

He blinked at her. "Of course you're not. My house is a hundred feet away."

"You know what I mean." She couldn't help herself. "It's still a long way for an octogenarian to hobble."

He patted the head of his cane. "Yes, well, if it's to save a lovely damsel in distress, I can do a hundred-yard dash now and again. What was your nightmare about?"

"Don't remember," she said shortly.

"Fair enough if you don't want to tell me." He set aside his empty cup and rubbed his hands wearily over his face. Then he looked at her, and she knew he was taking in her bloodshot eyes, the pinched look she could feel on her thin face, the nervous drumming of her fingers on the chair's arm. "You want me to stay or go?" he asked quietly.

"I'm okay now," she said.

"That didn't answer my question."

Grace thought about it, then stood. "Stay. How about a game of chess? I think I saw a board in the living room."

"Prepare to be pulverized," he said brightly. "I'm the world's chess expert."

"You're on."

It was all Grace could do to stay awake in church the next day. She and Toby had stayed up the remainder of the night, stoking the stove and playing chess and eating cookies, which had eventually turned into breakfast, and chatting about nothing and everything. She had finally shooed him home so she could get ready for the ten o'clock sacrament meeting, but not before thanking him again for coming over to check on her.

"It really is nice knowing someone's watching out for me," she'd told him as she'd seen him off at the back door.

He'd hesitated, then looked out over the yard and replied, not looking at her, "It's really nice having someone to watch out for."

She had watched his tall, lean figure stride across the yard toward his house hardly using his cane, and she'd chuckled softly to herself as she'd headed for her own apartment over the garage.

Church was pleasant but unremarkable. Grace caught a glimpse of her new friend Annie Fisher in sacrament meeting but lost sight of her after that. And then came Relief Society, when the person conducting asked Grace to introduce herself.

"I know you introduced yourself last week, and you don't really count as a visitor anymore," the woman said kindly, "but some of us are in our declining years and can't remember your name, so repetition never hurts."

"Speak for yourself, Marlene," someone muttered, and the roomful of women laughed.

Smiling, Grace climbed to her feet and repeated what she had said the previous week. "My name is Grace Whittaker, and I'm here just for the summer," and added, "working on the farm at Copper Creek Pioneer Village."

She sat again, but this time someone in the front row craned around and asked her, "Where are you from originally?"

"I live in Utah. Salt Lake City," Grace answered.

"No, I mean before that," the woman said. "I recognize you. Weren't you that little Harper girl?"

"Yes, that's it!" another woman declared. "Grace Harper, all grown up. I thought I recognized you, but I couldn't place it."

Grace sat stiffly with the smile congealing on her face, not sure what to do or think. She glanced around the room but couldn't see Annie anywhere. She cleared her throat and nodded jerkily. "Yes. My family lived here when I was very young. We moved to Utah when I was twelve."

"I thought so," the woman in the front row said, nodding with satisfaction. "You all remember Kate Harper, don't you? That was her mother. Kate and Jared Harper."

"Yes, now I remember," someone else joined in. "How is your mother, Grace?"

"I—" Grace looked around at the sea of expectant faces and wanted the teacher to jump up and begin the lesson, the fire alarm to go off, the roof to cave in—anything to stop this conversation from ponderously rolling forward into dangerous territory. "I'm sorry to tell you, she died almost ten years ago of a stroke."

"Oh, what a shame! She was always such a friendly, helpful woman." The elderly woman next to Grace put her hand warmly on Grace's arm.

"It's nice that you remember her after all this time," Grace said.

"And your father, Jared?" the first woman persisted.

Grace swallowed. "He passed away not long after. Pancreatic cancer." *Please let them stop the questioning right there*, she prayed silently. *Please,*

please. She could feel the panic rising in her chest, squeezing her lungs. The peace she had felt the last few days fled entirely.

"You poor dear, losing them both so young like that," the woman in the front row went on inexorably.

Can't she turn back around and face forward? Doesn't it hurt to sit all screwed around in her chair like that? Grace thought angrily.

But the woman was relentless. "I guess you're married now, then. You said your last name is Whittaker now?"

"I—yes."

"Is your husband here for the summer too, or is he still back in Utah?" There was something slightly disapproving in the woman's tone, poised and ready to judge, as if Grace were very irresponsible to be gadding about Canada for the summer without her spouse.

Grace opened her mouth, but nothing would come out. She sat frozen, her mouth opening and closing, but nothing happened. She felt as if she were drowning. Her breath began to come in short gasps. A high-pitched humming started in her head, driving out all thought. But then the elderly woman next to her put her warm hand on Grace's arm again and said brightly, "We shouldn't take up all of Sue Ellen's lesson time, should we? We can catch up with Grace afterward."

Her panic faded. The class resumed good-naturedly, and Grace felt the pounding in her chest begin to slow. She looked at her neighbor gratefully and saw her watching her with a kindly, knowing expression in her faded-blue eyes.

"All right?" she whispered to Grace. And without waiting for an answer, she tucked Grace's hand between both her own and held it gently for the rest of the meeting. Grace, feeling the comfort of it deep in her bones, found herself fighting tears. The simple gesture steadied her, let her breathe again.

At the end of the meeting, the woman bounced to her feet with a spryness that belied her age while the amen was still being said and pulled Grace up with her.

"If you run for the door, I'll cover for you," she hissed in Grace's ear. So Grace went as swiftly as she could without actually hiking up her skirts and running. But she didn't go far. She lingered in her car in the parking lot, scrunched down in her seat as she watched the people disperse in trickles and clumps from the building. After a few minutes, she saw the elderly woman, her rescuer, come out of the church and walk purposefully toward a little blue Nissan. Grace slid out of her car and went over.

The woman saw her coming and smiled, her face a relief map of wrinkles, and said simply, "Better?"

"Yes, thank you. How did you know?" Grace asked.

"You had that hunted look a sheep gets when it's surrounded by shearers determined to corral it." She laughed, a bell-like sound from deep in her chest. "You have to forgive them. They mean well. But they can be a bit too nosy sometimes." She took Grace's hand in both her own again, tipping her head back to look up at her. "I'm Margaret Hanmer. I didn't know your mother well, but I liked her."

"Thank you. I'm Grace. Well, you know that."

"Yes. I remember you as a girl. You had a lovely singing voice. You sang at a Christmas pageant once."

"Er—yes."

"All those little kids trudging around in their fathers' bathrobes, and an eight-year-old Mary with a pillow stuffed in her costume to make her look pregnant. I thought it was pretty silly, really, and wished I could sneak out early and go home, except I'd promised to help with the refreshments after. And then you stood up on a chair in a white dress and sang "O Holy Night," and the whole evening magically changed. Even the littlest children grew still to listen. When you got to 'Fall on your knees,' it nearly brought me to *my* knees."

Grace didn't know what to say. As she listened to this reverie, her breath once again caught in her chest as if she might suffocate.

But then Margaret chuckled, and the moment passed. "I live on Derry Street, not far from where you're staying," she said.

"Oh, good," Grace said. "It's nice to know there's a friend nearby."

Margaret's eyes nearly disappeared into her smile lines. "It certainly is. And you should also know that I'm a widow too these five years now."

Grace gaped at her, then looked down at her hand—her left hand—still caught in Margaret's grip, and saw the thin white band of skin where her wedding ring had once been.

"How did you know I wasn't just divorced?" she asked softly.

"You have the look about you," Margaret said, shrugging. "Was it recent?"

"Eighteen months ago."

"Ah. Just yesterday, then." Margaret nodded.

Grace smiled and impulsively leaned down to give the petite woman a brief hug. "You understand."

"I do."

"I owe you lunch. Would you like to come over?"

"What, you mean now?" Margaret asked.

"Sure. I'm on my own today, and I'd like the company. I have cold chicken and potato salad."

"You don't have to ask me twice. I have yesterday's cabbage soup and only a cat to converse with." Margaret wrinkled her nose in distaste. "I'll follow you in my car."

So Grace drove home, with Margaret following. At first she went slowly in case Margaret was a timid driver, but after awhile of watching in the rearview mirror as the woman wove confidently in and out of traffic, skidded her wheels rounding a corner, and honked at a car that was going too slowly, Grace laughed and sped up. She opened the front door of the Whelans' home with the delicious feeling of sneaking a friend into the house while her parents were away.

Margaret admired the beautiful kitchen and authentic woodstove, then took down an apron from its hook without asking. Within minutes, the two women were comfortable at the table with their chicken and salad and an apple pie Margaret had produced from her car.

"It was meant for the missionaries," she confided. "I was going to give it to them after church. But we'll enjoy it instead, and I'll make them another one next week."

They were halfway into their meal, laughing and enjoying each other's company, when the back door opened and Toby strode in.

They all regarded each other with some surprise, and then Grace jumped to her feet. "Terrific! Have you had any lunch yet?"

Toby eyed the pie, then wordlessly picked up a clean plate and came to join them at the table. Grace made introductions all around and watched with amusement as Toby made a courtly bow low over Margaret's hand and Margaret blushed undeniably pink. When they were all seated again, Grace resumed the conversation, but after a few minutes, she realized she was the only one talking. Margaret appeared to be suddenly tongue-tied. Grace watched her from the corner of her eye, surprised anyone could make the feisty woman shy. But shy she was, without a doubt. The older woman's eyes kept sliding over to Toby, and, Grace noted with something between incredulity and joy, Toby's eyes kept sliding toward Margaret.

Well, well. Who would have thought? But something had definitely instantly captivated both of them. Grace wondered if she should find an excuse to leave the room to let this unforeseen development carry on without her. But then Margaret seemed to shake herself and returned to the conversation as if she'd never lost the pace of it.

"I liked Sue Ellen's lesson today," she said, reaching for the glass of milk Grace had poured her. She added for Toby's benefit, "It was about enduring to the end."

"The end of what?" Toby asked cheerfully.

"Well . . . the end of our lives, I suppose," Margaret explained.

"Well, of course we endure to the end of our lives. When we stop enduring, we're dead. Life ends at that moment." Toby took a bite of apple and looked pleased with himself.

"That's not what I meant," Margaret said, frowning now. "You know the phrase 'enduring to the end.' It means not just living to the end but living well. Living *right*."

"Ah. And this Sue Ellen person told you how this was to be done?" Toby asked peacefully.

"We know how it's to be done," Margaret said. "Today was more of a pep talk to keep at it. Not give up."

"Why?"

"Why?" Margaret blinked at Toby, stumped.

"Why not give up? Why keep at it?" He grinned as confusion and indignation raced across Margaret's pretty face. Grace thought it made her eyes bright as stars.

"Well, for the reward, of course," Margaret said.

"Ah, yes, the reward Christians are always singing on about. Heaven and harps and joy in the world to come." There was more than a touch of cynicism in his voice.

Oh, don't be like that, Grace thought.

"Well, that's a part of it but not my personal motivation," Margaret said thoughtfully. She poked at her plate, pushing stray crumbs around with her fork. "I think we talk too much about the world to come and forget to pay attention to the world we're in, the beauty and opportunity around us right now. The reward to me is happiness and peace in this life too, here and now, and not just some vague someday." Margaret looked up, smiling, her face radiant with just the sort of joy she'd been describing. Her skin was clean pearl, her cloud of white hair floated around her face like floss, and her pale eyes were alight like crystal.

Toby stared at her a moment, his fork forgotten halfway to his mouth, and then he set it down on his plate without taking the bite. He cleared his throat. Grace watched silently as he took this in. "You sound as if you're familiar with that sort of happiness and peace here and now," he said, his gruff voice grown soft.

"I haven't always been. And I'm not always now," Margaret replied simply. "But I have my moments."

Toby, gazing at her, nodded and said, "That you do. You certainly do."

Grace stood and carried their empty plates to the sink, then returned to the table. Toby and Margaret had both dropped their gazes.

Margaret sighed and reached over to touch Grace lightly on the arm. "I want to thank you for a perfect meal and terrific company," she said lightly. "But I'd better go home now. I always take a nap after church, and Simon will be missing me."

"Simon?" If Toby had been a dog, his ears would have perked.

"My cat," Margaret told him, eyes twinkling. "We never miss our Sunday nap."

Grace started to see her guest out, but Toby was on his feet before her, helping Margaret from her chair, retrieving her sweater for her, picking up her pie plate, and walking her to the door. Grace hung back and let him do it, smiling to herself. At the door, Margaret called, "I'll see you next Sunday, Grace!"

"Oh, sooner than that, surely," Toby said, and then their voices were lost to Grace as they went out. It was almost ten minutes before Toby returned to the kitchen smiling smugly.

"That took awhile," Grace remarked, straight-faced.

"Just walking her to her car," he said.

"Margaret's nice, isn't she?"

"That she is."

"And you were able to talk to her," Grace pointed out innocently.

Toby tipped an invisible hat to her and went to the back door. "What time shall I come over for supper?"

"Oh, you're coming for supper?"

"Yes. And I'm bringing the salad. Shall we say about seven?"

"Sure." Grace laughed. "But you don't have to go now. Do you want to stay for some more chess?"

"After supper," he said. "Right now I have some harnesses to mend in the barn. See you tonight, then."

CHAPTER TEN

GRACE OPENED THE DOOR OF the barn that evening and paused, letting her eyes adjust to the dim light after the brightness of the sunset in the yard. The golden glow of the work lamp surrounded her, drawing her in. Toby looked up from the workbench, and Grace went to stand beside him. He was mending a leather strap from the horses' harness, splicing a new piece where the old had snapped. Grace couldn't imagine the strength it had taken to snap the thick, wide band.

"Supper will be on in about fifteen minutes."

"Thanks. I'll wash up in a second and go fetch my salad. It's ready in my fridge."

Grace watched his gnarled hands working deftly at their task. So he really did know what he was doing; it wasn't just show for the tourists. She breathed in the scent of leather and straw and dust and horse. That distinctive barn smell had become one of her favorites.

At her silence, Toby glanced up at her, his hands never stopping their movement. Grace tipped her chin and met his gaze.

"It was a car accident," she said.

Toby straightened, and his hands grew still as he turned all his attention to her. Grace drew a deep breath.

"I had to go into the school one Saturday to rehearse. I was the director of a music school. Ordinarily I wouldn't have been there on a weekend, but we had a big concert coming up. Greg was going to take the kids over to see his mother and have lunch there. They were merging onto the highway. A transport truck was trying to get over to exit and was going too fast. The driver said he didn't see them. He was busy looking in his rearview mirror in order to change lanes, and he just didn't see them."

Toby visibly tensed as if against an unexpected and violent blow. "And you lost all four of them at once?" He didn't hide the horror in his voice.

"Greg and Mark died instantly at the scene, Sam and Molly about half an hour later at the hospital. I didn't get there in time." Grace swallowed back the tremor in her voice. "It happened eighteen months ago, and I still can't really accept it."

"I should think not." Toby looked down at the leather in his hands, then set it carefully on the workbench, wiped his hands with a grimy rag, and turned to put his hands on her shoulders. Their weight was comforting, like a warm blanket around her. It seemed like the most natural thing in the world to take one step forward and let his arms envelop her. In spite of his age, his arms were hard with muscle, like tough tree roots, and she felt entwined in them, as if an oak tree were embracing her. Grace let her cheek rest against his hard chest and closed her eyes. For a moment, she was afraid she would weep, but no tears came. She stood still, listening to the steady thump of his heart and feeling his hand rubbing her shoulder blades.

"It feels like I'm holding glass," Toby murmured as if to himself, "but you must be made of iron underneath. I'm so sorry. You poor little girl."

"I'm okay," Grace said. She didn't want to move out of the comfort of his gentle embrace, but after awhile, she straightened and stepped back to look up at him. "I mean, I'm not okay at the moment, but I will be. It's going to take awhile, but I know I will be one day."

He nodded. "That's a start, then."

"I believe I'll be with them again someday. That there's a life after this one, and they're all right, even if I can't be with them right now. At least they're all together, and my husband is there to watch over them." She stopped, her throat threatening to close over.

He thought about this, then said slowly, "I believe the same thing. But it doesn't entirely take away the grief of the day to day, does it? Even knowing what you know, you still have to get up and face each day without them."

"You're right," Grace said. "It makes it easier to bear, I guess, knowing the separation is temporary. But no, it doesn't make the grief go away."

"But where there's hope, healing will follow. Remember that."

"Yes. I know."

He nodded and turned back to his work. Grace leaned on her elbows beside him, watching. After a moment, Toby said quietly, "What made you tell me today?"

"It was something someone said in church this morning," Grace said. "A woman was teaching our lesson, and she was talking about how excited she is at the thought of someday returning to God when she dies. She said she looked forward to being able to run up to Heavenly Father and give Him a big hug and tell Him all about her adventures."

Toby gave a low chuckle. "Like Lark rushing home from school with a crayon drawing, shouting 'Looky what I did!'"

"Exactly. The whole image didn't sit well with me." Grace hesitated, not sure how to phrase what she was feeling. "I guess it would be a great thing to be able to rush up to God like that with full confidence that you'll get a warm welcome. But somehow, I can't see me doing it. And I should be able to, shouldn't I? I should be eager to see Him."

Toby let out a long breath and reached for the awl to bore a hole through the new strap. "Maybe, but I don't see us rushing up to God like schoolchildren either. I think we'll come to Him limping, battered, and bruised, maybe even crawling, and we'll have clutched protectively in our hearts the one or two simple truths we've managed to glean from this whole life's experience. We'll have only that to kneel and offer Him." Toby looked at Grace, and the tender look on his face was something she had never seen before. "And then I think God will come running to us."

This image made Grace catch her breath. "Yes," she said, nodding.

"He'll reach down, pick us up, dust us off, and tend to our wounds. We'll maybe both of us have a cry. And we'll be comforted and healed."

Grace couldn't swallow away the tightness in her throat this time. "Yes," she whispered. "That's more like what I imagine." She put her hand out to cover his own. "You understand, Toby, in a way no one else ever has."

He looked down at their two hands, a soft smile on his mouth. "I haven't gone through the same war you have, Grace, but I suppose I've gone through my own."

"Is there anything I can do?" she asked.

He looked at her in the lamplight for a moment before he spoke.

"You're doing it. You're being kind to a lonely old man." He gave a low chuckle and tossed aside the harness. "Let's go see about that supper."

"Toby—"

"Yes?"

"I haven't told Laura or Martin. I'd rather not have *that* be the thing they think of first when they look at me . . . you know?"

"Don't blab. I get it."

"I mean, I suppose it's not a big deal if you tell them, but—"

He put his arm around her shoulders. "I said I get it. Let's go eat."

As they left the barn, a phrase from the poem on her mirror came to Grace's mind again, and she let it turn over and over in her thoughts as they walked to Toby's house. *At the crossroads . . . she took her first steps.*

The Whelans returned home late that night, Martin carrying a sleepy Lark draped over his shoulder. But the little girl revived when she saw Grace and was eager to tell her about their adventures. They had been *bored*, she reported cheerfully, while their grandparents had sat and talked for *hours* with their friends, but the friends had had an English setter that had had puppies, and that was all right. Lark went into raptures describing how cute the puppies had been. And there had been a rope swing to play on in the backyard and a real campfire to sit around while the older people were talking. And she got to sleep in a sleeping bag on the attic floor and could see the moon through her window.

Smiling and nodding, Grace let her rattle on for a while,and then turned to Declan. He was hovering near her elbow, looking as if he wanted to speak but overwhelmed by his sister's sudden talkativeness. As soon as he was given an opening, he jumped in, his face alight in a way Grace hadn't seen before. "We had pulled pork for supper last night, on buns, with barbecue sauce, and I made the tossed salad all by myself. Grandma let me use the knife when she saw how good I was at it."

"It was the best salad I ever had," Laura said, nodding. Over the children's heads, she and Grace smiled at each other.

"That's terrific!" Grace cheered. "Maybe you'll be a famous chef one day."

"I could have made them that carbon stuff, you know, that pasta, but I couldn't remember all the stuff you put in it," Declan went on.

"We'll make it again, and this time you'll do all of it so your hands will remember," Grace told him.

"Can we do it tomorrow?"

"Yes," Laura said. "We'll have that for supper. That will be good because I missed it the last time Grace made it."

"Do you know how to make breadsticks?" Declan asked, his eyes earnest. "It would be really good with breadsticks. They're my favorite."

"Chewy ones or crispy ones?"

"Chewy."

"Yes, I know how, and I'll show you tomorrow," Grace assured him.

"Now bed, both of you," Laura instructed. "You have school tomorrow. We'll unpack your overnight bags in the morning. Run up and get ready."

Lark kissed her grandparents and went up the stairs. Declan hugged Laura and Martin and then, on an impulse, came over and hugged Grace as well. She found herself hugging him back, no flinching, no hesitation.

"Good night," he told her and followed his sister up the stairs.

Grace looked up, smiling, to see Laura and Martin staring at her.

"Well," Martin said in surprise. "He's really warmed up to you."

"Lark too," Grace said. "She's not shy at all anymore."

"No, I mean he's a different child around you."

Grace shrugged. "I don't know. Maybe this cooking thing has just sparked his interest."

"Whatever it is," Laura mused, "keep it up. I haven't seen him this cheerful for a long time."

Mason came the following Saturday and whisked the children away to visit friends in Woodstock. He came and went while Grace was out in the greenhouse, so she didn't see him, and the place felt quiet and empty without Lark and Declan underfoot. She had grown used to them and missed them when they were gone.

That afternoon, Laura went off to do a spinning demonstration, and Martin went out to the fields, leaving Grace shelling peas at the table. She was still at it when Mason and the children returned home, clattering into the house in a whirlwind of noise and discarded shoes. Declan snuck a handful of raw peas and went off to watch television, but Lark contentedly plopped herself into a chair beside Grace and proceeded to tell her all about their day with their friends and what sounded like a menagerie of assorted pets.

Mason washed at the sink and then sat at the table too, idly reaching for a handful of pea pods. He snapped them open and swept the peas into the bowl with his thumb in one practiced movement, and when at last Lark paused for breath, Grace inserted, "You've done this before."

"I have indeed. And so have you, Lark, so get helping."

Lark jumped up from her chair. "I have to tell Granddad about Jenny's new bunny." She ran outside, slamming the screen door behind her.

Mason shook his head. "Anything to wiggle out of work." He sighed. He reached for another handful of pods. For someone with such large hands, he did the delicate work quite deftly.

"So today was a success, from the sound of it," she said.

"Yes. Except the Laytons, the people we visited, seem to collect animals the way other people collect stamps. You can hardly move for fear of sitting on a cat or stepping on a guinea pig. And the dog hair! Mom could roll it up and spin with it, there was so much of it around the place."

Grace laughed. "I'll keep it in mind in case Toby's sheep ever go bald."

"The Laytons are great people though. We knew them before they left Toronto. They have four kids. Lark and Declan loved it. What kid wouldn't? It was bedlam. Though they begged for a pet of their own all the way home."

Grace blinked. "They have chickens. And Toby's sheep. And there are barn cats; I've seen them."

"It's not the same as having a Labrador."

"No, that's true."

Mason finished the last of the peas and swept the empty pods into their bowl. Brushing his hands together, he glanced around the kitchen. "What's next?"

"That's it. My tasks for the day are done."

"What, you mean you actually get a break?" Mason's smile flashed in his beard. "Don't say it too loud, or Dad will be in here asking you to dig a new well or fence the back forty or something."

Grace went to put the bowl of freshly shelled peas in the fridge. "He's not that much of a task master, really. I mean, yes, he asks me to do a lot, but he's out there doing it right along with me."

"True. He wouldn't ask a person to do anything he wouldn't. But he can be a workhorse. Trust me; I know. Don't let him wear you out."

She tipped her head to one side, considering this. It felt *good* to be worked hard. It was nice to tumble with numb exhaustion into bed at night, too tired to think or even to dream and knowing you'd spent the day doing something useful and important. She wasn't sure how to explain this to Mason, though, so she just nodded.

Saturday evening, the Whelans were invited out to dinner with friends, so Grace was on her own again. She couldn't find Toby anywhere, and the idea of cooking just for herself didn't appeal to her. Instead, she took a book and drove into town, intending to grab a Subway sandwich and sit and read in the park until the light faded. She had just settled on an iron bench under a blossoming maple tree and was fishing her turkey sandwich out of the paper bag when a voice called, "Hello again!"

She looked up and saw the tall schoolteacher she had seen swimming through his students at the museum. He had paused on the sidewalk in front of her, his hands in his jacket pockets. His face was as interesting as she remembered.

When she smiled in recognition, his cautious expression cleared. "You remember me," he said.

"I do. Grade-ten history, isn't it?"

"It is." He nodded at her book. "Lindbergh? I remember my mother reading that. I never have."

"You should. I reread *Gifts from the Sea* about once a year. I find it soothing. And somehow it always seems best to read it outdoors."

"I won't interrupt you, then. Just wanted to say hi."

Grace opened her mouth to say . . . she wasn't sure what. *I don't mind your interrupting. Join me. Talk. Share my bench. Share my sandwich.* But he had already turned and was continuing down the walk, rounding the corner, and the opportunity was gone.

Somehow she couldn't quite concentrate on her book after that.

* * *

As April turned into May, the days fell into a comfortable rhythm. Grace spent most of her time in the greenhouse or out in the fields with Martin, learning from him and helping however she could. In his soft Irish voice, he told her how to transplant the seedlings, and it was how she had anticipated, crawling along on her hands and knees, transferring the delicate plants from the trays to the earth, until her knees and back screamed in agony. She dragged herself along, thinking fiercely that authenticity was only good for so much and surely there had to be an automated way to do this . . . But then she only had to straighten, her hands on her hips, and look around at the great distance she had come, the tidy rows of baby plants as neat as quarter notes on a staff, the sun shining down on the work of her hands, to feel completely at peace again, pain and creaking bones forgotten.

Her hands began to toughen and her skin to tan. Her fingernails gained a permanent brown outline, and she discovered newly sculpted muscles developing in her arms. She remained as slim as ever, but now there was a toned hardness to her body that hadn't been there before. She slowly grew used to being watched by the museum patrons who shuffled by, gawking at her as if she were some sort of being from another planet. There were times when she was trudging through the fields, tamping down grass-clipping mulch between the rows of vegetables, that she felt she *had* come from another planet. What was she doing here? How had it come to this? And yet, why had it taken her so long to come? She knew deep down that it was what she had needed, what her weary soul had craved. As she stooped and touched and dug, as she hauled and plucked and nourished, she could feel the warmth of the sun, the healing strength of the earth itself seeping into her heart, nourishing her very bones. Once or twice she even caught herself softly humming.

Grace still spent time with Laura in the wool room perfecting her spinning and forming skeins of thick, warm yarn. She never dressed up in nineteenth-century costume and helped with Laura's demonstrations, but she did come to observe sometimes, and she helped by processing the Internet orders Laura received on her website. Sometimes she carried the basket of heavy skeins down to the gift shop at the visitors' center for Michelle Dalby, the curator's wife, to sell. The other woman who helped in the gift shop, Jane Persaud, dipped candles, and Grace would linger to watch the older woman and chat, breathing in the sweet smell of beeswax. Sometimes she would stop in at the general store to see Sarah, who invariably let her choose a candy from one of the glass jars as if she were a five-year-old, and which Grace never turned down. She got to know the friendly but rather vague Rainbow Warner, who looked completely incongruous in her time-period outfit, her dangling crystal earrings, her long hair loose on her shoulders. She looked like a throwback to the sixties who had somehow become entangled in her grandmother's dressing-up box.

Grace enjoyed her pleasant visits with these friendly women as she wandered down the gravel road, content with the knowledge that there were no deadlines, no staff meetings, no contracts to work out, no commute, no performances. Her work was waiting right there, patiently, outside her own door, and she had all the time in the world.

And now she had friends to spend it with. She knew that was also part of the healing happening. Not just Laura's family and the people from the museum but Annie Fisher and Margaret Hanmer too. She saw them frequently, sometimes just bumping into them accidentally about town or sometimes arranging to meet them for lunch or a walk along the shore of

Lake Erie. She had always had plenty of acquaintances in her life, fellow music instructors and women at church, but she hadn't really felt the need for deep friendships before. She had always been so busy and preoccupied and independent. She hadn't thought of herself as isolated before, but now she realized she had been without the real companionship of women friends. She could feel her heart thawing and warming under their affection, and she knew it was something she had long been in need of. She looked forward to time spent with them. She didn't let herself think about the end of the summer, but she also didn't let herself hold back just because their time together was limited. She only let herself—tentatively but steadily—love and be loved.

She also found she was changing in other ways. In her former life, she had been wrapped up in her music and teaching. Now she was surprised to find she was developing a real love of working with her hands, especially with the spinning, despite her rocky start. There was something very satisfying about turning the bulky, disorganized fibers into something useful and pretty. It was another miracle, she mused—the earth, or in this case, Toby's sheep spontaneously producing whatever a person needed. The lanolin in the wool helped keep her overworked hands from turning to leather, and gradually her yarn began to look more like Laura's until finally they couldn't tell whose was whose.

Evenings, when the work was done for the day and the museum was closed, the family played games or watched DVDs, and Grace was included among them as if she belonged there . . . as if she had always belonged there. She found she was able to relax and immerse herself in the moment, play with the children, bake and eat—admittedly more eating than baking—and just soak up the feeling of friendly contentment that surrounded her.

* * *

Martin tried not to look obvious about it, but he was watching Grace's unfolding with interest. It was like watching a flower slowly bloom. The pinched look was gone from her face, her skin was a healthier color, she had gained some muscle, and that haunted look around her eyes was nearly gone. He rarely saw it now, that pause, that gazing off into the distance when she thought no one was observing. He didn't know what had brought her to them, but he suspected it was something to do with that fragility that now showed itself only infrequently. He didn't discuss his observations with his wife and didn't know if she had noticed the changes in their guest. He didn't know what was making Grace thrive—the good, wholesome food they ate, the hard physical work, having something useful to contribute, or just simply being surrounded by people who loved her. Because they did love her now, especially the children, and Laura seemed happier with another woman around. Martin tried not to look too far ahead to when Grace would leave them. His initial doubts about her ability to be useful had dispersed quickly, and he wasn't enthusiastic about the idea of her going. Much as he hated to admit it, he was feeling his age lately, and it was nice to have the extra set of hands around to help. And though she'd never admit it, he suspected Laura felt the same way.

* * *

Grace couldn't help but notice during Mason's visits that even while he was laughing with Lark or kidding with his mother in the kitchen, he held himself back from fully entering into the life of the family or the farm. There was always the knowledge that he would be leaving again Sunday evening, and though Grace couldn't put her finger on it, it was as if something kept him always just a little apart from the rest of the group. It wasn't just his size that made him stand out. His laughter seemed genuine enough. But there was something in him holding him back, a sort of shield or layer holding the affection of his family at bay. A discordant note in the family harmony. And a bit of it seemed to have rubbed off on Declan.

It saddened Grace whenever she noticed it. She thought Laura was probably aware of it too, though she never mentioned it, and Grace did not feel it her place to bring it up. But she began to include Mason in her nightly prayers because she sensed that he, like her, was in need of healing. She thought that perhaps if Mason could find some peace, then possibly Declan might too.

CHAPTER ELEVEN

ONE FRIDAY AFTERNOON, GRACE WAS carrying a trash bag out to the bin when she saw Margaret's little Nissan pull up the drive. She closed the bin lid and walked down the lane to meet her. Margaret rolled down her window and gave a cheery wave.

"Good to see you! What brings you all the way out here?" Grace asked.

"I ran out of that nice dark wool I'm making a shawl out of," Margaret told her, parking and opening her door. "I thought I'd drop by to see if there's any more of it around. I just need one more skein to finish."

"I'm sure Laura has some, but I can't guarantee it will be the same color you're already using," Grace said.

Margaret waved her hand airily. "I'm sure whatever she has will be fine. It's just a shawl for myself, and I don't mind a bit of variety." Grace saw Margaret's eyes look nonchalantly around the yard. "You know, my father raised sheep, and I surely would like to see the sheep this great yarn comes off of. Do you think maybe I could see them sometime?"

Grace hid her smile. "I'm sure Toby wouldn't mind giving you a personal tour."

"Toby? Oh yes, your tall friend . . ." Margaret said casually. "Is he the one who raises the sheep?"

"You know he is, and if you wanted to see him again, all you had to do was say so," Grace said, trying unsuccessfully not to laugh.

"That's not my motivation at all," Margaret protested. "I just like sheep, that's all. My father raised merinos."

"I'm sure he did." Grace linked arms with her friend and walked toward Toby's place. "Let's go see if he's in."

Margaret hung back a little. "Am I that obvious? Will he mind awfully?"

"Not at all. He'll enjoy seeing you again," Grace said.

"Will he even remember me?"

"For certain. I'm sorry, I should have thought to arrange another meeting sooner."

"Well, if you don't think he'll mind . . ."

"I bet if we linger long enough over the sheep, we might be able to finagle a supper invitation from him too. He's a pretty good cook, you know."

"Is he?" Margaret looked pleased.

"And if you like, I can conveniently remember I'm supposed to be somewhere else, so you can have him to yourself . . ."

Margaret gave Grace a hard tap on the arm. "Don't you dare. He'll see right through it. Besides, we need you as a chaperone."

Grace snickered, and Margaret sniffed.

"Do you think that's ridiculous? Just because we're over eighty . . ."

"No, no!" Grace said hastily, anxious not to offend even while she choked on her laughter. "I'll be very happy to act as chaperone."

Margaret patted her hair into place as Grace raised her hand to knock on Toby's door.

"Just remember," she hissed in a stage whisper. "We're here to see the sheep!"

"Of course," Grace said demurely. "That's the only reason you came. And that's why you're wearing your best dress and leather pumps. So you can traipse around the sheep pasture."

Footsteps sounded within, and she smiled up into Toby's delighted face as he swung the door wide.

* * *

Saturday morning, Laura came out to the greenhouse to let Grace know she had a phone call. Grace followed her back to the house. Who would be trying to reach her? Unexpected calls always slightly unnerved her; it was an automatic reaction. She took the receiver and said a cautious hello.

"Grace? It's Annie Fisher."

"Annie!" Grace felt her face split into a smile, and she nodded to Laura, who was hovering nearby, to let her know all was well. Laura nodded back and went off about her business. Grace leaned against the wall. "How did you get this number?"

"It took some detective work, let me tell you. But fortunately I excel at that. Why don't you have your cell phone on?"

"Sorry, I must have forgotten it back in my room. I was out in the greenhouse."

"I hope I'm not interrupting your work," Annie said. "I debated about when to call. Too late and you'd already be at work, and too early and you'd be asleep."

"I don't sleep much," Grace replied cheerfully. "And anytime is a good time to hear from a friend."

"I always thought that was a cruel part of life," Annie remarked. "By the time your kids are sleeping through the night and your teenagers can drive themselves places and life is slowing down its pace and you finally have time to sleep, menopause hits and you're wide awake at three in the morning. What kind of sadistic joke is that? God has to be male because no woman would have thought that up. But *that* isn't what I called to discuss!"

"Okay. What's up?"

"Victoria Day."

"Yes?"

"We always throw a big shindig at our house in honor of Queen Victoria. We have a potluck dinner and then go down to the beach to watch the fire department shoot fireworks off over the lake. It's this Monday. Want to come?"

Grace grinned. She'd forgotten about Victoria Day. How could she have forgotten? She'd loved the holiday as a child—family picnics, sparklers on the lawn, and the delicious feeling of waking up Monday morning and knowing school was canceled.

"I'd love to come. What time?"

"Six o'clock dinner, and you don't need to bring anything; you're our guest."

"Of course I'll bring something. Laura will let me use her kitchen. What shall I cook?"

"Whatever you like, then. Newton is doing up burgers and polish sausages on the barbecue, and I know Patty Henderson is bringing meatballs, so the carnivores are covered."

"How about a fruit salad and cookies of some sort?"

"Perfect." Annie gave her the directions to the Fisher house, and Grace jotted them on a paper plate sitting conveniently on the counter.

"Thank you for inviting me," Grace told her before hanging up. She folded the paper plate into her back pocket and went back out to the greenhouse where Martin was waiting. She felt ridiculously excited about the potluck. And the idea of fireworks over the lake made her feel like a five-year-old.

Monday the museum was closed for the holiday, and Laura and Martin were taking the children to Toronto to visit Mason for a rare day in the city. Declan had plans to meet up with an old school friend, and Lark was squirrelly with excitement over their plans to visit the Ripley Aquarium, which was having a Victoria Day special opening. Grace waved them all off on their journey and then spent a couple of hours in the kitchen getting the salad and the oatmeal-pecan cookies ready for that evening. The cookies turned out smelling heavenly, and on a whim, she put some on a plate and carried them to Toby's house.

When he opened the door, he threw his arms wide and proclaimed, "A lovely young woman bearing food! What more could an old man ask for?"

"I'm hoping you aren't allergic to nuts," Grace said, giving him the plate.

"If I were, I would have broken into hives living in this madhouse long ago," he replied, and popped an entire cookie into his mouth. "Marvelous! Come in and join me. I'll get some milk for these cookies."

"Oh, I'm not eating them with you. They're for you," Grace said, but he swept her in anyway and closed the door. Setting the cookies on the kitchen table, he busied himself setting out two glasses and a pitcher of milk, and Grace took the opportunity to look around his cabin.

She had never been beyond the entryway before, and now she couldn't help her curiosity as she examined the snug kitchen and adjoining living room. She felt as if she had stepped into a movie set. The image of a nineteenth-century log cabin didn't stop at the door. From the iron stove to the patchwork quilt thrown over the wooden bedframe beside it, the cabin looked as if it were unchanged from the time it was built. Instead of kitchen cupboards, Toby had wooden shelves. His dishes were ceramic crockery, and large glass canisters in a neat row on his wooden counter held flour, beans, and brown sugar. The floor was of wide pine planking, and a willow-twig broom stood against the smoke-darkened stone fireplace, where an old-fashioned iron spit big enough to hold a whole pig stood over recent ashes. Even the glass in his windows was wavy with age.

Grace turned to see Toby standing beside the table, watching her.

"You're thinking to yourself 'He's in his natural habitat,' aren't you? You probably think I built this place myself as a young man."

Grace laughed. "It's got to be two hundred years old."

"Just over. Built in 1810. And no, I'm not the original occupant."

"I didn't think you were. But it does suit you somehow. It *is* your natural element."

They sat at the table and munched their cookies and milk, chatting about anything that came to mind, from the research conducted at Ripley's Aquarium to the cost of pecans.

Grace also told him about the potluck supper at the Fishers'. "I'm sure they'd be delighted if you came too," Grace told him. "Why don't you come with me?"

"I don't want to impose."

"Believe me, the Fishers aren't the sort of people you can 'impose' on. Their philosophy is the more the merrier. They have eight children."

"Sounds crowded."

"And then we're going to the beach to watch fireworks when it's dark. Say you'll come." Grace added, "Margaret might be there."

He slid his gaze toward her. "Was she invited too?"

"I don't know, but I would think so. The Fishers are friends with everyone. They probably invited the whole church."

"So I'd be surrounded by a bunch of Mormons?"

"And good food and fireworks. You can't say no to Firecracker Day."

"I'll think about it."

"Shall I call Margaret and ask if she'll be there?" Grace asked innocently.

"Hmmph," he replied and pushed another entire cookie into his mouth.

Margaret herself was the one who opened the door to them at the Fisher home that evening. She was wearing a woolly baby-blue sweater and jeans with sneakers, which made her look ten years younger. She gave them each a vigorous hug, having to stand on tiptoe to hug Toby. Grace was a little surprised to see Toby respond with a hug back that nearly lifted Margaret from her feet. A little breathless, the older woman brushed her hair out of her eyes and pointed toward a path leading around the side of the house.

"I'm just on door duty to let everyone know to go around to the backyard," she said. "The potluck is on the back patio. I'll come myself in a few minutes, as soon as I find something to make a sign with to put on the door."

"We'll see you there, then," Toby told her.

They proceeded to the backyard, where they found about fifty people milling around the expansive patio. Billows of gray smoke rose from two silver barbecues, and trestle tables held an array of covered dishes and Saran-Wrapped plates. A third of the gathering appeared to be under the age of twelve, with hordes of children running around the lawn with sparklers even though the sun was still high over the horizon. Buckets of water stood at the end of the lawn, already sprouting with spent sparklers.

The Fishers' big white house and massive yard suited a family with so many children. A trampoline stood in one corner, a volleyball net stretched between two poles, a cavalcade of Tonka trucks crawled through a sandbox the size of a small desert, and a bocce ball game on the grass entertained a group of teenagers.

Annie Fisher extracted herself from the crowd to greet them. She wore a red blouse with white jeans and had an unlit sparkler stuck behind one ear like a flower. Grace wondered if she was going to light it later.

"I'm so glad you came!" Annie said, arms outstretched. "Welcome to the Fisher house. This has to be Toby. Margaret's told me all about you."

"She has?" Toby looked pleased.

"I hope it's okay I brought him without ask—"

"Of course! I'm happy to meet you at last, Toby. You can put the cookies on the table there. My, they smell wonderful, don't they? And the fruit looks lovely. Jane, set this somewhere, would you? There might be room on that table there." Annie whisked the bowl away from Grace and handed it to a young girl at her elbow. The girl dutifully trotted away with it.

"Have you met Newton yet? You need to meet my husband, Toby. He's a great history buff and would love to talk to you." Annie glanced around. "I invited a friend of mine I want you to meet, Grace. His name is Angus. But I don't see him here yet. I always get nervous when he's late for something . . ." She wandered away, looking distracted, and left Grace to locate Newton Fisher and introduce herself and Toby.

Manning the barbecues, Newton was a tall, distinguished-looking man who, Grace had learned at church, was a psychiatrist and one-time university professor.

Newton shifted the barbecue tongs to his left hand and shook hands with both of them. "Excellent! Glad you could make it. Make yourselves at home. Grab a plate. Where has Annie gotten to?"

"She went wandering off looking for someone named Angus," Grace told him. "It seems he hasn't arrived yet, and she looked a bit worried about it."

"Ah. Yes. Um."

"Is something wrong?"

"Well, no. It's just that Angus got himself kidnapped last year and—"

"Kidnapped!"

"Twice, in fact. Oh, it all ended well. But since then we tend to be a bit jumpy when he can't be easily located."

"My goodness!"

"I should go double-check. Do you mind awfully?" Newton said, and handing the tongs to a startled Toby, he strode away into the crowd.

Bemused, Toby took over the barbecuing.

"Are you okay with that? Do you know how to . . . Oh. Stupid question, I suppose," Grace said, catching herself. "You're a blacksmith. You're used to open fires and all that."

"I think I can manage," Toby replied wryly. "A bit eccentric, these friends of yours, aren't they?"

Grace looked at Toby standing there with tongs upheld, white hair wild about his ears, his brown trousers, high leather boots, vest, and long-sleeved peasant shirt straight out of the Victorian era, and struggled hard not to giggle.

"A bit, yes," she conceded. "Most of my friends seem to be."

CHAPTER TWELVE

THE EVENING WAS A PERFECT success. Filled with good food and warmed by exuberant friendship, the entire crowd headed down to the beach as darkness fell, guided by LED flashlights—Grace hadn't thought to bring one, but Annie loaned her and Toby one of several spares. The moon was half full, and the silver light on the lake was entrancing. Grace linked elbows with Caleb Fisher on one side and Margaret on the other—Toby being on Margaret's other side—and watched the blossom and sparkle of the noisy fireworks with a deep sense of contentment. It seemed as if most of the town of Port Dover had turned out for the event, filling the beach, the splash of LED lights like fireflies here and there, illuminating the hundreds of upturned faces. Listening to their appreciative murmurs and "oooohs" was almost as entertaining as the light show.

Grace spied Sarah Carson-Flake in the crowd, holding hands with a nice-looking older gentleman who had to be her husband, and waved a cheery hello. Sarah saw her and waved back, then turned her attention back to the brilliant sky. Grace listened to the thunder of the fireworks roll out over Lake Erie, and she couldn't remember being this at peace in years.

There was only one awkward moment the whole evening. After the last, best firework, which looked like a great white dahlia, signaled the finale, a brass band positioned in the middle of the beach launched into "God Save the Queen," and the crowd began to sing together. Grace stiffened, still linked by the elbow to Caleb and Margaret, and her throat constricted in a wave of sorrow. Standing on this chilly beach with her friends, Grace realized she had been hoping somewhere hidden deep in her heart that the progress she had made over the past few weeks would unstop her voice. She *wanted* her ability back, to be able to sing with her heart really in it. She didn't want to grieve anymore. She missed music. But the sorrow was still there, a tight little ball at the base of her throat, and she knew if she tried to really sing, her voice would fail her.

Caleb shot her a curious look, and Grace summoned an apologetic grin.

"American. Don't know the words," she mumbled, lying, and he nodded in understanding.

* * *

At the end of May, the CSA enterprise kicked in. Martin pulled four hundred blue plastic bins out of one of the sheds, and they spent half a day scrubbing them clean. Each was just smaller than a laundry basket, and there were numbers written in black permanent marker on their sides.

"There are two bins for each CSA customer. Each person has an identifying number," Martin explained. He rubbed his hands together with relish. "I love this part of farming, when I get to start sharing the bounty with others."

Grace laughed, feeling his infectious good cheer spring up within her but also feeling a bit daunted by the towers of bins. "This looks like a big enterprise," she said.

"Laura keeps track of it all on the computer. For the most part, each person gets the same thing, and it's pretty straightforward, but we have a few customers who have special instructions we have to be mindful of. For example, a couple of them are allergic to peppers, and one has a strict aversion to garlic. Personally, I think that one's a vampire. How else could someone live without garlic?" He chuckled. "We fill the baskets Friday mornings. The customers come drop off their empty boxes and pick up their filled ones by six o'clock. If someone doesn't show, we know who by the number."

"It sounds like a slick operation," Grace said. "And for the most part, they don't know what they're getting each week?"

"Whatever's in season. If it's something unusual, like an Asian green or a special kind of squash no one has seen before, Laura will include a recipe. And I like to toss in a little something to pretty it up when I can—a bunch of tulips in the spring, some lavender in the summer, a handful of daylilies in the fall."

"That's a nice touch. What happens if someone doesn't pick theirs up?"

"I'll phone them to remind them. But they sign an agreement that if they don't pick it up by Saturday at noon at the latest, it goes to the food bank. You can't let fresh vegetables sit long, and it's a crime to let them go to waste."

"That's reasonable," Grace said. "This whole idea sounds fun. I'm happy to help."

"Yes, well, you tell me if it's still fun after you've loaded up the two hundredth bin," Martin said with a wink.

Grace got her first taste of how it all worked the following Friday. She was up at dawn with Martin to harvest and wash the produce ready for the bins. Laura helped too, wearing faded blue jeans and rubber boots, her unruly hair tied back in a bandana. It being early in the season, each CSA bin received a paper sack of snow peas, a pound of regular peas still in the pod, a head of lettuce, a bunch of mustard greens and arugula, a pint of strawberries, radishes, young broccoli, a bouquet of garlic chives, some green onions, three thick stalks of ruby-red rhubarb, and a bundle of asparagus. Laura added a recipe card to each bin for strawberry-rhubarb pie.

To Grace, this was a wealth of food, well worth the amount of money each customer paid. They would have spent far more in the grocery store for the same amount of produce, and it wouldn't have been as fresh and lovely as what they got from the farm. It was fiddly washing the greens, but as they walked down the aisles of bins, filling each to overflowing, Grace felt a surge of happiness—and, yes, pride—imagining how pleased the customers would be.

"I don't even know how to describe what I'm feeling," she confessed to Martin as they made their way back to the house. She walked with her head thrown back, gazing up at the treetops and the crystal sky, her hands shoved into her jeans pockets. "What's the word for it?"

Martin gave her a quiet smile. "Abundance," he suggested. "Seeing all the work starting to pay off."

"Yes. And I think it's . . . gratitude," Grace decided. "All this is provided for us; the earth will give us whatever we need. All we have to do is get our hands a little dirty."

Martin glanced at her, and from his expression, Grace knew what he was seeing. There was mud caking her shoes and streaks of dirt on her jeans, embedded in her skin, and she knew it was probably smeared across her forehead where she'd swiped at a stray wisp of hair with her wrist. There was a wilted strand of chive snagged in her hair, and crushed strawberries stained her knees. "A little dirty," he agreed and laughed.

* * *

One evening, Lark sang them all a song she had learned in school that day, her voice high and pretty but admittedly a bit off-key as she belted out the French rhyme. Everyone clapped for her, and then in the pause that followed, Toby let drop offhandedly, "You know, Grace used to be the director of a music school."

They were sitting in the living room after supper, Grace with a lap full of peas she was shelling into a bowl for tomorrow's meals. She felt her ears heat up as everyone turned to look at her as if Toby had just announced she was some exotic new tropical bird.

"I didn't know that," Laura exclaimed, her hands growing still over her own pea-pod bowl. "How interesting! What instruments do you play?"

"Well, actually . . ." Grace had to swallow to get her saliva working again. "I was an opera singer. I trained singers." She tried to direct the attention away from herself by adding brightly, "You sing very nicely, Lark. You carry a tune well."

"No, she doesn't," Declan remarked. "She goes squeaky on the high notes."

"That's because she's still very little," Grace told him. "She'll have a great voice when she's older. And the important thing is that she loves singing. That's really all that matters."

"You sing a song for us, Grace," Declan prodded, coming to sit beside her on the couch.

Grace's breath caught. "I—I don't sing anymore," she stammered. "I haven't in a long time."

"Why not?" Lark asked. "Don't you love to sing too?"

"Well, yes, I do. I did . . ."

"Then why don't you sing?"

Grace cast an agonized look at Toby, who was reading a book in the chair by the woodstove. He looked at her over the edge of his thick reading glasses. "Laura, do you have any more of those brownies?" he asked abruptly. "I could use another one with a big glass of milk."

"You've already had two," Laura chided, but she was smiling as she put aside her work and went to fetch a plate.

"I want another one too!" Declan shouted, and mercifully, the general stampede toward the kitchen shattered the conversation.

Grace looked at Toby. "Thanks," she whispered.

He couldn't have heard her from across the room, but he nodded and winked and went back to his book.

* * *

One morning, while the horses were out in the paddock lazily grazing, Grace helped Martin muck out the stalls and put down fresh sawdust. She didn't mind the work, even though Declan had teased her all morning before he'd left for school about having to do it. She always liked being in the barn, with its welcoming smells and the taste of hay in the air.

"I'm going to hitch the horses to the wagon and go fetch a load of grain from the feed store," Martin said, setting aside his rake. "Want to come?"

"Why don't you just take the pickup?" Grace asked.

"It's more fun to drive the wagon," he said. "Besides, it doesn't hurt to take the horses through town once in a while to stir up interest in the museum among the locals. They forget we're here sometimes, and everyone likes to see the draft horses."

Grace wasn't sure about the idea of driving the huge team down a city street, and she suspected she would be given the task of following behind with a shovel and bucket, but she agreed good-naturedly. Martin went out to the paddock, caught the two mares, and led them out to where the buckboard wagon waited in the drive shed. It wasn't one of the fancy ones you'd see at a country fair, all painted and shiny and showy. It was a working wagon built of unvarnished wood now gone gray and splintery, the wheels caked with dirt, and bits of straw clung to the corners of the bed.

"It's not elegant, but it's serviceable," Martin said. And then he stopped short, blinking in surprise. "I forgot to harness them first. Well, no matter. Here, you hold them while I run back to the barn and fetch the harness."

And before Grace knew it, she was standing holding their two lead ropes while Martin disappeared around to the front of the barn. Her first thought was to yell, drop the ropes, and run. But, of course, she didn't. She stood stiffly, not moving an inch, staring at their great shaggy feet the size of dinner plates and waiting for them to rear up and crush her. And, of course, they didn't. They ignored her, standing patiently with their warm breath slowly blowing in and out.

Martin came back, waddling under the weight of the pile of leather and metal he carried. Grace watched without sympathy as he approached.

When he was within earshot, she said dryly, trying to keep the tremor out of her voice, "That was pretty obvious of you."

Martin grinned and laid the harness out on the grass to sort it. He laid the Irish accent on thick as he replied, "But they didn't kill you, did they?"

"No. Not yet, anyway."

"Then my work here is done." He straightened and grinned at her. "They really are just gentle giants, you know."

"*Giant* being the operative word," Grace replied.

"It's time you learned to harness a horse."

"No."

He shook his head. "You're the most stubborn employee I've ever had."

"Harnessing a horse is not a skill I will need in the future."

"You never know."

"I know," Grace said firmly.

Martin stepped closer, his voice dropping to a gentle murmur. "Learning to trust *is* a skill you will need in the future, Grace. Just let go, and be brave. It's the next step. I won't let anything hurt you."

For a long moment, they eyed each other, and then Grace drew a breath and gave a short nod. "Show me," she said.

So he showed her, moving carefully and slowly, easing her through the steps with minimum fuss. Grace let him guide her through the maze of seemingly incomprehensible straps and buckles, and when he took her hand and placed her palm on one of the horse's necks, she let it rest there. The horse's coat was soft, and the warmth of its big body crept through her hand and up her arm. The horse turned its head and blew softly at her through its nostrils.

"You know, I've never asked what her name is," Grace said quietly, gazing into the wide brown eyes.

"That one's Death."

"What!" Grace jerked back, startled.

"And that one's Taxes. The only two things in the world you can count on."

Grace felt herself begin to chuckle. "You've got to be kidding."

"Blame Toby. He's the one who named them."

Grace rubbed her hand gently over the mare's wide nose. "I dread thinking what he named his sheep."

* * *

It was a weird experience, riding in the old wagon through the wide, tree-lined streets of Port Dover. It felt almost wrong to see modern, glassy storefronts and cars lining the road. Somehow it wouldn't have surprised Grace to see old wooden boardwalks, hitching posts, and a swinging-door saloon instead of Boston Pizza and Banana Republic. The horses' hooves made hollow clopping sounds on the blacktop, and their heads nodded in rhythm. Grace sat on the wide seat beside Martin and held the reins as he murmured quiet instructions. People looked out of store windows and came out onto the sidewalks to watch them go by. Grace fought the urge to raise her hand in a dignified wave, like Queen Elizabeth acknowledging a crowd.

"There are cars backing up in a line behind us," she told Martin as they rounded the corner in front of the police station. "Should we pull over and let them get past?"

"Naw, it's good for them to have to slow down their busy lives for a minute," Martin said. "We're doing them a service."

"I hope the police agree with you," she muttered.

He waved an airy hand. "The police are used to us."

The feed store was on the far side of town beside a gas station. Martin nodded at the gas pumps cheerfully. The sign on the pole announced that gas was $1.28 a litre. Grace did a quick calculation in her head. Over five dollars a gallon.

"Don't need to stop there. Isn't that a nice feeling?" Martin asked.

"Yes, actually, it is."

When they reached the feed store, Martin jumped down and left Grace holding the horses steady while he went inside. Grace sat feeling very tall and nervous, watching the horses' ears for any sign of jumpiness, any indication that they might turn and run off with her. But they stood placidly chewing on their bits and nosing each other and, from time to time, shifting their weight from one massive hip to another and flicking their tails with swishy sounds.

After what seemed a long time, Martin reappeared and waved to her. "Drive them around to the back loading dock," he called. And then he went back inside, leaving Grace to follow orders.

Uncertainly, she shook the reins and made the chirping sound Martin made, and to her delight, the horses obeyed her as if she were Martin. They walked ponderously around the side of the building and stopped where she told them to.

When Martin came out of the loading door, Grace gave him a triumphant smile. "I can speak and mountains are moved!" she declared.

He laughed. "It does feel like you're holding an awesome power in your hands, doesn't it?"

"Yes, it does."

He and two other men quickly loaded heavy sacks of oats, barley, and chicken feed into the back of the wagon. Martin gave the men each a friendly handshake, and then he climbed up beside Grace on the wagon seat. "Take us home," he said.

And she did, feeling very smug.

* * *

Grace brushed away an inquisitive bee and pulled up a fistful of stubborn grass. She didn't know the names of Laura's flowers, but they were a pleasant pink and white and were shaped like something a child would draw—a circle center with six loopy petals splayed around it. To her, they appeared thankful when she liberated their choked stems from the weeds. It gave her a benevolent feeling. They needed her.

Behind her, the screen door snapped closed with a bang. She looked up to see Mason crossing the lawn with two tall glasses in his hands. She sat back on her heels and squinted up at him against the sun as he approached. His lumbering bearlike size still astonished her, no matter how many times she saw him.

"I brought you some cold apple juice," he said, giving her one of the glasses. "I thought you might be hot working out here."

"Thank you. That was thoughtful," Grace said. It *was* hot. The skin on her forearms and on the back of her neck, though already deeply tanned, was beginning to tingle with the hint of imminent sunburn. She took a long drink, savoring the cold liquid in her throat.

"I thought you'd be out working with Dad somewhere," Mason added, sitting beside her on the grass and taking a swallow from his own glass. "It's the garden's height of production, isn't it?"

"He went up to the visitors' center to watch your mom's demonstration," Grace said. "He said he likes to go be supportive now and then."

"So while he's gone, you thought you'd kick back and relax and do a spot of weeding," Mason observed.

"Yes, well, I'm not good at holding still." Grace returned his smile.

Mason eyed the long stretch of flowerbed she had already weeded and the pile of greenery she had collected.

"You've been out here awhile," he remarked. "Mom will be grateful to you. She loves her flowers, but she's always saying she doesn't have time to get to them. There always seems to be something more pressing, and the serious business of vegetables trumps frivolity every time."

"I wouldn't call flowers frivolous," Grace said and took another swig of juice.

"They're nice to look at, but they don't put food on the table," he said, running his fingers through his beard.

Grace thought about this. To her mind, beauty was just as important as food. Surely the world needed both. Life was more than earning a living, after all. It had to be *worth* living. But she didn't imagine Mason would understand if she tried to explain. So instead, she shrugged and said, "They attract pollinators, like this bee here that keeps dive-bombing my glass. And you need *those* to grow vegetables."

"True," Mason conceded. He finished his juice and set his glass aside in the grass. Leaning back on both hands, he looked up at the blazing sun and deep-blue sky. "It sounds like you've been taking your gardening lessons to heart. How are you enjoying it here with my folks?"

"It's perfect. It really is. I think this is a beautiful place, and your parents are the kindest people in the world. Martin is teaching me a lot."

"And will you go home and be a farmer when the summer is over?"

She laughed. "Probably not. I'll probably go back to Salt Lake and get a dreary office job and raise nothing more than an African violet on my windowsill."

"Then why put yourself through all this if you won't use it later?" Mason asked, frowning at her.

Grace shrugged. "Because I'm using it *now*."

"What do you mean?"

Grace set her glass aside and reached for another handful of weeds. She tried to think of how to explain herself. "What I'm doing and what I'm learning serves a purpose now. It was just what I needed. Because of this summer, I'll be *able* to go back to Salt Lake and resume some sort of life." She glanced up and saw him watching her carefully, and she knew he couldn't understand because he didn't know her full story. He didn't know the progress she had made and the healing she had begun to find here in this magical place this summer. She shrugged again. "Well, and at least if I ever do need to know how to raise my own food, I'll be prepared, right? I may not need that skill, but if I ever do, I'll know how."

"I guess that's worth something," Mason agreed. "Learning any new skill gives you confidence to tackle whatever lies ahead. If nothing else, you've learned that you're capable of learning."

Grace laughed. "Yes, I am. Martin has made sure of that. And he's taught me I'm braver than I thought I was, which is always a good thing." She tossed a dandelion onto her pile and rubbed her nose with the back of her hand. "Where are Declan and Lark this morning? I thought they'd be out with you."

Mason waved a hand vaguely toward the house. "We're going into town later, but right now, it's vitally important that they finish the DVD they're watching. The planet will grind to a halt if they don't see how the movie ends."

"Ah."

"Despite the fact that they've seen it a hundred times already."

"Yes."

"We'll probably take a picnic down to the park later, and then maybe go swimming. Lark swims like a fish."

"And Declan?"

"He's a bit more cautious. He could be good at it if he'd relax and let himself enjoy it. But he's . . . kind of a tense kid. You may have noticed."

"Mmm," Grace said noncommittally. "Did your mother tell you the funny thing Declan said this morning?"

"No. What?"

"She was looking at her website, processing wool orders, and she said she was surprised by how many hits the site was getting. She didn't know where they were coming from. And Declan said, 'Don't worry, Grandma. We'll find out who it is and hit them back.'"

Mason sighed. "That's my son. Always ready for a fight."

"Always ready to defend his grandma," Grace corrected. Couldn't Mason see the love and humor in what Declan had said?

Mason pushed himself to his feet and picked up both their glasses. "Well, enjoy your weeding. Don't stay out in the sun too long. You'll burn on a day like this."

"Too late for the warning," Grace replied. "But thanks. Enjoy your picnic. And thanks for the juice and the company."

He studied her a moment with his steady blue gaze. "My pleasure," he said and went back to the house.

CHAPTER THIRTEEN

At first, Grace wasn't sure if she was dreaming or awake. There was a low droning, a sort of buzz that grew gradually in pitch, louder, louder, disturbing her sleep. Then it rose to a wrenching scream that catapulted her out of bed and across the room to the window. Heart hammering, she yanked open the curtain and peered out into gray predawn light.

There was a flash of white light and another roar, and Grace jerked back from the window. She fumbled for her shoes and robe and hurried down the stairs to the yard. Martin, Laura, and Toby were just coming out their doors, astonishment on their faces from their rude awakening. Even in her fright, Grace couldn't help noticing Martin's hair standing up on one side like a turkey's fan and Toby's skinny bare legs sticking out below his disreputable bathrobe.

"What is it?" Grace cried, hurrying to join them.

Laura gripped her arm with both hands, the two women clinging together. "I don't know. It sounds like a battle."

The group moved cautiously toward the source of the noise and lights, coming to a stop against the rail fence by the barn. Martin let out a shout of dismay, and Laura gasped. A large, black SUV was roaring in wild circles around the vegetable field. They all watched in horror as the great machine spun crazily, kicking up the earth in sprays with its tires. The headlights illuminated the ground, the barn, their frozen faces in flashing bursts as the SUV swung around.

"The vegetables!" Laura wailed.

"We've got to stop him!" Grace cried over the roar of the engine.

"He's going to hit that barn if he isn't careful," Toby added.

"Careful? Look at him!" Laura snapped. "He's destroying everything."

"What do we do?"

Martin, watching with hands on hips, shook his head. "Call the police," he said grimly, "and wait for the idiot to run out of gas."

Laura dashed back to the house. Grace gripped the top rail of the fence, tears streaming down her face. All that work. The plowing, the horses, the backbreaking transplanting of all those delicate seedlings. The beautiful abundant harvest that was just beginning. Gone. She wasn't aware she was crying until she felt Toby put an arm around her. Gently, he lifted his terry bathrobe sleeve and wiped her cheek.

"Why would someone do such a thing?" she cried.

He didn't respond, only tightened his arm about her shoulders.

Grace took a shuddering breath and nodded jerkily. "I'm all right. You don't need to—"

"Yes, I do," he replied calmly. "I ran out of the house without my cane."

She couldn't help smiling. Even during disaster, he found a way to make her feel she was doing him a favor, even as he comforted her. She leaned against him, and they watched as the SUV began to slow, gave a final spin and whine, and rocked to a stop. The engine continued to growl, though at a lower pitch now, and the headlights fixed on the jagged ruins of the ground.

When nothing more happened, Martin carefully climbed over the fence and walked toward the vehicle. Grace gripped Toby's hand. But nothing happened. Nothing moved. Martin cautiously approached the driver's door, pulled it open, and looked inside. After a moment, he reached inside and turned the key off. There was a deafening silence, soothing to Grace's bruised ears. The engine ticked, cooling. Martin walked back toward them, pocketing the key.

"Don't know who he is," he reported, "but he's asleep with his head on the steering wheel, and the interior of that truck smells like the inside of a whiskey bottle."

By the time the two police cars arrived, dawn was coming over the horizon and the birds were beginning to sing. It seemed somehow unfair to Grace that they could sing and go on with their normal morning when hers and the Whelans' had been shattered. As the sunlight grew, the devastation became apparent. The black truck sat quietly in the middle of a series of concentric rings, deep gouges in the earth, where the vehicle had spun. The neat, careful furrows were obliterated. Bits of smashed and broken plants—the Whelans' livelihood—lay scattered over the surface, unrecognizable.

One of the police officers handcuffed the unconscious driver to his steering wheel while the other three surveyed the damage with Martin.

"I suppose it could have been worse," Martin reported to Laura and the others afterward. "He confined himself to this one field. We didn't lose everything. And he came through the gap instead of taking out the fence."

"The CSA," Laura murmured. "Do we have enough left to go on with?" She was watching her husband's face closely.

"We'll manage," Martin said firmly. "The important thing is no one was hurt. Imagine if he'd come during the day when there were children visiting the grounds."

"You're right," Laura said, nodding and wiping at her tears. "It could have been much worse."

The police were on their radios, and one was going through the truck's glove compartment, looking for identification.

Toby squeezed Grace's shoulders. "Help me back to the house," he said. "We can do no good standing here."

Grace silently walked with him back to the Whelans' house and settled him in an armchair. He seemed to have aged overnight, his craggy face weary. He ran his hands through his tousled white hair and sighed, but when he looked up at Grace, there was no grief in his eyes.

"A farmer's life is never predictable," he said. "They've lost crops before, and will again, no doubt. Ice storm or SUV, there's no difference."

"All that work though," Grace mourned.

"No use thinking about it." He hit the arms of the chair lightly with his fists. "Let's get breakfast on for everyone and get the kids to school. The less Laura has to deal with, the better."

"Good idea," Grace said. "But sit here and rest, and I'll make breakfast."

"Are you saying I'm not up to it?" he asked, eyes sparking.

"No, I'm just saying you've had a rude awakening and you've been on your feet awhile. I'll handle it."

Toby pulled himself out of the chair and headed for the kitchen. "You were equally rudely awakened," he replied. "And we'll handle it together."

Declan and Lark came scampering down to breakfast with wide eyes. "There are police cars in the yard!" Declan announced. "What's going on?"

"I'm surprised you two slept through the noise," Grace told them. "Someone drove an SUV into the field by the barn and messed up the vegetables. The police are arresting him."

"Why did he do that?" Declan stopped short, staring.

"I think he had too much alcohol, and it made him do something foolish," Toby answered. "He shouldn't have been drinking and driving. You two get ready for school, and Grace will drive you into town this morning, okay?"

Lark agreed and went back upstairs, but Declan lingered in the kitchen, coming to stand beside Grace as she whipped eggs in a bowl. He said nothing, but he leaned against her just a little, and Grace put down her whisk and gave him a gentle hug. Then pulling back from him, she put her hands on his shoulders and looked into his dark eyes, reading the trouble there. Understanding.

"Everyone's okay," she told him. "No one was hurt."

"Where are Grandma and Granddad?" he asked in a small voice.

"They're outside with the police, looking at the damage. They're all right. The police are handling it."

Declan licked his lips. "When I saw the police cars' lights, I thought—"

Grace hugged him again. "Everyone is okay, Declan. I'm telling you the truth," she assured him. "Now run and get ready for school, and come back for your breakfast."

He nodded and went quickly up the stairs. Toby and Grace exchanged looks.

"I didn't realize he'd jump to the conclusion . . ." Toby murmured.

"Once you've experienced loss, you start expecting it around every corner," Grace said quietly.

* * *

The arraignment didn't happen until the next afternoon when the prisoner was sober enough to stand in front of the judge in his orange jumpsuit and look suitably subdued. Martin, wearing his only good suit, attended and was uncertain about what to expect. As soon as the judge entered the room, though, Martin relaxed. It was Norm Bayliss. Martin and Laura knew him from the curling club. A fair and soft-spoken man with several teenage children of his own.

The defendant looked a bit green around the gills and unshaven, but his longish blond hair was neatly combed. He stood with his hands clasped in front of him and didn't look at Martin. He looked more like a boy than a man, maybe twenty. He couldn't see the color of the boy's downturned eyes, but he did notice the flash of blue and red showing at his cuffs—the fellow probably had tattoos all up his arms. He looked too skinny to be a biker, too young to be a hardened criminal. Martin settled back with arms folded to hear the tale.

It was straightforward enough. The defendant spoke in a gruff voice little louder than a whisper, and what he left out, his dapper court-appointed lawyer filled in for him. The drunk driver's name was Matt Stevens. Age twenty-three, originally from London, Ontario. A previous charge of assault two years prior, and a couple of shoplifting charges. He had never driven while impaired before. He worked at a fish-and-chips shop on weekends and went to night school for his electrician's license. He recalled his girlfriend, Sylvie, had dumped him at a party on the evening in question. He recalled being angry and drinking a lot. He didn't recall stealing the SUV. He didn't recall driving it into Martin Whelan's field or what happened after that. He only remembered waking up to find himself handcuffed to the steering wheel. He regretted—here his gaze slid toward Martin and then quickly away—what he had apparently done, and he pled guilty.

Listening to the story, watching the faces of the people in the room, Martin felt a strange feeling come over him. He didn't want this sorry-looking, scruffy kid to go to jail. What would that do but derail him further from life? He wanted him to be able to finish night school. To get himself straightened out. The kid looked like he hadn't eaten well lately. He looked *unloved*. And he had just been dumped by his girlfriend on top of everything else. As the proceedings began to wrap up, Martin gathered his nerve, cleared his throat, and raised a hand to attract Norm Bayliss's attention. "Um . . . Your Honor? Can I have a word with you, please? Privately?"

Martin returned from the courthouse with a bemused look on his face. He told Laura, Toby, and Grace about it at supper as they sat poking unenthusiastically at their salads.

"He pled guilty even though he doesn't remember driving into our field or why he did it. He—er—also doesn't remember stealing the car."

"It was stolen?" Laura gaped.

"Apparently it belongs to the girlfriend's new boyfriend."

Toby gave a low whistle and shook his head. "He's dug himself into a good hole."

Martin shrugged. "He's a bit rough around the edges, and he's been in a bit of trouble before, but I think underneath all that is a good kid. Someone just needs to take a chance on him."

"What's going to happen to him?" Laura asked.

Martin gave her a sheepish look. "Norm Bayliss was the judge."

"Oh, really?"

"Well, I talked to him, aside-like."

Laura's eyes narrowed. "And what did you say to him?"

"I suggested the boy would benefit more from doing community service hours than from going to jail."

"Uh-huh." Laura's face tightened with suspicion. "And he would do these service hours . . . ?"

"I suggested he spend them helping restore what he destroyed."

Laura sat back from the table, her mouth open. Toby began to cackle.

"Absolutely not!" Laura cried, finding her voice. "I don't want him working here!"

"It's just for the rest of the summer," Martin told her. "It's a logical consequence, when you think about it. After a summer of hard labor, he certainly won't be in a hurry to do something like this again."

"Can the field be restored?" Grace asked doubtfully.

"It's late in the season, but there are things we can plant. It should be fine," Martin said. "And the more hands helping, the quicker we can replant."

"And he would come every day? I suppose I have to feed him?" Laura asked, frowning.

"Well, he's going to lose his driver's license," Martin replied. "He won't be able to drive himself from London every day."

Toby brought his hand down flat on the table. "He can bunk with me. I have a pull-out couch," he said.

Laura sighed and shook her head. "I suppose you're right," she said. "If the judge agrees, it's the most logical consequence. And goodness knows it *will* take a lot of help to get that field back into production."

Martin smiled. "That's my girl," he said.

"I don't have to like him though, do I?" she added poutily, and the rest of them laughed.

CHAPTER FOURTEEN

MATT STEVENS ARRIVED THE FOLLOWING Monday morning, driven by his self-conscious father, who only mumbled his thanks, shook Martin's hand, and zoomed off again, leaving Matt standing in front of the house with his gym bag and a suitcase. Matt watched his father's car disappear down the drive, then turned to look at the small group on the front steps.

Studying his eyes, Grace keenly recognized the embarrassment he must be feeling. It was bad enough being caught in the crime, but she imagined having to return and face—and live with—the victims was agonizing.

He was tall and thin, his elbows sharp below the sleeves of his blue T-shirt, his arms decorated with homemade-looking tattoos. Dragons and swirls, from the looks of them, in red and blue and green gave him a festive, almost Christmasy look. Two inches of his boxers showed above the waistband of his black jeans. His blond hair fell over his eyebrows, and his cheeks had the scraped red look of a fresh shave. He looked more like an abandoned little boy than a convicted vandal. He shuffled his tennis shoes, switched his gym bag to the other hand, and then, as if making a decision, raised his gaze to look Martin directly in the eye. "Put me to work," he said in a hoarse voice.

It was, to Grace's surprise, Laura who hurried forward first. She took the bag from him with her left hand, shook his hand with her right, and smiled warmly up at him. "We're glad to have you with us, Matt. I'm Laura. You've met my husband, Martin. That's Toby—you'll be rooming with him. And that's Grace. She's also here just for the summer, helping us out."

Matt blinked at Grace. "What did *you* do?" he asked.

Everyone burst into laughter before Grace explained her presence, and the embarrassment of the first meeting passed.

"Let's get you settled. Have you had breakfast?" Laura asked.

Matt shook his head.

"That's all right, then. Come, and we'll show you where you'll be staying."

Laura and Toby whisked him off, Matt with a suspicious expression on his young face, and Grace, still smiling, nudged Martin with her elbow. "I don't understand Laura's change of attitude," she said. "She didn't want him to come here, and now that he's here, she can't trip over herself fast enough to make him welcome."

Martin chuckled, gazing fondly after his wife. "I knew she'd take one look at that poor, skinny kid and every mothering instinct she had would kick into high gear. By the time she's done with him, Matt won't know what hit him. Come on, let's get to work."

* * *

Matt did not, in fact, know what had hit him. He had expected to hate this place and despise these people. He had reported on Monday morning with the determination to put in his community hours and get out of here as fast as possible. He was overwhelmed with resentment, embarrassment, and—though he'd never admit it—nervousness. He'd far rather do jail time than slave in some bumpkin farmer's field he himself had destroyed. He just wanted to get this over with and go back to his real life, useless as his real life was.

He hadn't expected to like it.

True, he wasn't fond of getting up at the crack of dawn every morning. By the end of his first week, he was exhausted and sore, muscles that he'd never even known he had complaining. But he liked the work itself. He had always liked the feeling of using his hands, of creating something useful or beautiful, and he supposed vegetables were both—something he had never considered before. He liked the feeling of purpose his days were taking on. He liked being outdoors away from the rancid-oil smell of the chip shop. He even liked—he grudgingly admitted to himself—being away from his video games, which lately had become suffocating and stale. He liked the thought that someone was counting on him to do his part. The following of a consistent routine. The idea that someone not only noticed but expressed approval of his progress. It didn't hurt to be out of the house and away from his father's depression and criticism either.

And in spite of himself, he liked these people too, especially the old man he was staying with. The guy could really cook, he was an undemanding companion in the evenings, he didn't talk too much, and he was able to turn leather and metal into important things, shape the materials into whatever his mind imagined or whatever the circumstances required. Martin was okay too, teaching him how to do a task and then walking away and leaving him to it, trusting him to be able to do it or expecting him to ask questions if he couldn't. Matt didn't even mind Laura fussing over him and talking about fattening him up. It kind of felt good to have a mother clucking around him. It was a far cry from the hands-off parenting style of his own mother, who had spent most of his childhood shopping or sitting at the bar in the Red Lion before she'd finally gone off and left when he was fifteen.

Yes, all in all, he thought he could have landed in a worse situation. He wouldn't mind putting in his time this summer. In fact, as far as he could tell judging from just one week on the job, he thought he might like to do this sort of work more than being an electrician.

* * *

"Declan! For the last time, come in and do your homework!" Laura bellowed out the back door. A group of tourists, a Japanese family with three children, turned from peering in the greenhouse windows to look at her. Laura ignored them. "If you don't come now, there will be no supper for you tonight!" she called. She came back into the wool room, shaking her head. "That boy! His teacher sent a note home today saying he had to send Declan to detention *twice* for acting up in class."

"What do you think is the problem?" Grace asked. They were sitting together, Grace spinning wool and Laura carding in the buttery late-afternoon sunshine spilling over the smooth wood of the floor. Laura had shown Grace how to use the proper spinning wheel, and it was tricky to get the rhythm right between her hands and her foot. It wasn't as easy as Laura made it seem. She loved the soft purring sound it made though.

"Mason's coming this weekend," Laura said. "Declan's always worse right before he comes. Like pressure building up in a bottle."

"I know it must be hard on both of them to be apart so much."

"Yes." Laura frowned over a stubborn cocklebur trapped in the wool fibers. "Mason's a good father. He's doing his best. He does what he thinks is best for the children."

"You don't need to defend him to me," Grace told her gently.

"I know. But I do feel—well, if Declan's grades drop while he's in my care . . ." She stopped, pressing her lips tightly together.

"You're doing your best too," Grace reminded the older woman. She stopped the spinning wheel and looked morosely at the bumpy string she'd created. It looked worse than what she could do with a drop spindle. It was like starting the whole learning process over again. "I'm not helping much here. I think I'll go out and see if I can talk Declan into coming in," she offered.

"Would you? You do seem to be able to get him to cooperate when I can't."

Grace abandoned the mess and left the room. As she stepped outside, she could hear the drone of the tractor like a legion pipe band warming up behind the barn. She wasn't used to the invasive sound. Martin had considered all his options, but with the planting season already past and time pressing to get more plants in the ground, he had opted for speed and convenience over authenticity. He'd left the horses idle and borrowed a Kubota tractor from a neighbor. It could plow the damaged area in triple the time Death and Taxes could. But it was an abrasive noise, and Grace could smell the fumes and diesel from here. She would be glad when the invading monster was gone.

She found Declan behind the hen house, not doing anything, just sitting on an overturned bucket in the chicken run, watching the big red birds milling around his feet. Once in a while when one got too inquisitive about his shoes, he would shift his position suddenly and send the hens squawking in alarm.

Grace let herself into the run and came to stand beside him. She had to watch where she stepped, and she didn't like the look in the hens' eyes, but she stood her ground. If Declan could do it, so could she.

"Your grandma sent you to collect eggs half an hour ago," she commented.

Declan didn't look at her.

"She'd like you to get your homework done before dinner."

"I know."

She poked him softly with the toe of her shoe. "Why so glum? Is something bothering you?"

"I dunno."

"You can talk to me, you know."

"I know."

Grace thought a moment. She could try to talk about what had happened at school today. About his feelings about losing his mother, about his father being so far away. She supposed she could try to smooth it over or talk about how difficult this was for his grandparents and how he could help the whole situation by doing what he was asked. Instead, she said simply, "Let's make lemon bars after supper."

He lifted his head and looked at her.

"Hurry and get your stuff done so there's time," Grace added.

Declan stood, picked up his empty bowl without another word, and went into the hen house to collect the eggs. Grace tiptoed back to the chicken-run gate and let herself out. She was halfway to the house when Declan caught up with her. They walked together the rest of the way, and Declan put the eggs in the sink for Laura to wash before they went into the fridge.

He started toward the stairs and then looked back at Grace. "With powdered sugar on top?"

"Sure."

Grace went back into the wool room and resumed her seat at the spinning wheel.

"Any luck?" Laura asked, not sounding very hopeful.

"He put the eggs in the sink, and now he's upstairs doing his schoolwork," Grace said, starting the wheel to spinning again.

Laura paused and then laughed, shaking her head. "You're a miracle worker, I swear," she said. "What are we going to do when you go?"

* * *

The next Friday afternoon, Martin sent Grace into town to buy gardening twine so they could tie up the beans. She bought the twine and wandered the hardware store a little while, enjoying the rare break in her work, and then stepped out onto the sunny sidewalk. It wasn't often she got to town on a weekday, and she found the traffic slow and the sidewalks nearly deserted. A cooling breeze rose from the lake, lifting her bangs from her forehead, and without really thinking about it, she turned right instead of left, away from her car, with the wind at her back. She walked along, swinging her shopping bag and looking in the storefronts as she passed, heading in no particular direction. Port Dover had no more than seven thousand permanent residents, and there was an eclectic collection of boutiques pandering to tourists who came for the beaches. She became engrossed in the sights and colors as she walked. Shops gave way to pretty homes with manicured lawns, shady trees, banks of spiky leaves that would turn to orange lilies in the late summer, and rose bushes. She knew she should head back to the farm—Martin was waiting for her—so she told herself she'd go one more block and then turn around.

A shrill bell startled her, and she looked around and noticed for the first time the large redbrick building across the road. The chunky white letters on the side said Reynolds High School. As she watched, the doors opened and teenagers began streaming out. Young people were alike the world over, she thought to herself. Shouting, rowdy, laughing, slinging backpacks over one shoulder, extracting bicycles out of the rack. Exuberant. Free. When was it that adults lost that energy and grew reluctant to make noise in public? she wondered.

Two boys crossed the street toward her, passing a soccer ball back and forth between them with their feet. The ball hit the curb and bounced up, nearly into Grace's face, and she jerked back, startled. Then she recovered herself in an instant and caught the ball at her thigh, dropped it to the ground, and kicked it back to the boys with the inner side of her tennis shoe. The boys laughed, called an apology and a thank-you, and continued on their way.

"That was slick," someone said.

Grace looked over her shoulder and found the schoolteacher—the one she had started to think of as *him*—watching from the schoolyard. She put one hand up to shield her eyes from the sun so she could see him better and waved her other hand. "High school soccer team," she called. "About a hundred years ago."

He crossed the street to join her, one hand in the pocket of his trousers and the other holding a leather satchel. Despite the warmth of the day, he wore a camel-colored corduroy jacket over his plaid shirt and a nice brown tie. He'd had a haircut, she noticed, and his ears seemed to stick out more than they had the day she'd seen him at the museum. His expressive face slid into a grin. She was surprised to realize how much it pleased her to see him again.

"We meet again," he said.

"Hello! Is this your school?" she asked.

"Not mine, personally. But yes, this is where I teach, though not for much longer," he said.

"Oh, why not?"

"They're closing the school next year—not enough enrollment—and bussing the kids to other schools. I'll be switching to Simcoe Composite."

"That's sad. Is that very far from here? Will you have to move?" She found the news upset her even though she told herself she was being stupid. What did it matter where he went? She would be back in Utah by then.

"It's not a bad commute, really. I'll still live here."

"Do you have a house?" She looked around as if expecting it to materialize on the sidewalk.

"Yes, an old Victorian about a block from here, on Rasmussen. Would you care to see it? I'm just heading home. I think I have some lemonade in the fridge."

She hesitated, wondering whether it would be a good idea. She studied his friendly face and told herself she knew his workplace and would know where he lived. She could pick him out of a lineup. There were fifty young witnesses who had seen them talking. She was probably okay. She felt a smile blossom on her face and knew she looked goofy but didn't care. "Thank you, I'd like that. I can only stay a little while. Then I have to get back to work." She jiggled the shopping bag. "I was just running an errand."

They fell in step, and Grace suspected he was shortening his long stride to accommodate her pace.

She nodded at the briefcase he carried. "Taking home homework to grade over the weekend?"

"Sadly, yes. Forty-five essays to mark."

"What's the topic?"

"'Analyze the tactics of Generals Wolfe and Montcalm at the Battle of the Plains of Abraham and discuss what would have made the battle end differently,'" he replied and shot her a look out of the corner of his eye. "Riveting stuff."

She shrugged. "I've always liked history. I've wanted to go see where that battle happened, actually, but I've never been to Quebec."

"Never?" His eyebrows shot up. "Well, you must certainly rectify that. It's a beautiful place. And not that far away. You can get there in a long day's drive."

"Maybe on my next trip to Canada," Grace said. "This summer is pretty full."

He came to a stop and looked down at her in surprise. "You're just visiting?"

"Yes, until September. I lived here as a child, but my home is in the States now."

"I didn't know. I thought . . ." He trailed off in some confusion. "But you said you had to get back to work."

"Yes. Just working here for the summer, staying with friends."

"Pity," he said and turned to push open the gate of the house before them.

Grace tipped her head back to look up at the graceful old Victorian house, admiring the pale paint, the arched windows, the drippy gingerbread trim. Even the yard was authentic Victorian, crammed with peonies and lilac bushes past their prime in a messy arrangement that perfectly suited both the house and its owner.

"You live here?" she breathed. "I can't imagine a more perfect spot for a history teacher."

"Thanks. It is nice, isn't it? It was in kind of rough shape when I bought it; whoever redecorated in the seventies had an unfortunate fondness for orange shag carpet. But I've restored it over the years, added on an office, and now I can't imagine living anywhere else." He paused on the wooden steps. "Let's sit out here on the porch though. The house is authentic right down to the lack of air conditioning. Out here, at least there's a nice breeze."

So she sat on the picturesque porch swing and contentedly listened to the fat bumblebees diving in and out of the flowerbeds while he fetched two glasses of lemonade and a bag of Oreos. They sat for a quarter of an hour, sipping the ice-cold drinks and licking the centers out of the cookies and chatting about nothing in particular—the movement of young people out of Port Dover to bigger cities, her work at the farm, the trials of the local school board, the cost of lemons, the proper way to prop up peonies so their shaggy heads didn't sag to the grass. He kept the swing moving gently back and forth with one foot on the ground, his other long leg drawn up with his foot on the swing and his elbow resting on his knee. Grace lost track of time and came to herself with a start when they reached the bottoms of their glasses.

"I should get back to work. Martin will wonder where I've gotten to," she exclaimed, jumping up from the swing and picking up her shopping bag.

"So soon?"

"Yes, sorry, I really should be getting back. Thank you for the lemonade and the pleasant talk."

"Do you want me to walk you back to where I found you?"

"No need, thanks. I can find my car."

He stood and accompanied her back to the sidewalk, hands in his pockets. "Well, you know where I live now, so you can come again."

She looked up at him, gauging how sincerely he meant the invitation. He bent to break off a sprig of orange avens growing in the bed near the gate and carefully tucked the tiny flower behind her ear. The gentle gesture startled her.

"Anytime," he said, holding her eyes with his.

Grace didn't remember the walk back to her car and only vaguely recalled the drive back to the farm. It wasn't until she was putting the little orange blossom in a cup of water in her room that she realized she still didn't know the history teacher's name.

CHAPTER FIFTEEN

GRACE AND LARK WERE SITTING on the front porch early the next morning when Mason drove up. Grace was snapping green beans into a bowl, and Lark was dancing impatiently with both hands on the railing. As soon as Mason was out of the car, Lark jumped off the porch and landed in his outstretched arms, squealing with pleasure, and Mason, following their usual ritual, scrubbed his wiry beard against her cheek. She shrieked and wriggled free of her father's bear hug.

"What did you bring me?" she demanded, yanking on his hand with both of hers.

"Greedy girl. Am I to bring presents every time?"

"Yes."

"What do you think I brought?"

Her fingers darted nimbly into his pocket and pulled out a lollipop bigger than her palm.

"Grape!" she cheered. "My favorite!" She unwrapped the cellophane and tried to stick the whole thing in her mouth at once.

"Easy does it," Mason said. "You probably haven't even had breakfast yet."

"Not yet, but it's almost ready. I've been waiting for *hours*." She ran ahead of him into the house.

Mason gave Grace a nod of greeting. "Seven in the morning and you're hard at work already, I see."

She smiled and set aside the bowl. "It's cooler working in the morning. If I get a lot done before noon, Martin lets me take a nap after lunch."

He chuckled, a warm, rumbling sound in his chest. "How are you surviving?"

She thought he appeared to be in the mood to talk, something that didn't happen often. "I'm well, thank you," she told him. "I fall in love with this place more every day. I don't know how you can stand to be away."

Mason drew a deep breath and looked up at the maple trees shading the house. A soft breeze was turning their leaves with a rustling murmur. "The city has its good points," he said. "I just can't think offhand what they are at the moment."

He opened the door for her, and they walked together into the kitchen, where Laura was making french toast and Martin was setting the table. Lark was peering into the frying pan on the stove.

"Yum! Can I have Declan's too?"

"No, it's for Declan," Laura said.

"He won't want it."

"Sure he will," she remonstrated. "Go and tell him it's almost ready."

"He knows," Lark said, sucking noisily on her candy. "He's up in the loft again and won't come down."

"Again?"

There was a pause, and Mason and his mother looked at each other over Lark's head.

"I'll get him," Grace said quietly.

Mason's reddish-blond eyebrows rose.

Laura shrugged. "He seems to respond to her better than to the rest of us lately," she said. "She can get him to do things none of us can."

Grace pushed on her shoes at the back door and strode toward the barn. When she returned with Declan five minutes later, Mason greeted him sounding a bit subdued. Perhaps even cautious. Declan gave his father a perfunctory hug without really looking up at his face, then sat at the table next to Grace. The others took their places, and Laura brought the platter to the table.

"Oh, good, french toast!" Declan cheered, suddenly animated.

"You don't sound as if you like it at all," Grace teased.

"Can you teach me to make it sometime, Grace?"

Mason looked up from cutting Lark's toast for her, his gaze shifting from his son to Grace.

"If you had come in when you were called, you could have made it with your grandma this morning," Grace said.

"Yeah, I know." Declan waved this off. "But do you know how to make it? Can you teach me how tomorrow?"

"Sure, I don't mind french toast twice in a weekend," Martin said.

"All right," Grace said. "If you'd like."

Declan turned to his father with a grin. "Grace is teaching me how to cook all sorts of stuff," he said.

"Is she now?"

Martin ruffled Declan's hair. "He's quite good at it. We have a budding chef in our midst, I think."

Declan squirmed with the compliment and turned a pink and smiling face toward Grace, who smiled back. Mason picked up Lark's fork and knife and resumed cutting her breakfast for her.

"The police came here last week," Lark informed him cheerfully.

Mason looked up in surprise, then looked at his mother for confirmation.

"A little trouble," Laura said nonchalantly. "A drunk driver tore up one of the fields with his SUV. Or rather, a stolen SUV."

"Oh! Did he do a lot of damage?" Mason exclaimed.

"Nothing that can't be repaired. We've almost finished replanting, in fact," Martin said calmly. "It has set us back a bit, but it couldn't be helped."

"And where is this drunk driver now?" Mason demanded. "Did they catch him?"

"He's over having breakfast with Toby," Lark replied, reaching for her milk.

Mason looked at his mother again, mouth open.

"His name is Matt. He's staying with us over the summer to do his community service hours," Laura said. "Helping your dad repair the field. Do you want another serving, dear?"

"No. I mean, no, thank you. But, Mom, is it—is it entirely safe to have him living here on the grounds?" Mason asked, waving the knife and fork. "I mean, who is he? What do we know about him?"

"Just a student from London. It's fine, dear. It's not like he's a serial killer. Just a young man who made a wrong decision. And we're helping him to right it."

"And the damage was limited to one field," Martin added. "It's nothing to be concerned about."

Grace ducked her head to hide her smile. It certainly hadn't been a small deal when it had happened. But she understood Martin's need to reassure his son, especially with this stranger now on the property where Mason's children lived.

"I've been working with him," Martin added. "He's quiet, doesn't talk much, but he's a hard worker and learns quickly. I like him."

Grace felt an odd little response in her chest that faded as quickly as it had come. Was it jealousy? Surely not. It was okay to share Martin with Matt. The farm had given her so much, had helped her in ways she hadn't even known she'd needed. Now there was an opportunity to share that magic with someone else who also needed it. It wasn't as if Matt was taking her place—on the farm or in the family's affections. There was plenty of work and love to go around, and always room for one more. That thought caused a light little bubble of happiness to rise within her, and she looked up, smiling.

Across the table, Mason looked up just as she did, and when their eyes met, he paused as if discovering something in her face that surprised him. His mouth opened to say something, but then he hesitated.

The moment was gone then as Lark demanded with her mouth full, "What are we going to do today?"

Mason looked from her to his father, uncertain. "Dad, do you want me to stay and help with—"

"Not at all." Martin waved him off. "You only get so much time with the kids. There's nothing you need to do here."

"You're sure? I want to help if I can."

"Positive. It's all taken care of. Matt's a good worker. Like I said, we're nearly finished."

"Well," Mason said doubtfully, "then maybe I'll take the kids down to the beach. What do you think?"

"Yes!" Lark shouted. "I love the lake."

"Can Grace come too?" Declan asked.

Mason looked startled, unsure what to say.

Grace could sense his discomfort and hurriedly came to the rescue. "Thank you for the invitation, Declan, but I was going to meet my friend Margaret today for lunch." She didn't add that lunch was to be at Toby's.

"Aw, can't you move that to another day?"

"I don't want to disappoint her. Besides, this is your time to spend with your dad. I don't want to intrude," Grace said. "But I'll see you tonight, and you can tell me all about it."

Declan nodded and reached for the milk. Grace looked at Mason and saw him watching her thoughtfully. She wasn't sure she could read the expression on his face.

After breakfast was over, the children ran upstairs to fetch their bathing suits and towels, and Laura went to hunt for sunscreen in the bathroom cupboard. Martin disappeared outside as Grace carried the dishes to the sink and began to wash up.

"Declan's taken a shine to you," Mason remarked, putting away the maple syrup and milk jug.

"I guess so. He's really been enjoying cooking with me. It's not something I usually enjoy, actually, but it's more fun with him helping in the kitchen."

"It's good to see him enthusiastic about anything these days." Mason hesitated and came to stand beside her at the sink. "Listen, about Declan's invitation, I hope you didn't mind—"

"Not a worry," Grace said. "This is your time with your children. I don't want to interrupt that. And I really do have a lunch date with Margaret. And Toby," she added.

"You're having lunch with Toby?"

"Truth be told, it's more like Margaret and Toby have a lunch date, but they invited me in order to keep it casual so that neither one of them has to admit to liking the other."

Mason's mouth fell open again. "Toby has a *girlfriend*?"

Grace laughed and looked around to make sure no one else had overheard. "Shh. We're not supposed to have noticed. And he'd deny it if confronted. But yes, he likes this friend of mine. She's about his age, a widow, and very nice."

"Well, well. Good old Toby." Mason shook his head. "It is a morning full of surprises."

"What's a surprise?" Declan reappeared carrying his things for the lake.

"That you beat Lark down the stairs," Mason said. "Run and let Grandma lather you up with sunscreen, and we'll be off."

* * *

That afternoon, Grace made time to go down to the gift shop to visit Michelle Dalby and Jane Persaud. She never knew what state she would find them in; it depended on the number of museum patrons at any given moment. Sometimes the shop was quiet as a library, and other times it was packed and noisy. Today there was a crowd of customers at the counter, and Michelle and Jane were looking harried. Grace hung back and examined a rack of pioneer recipe books while she waited.

But another busload of tourists was deposited in front of the visitors' center before the last wave had finished with their purchases, so it didn't look as if things would calm down anytime soon.

She was about to wave a good-bye and go on her way when a flustered-looking woman in a floppy straw hat with a camera around her neck saw her standing idle and pounced. "Do you work here? Can I get a price check on these quilted place mats?" She waved the fabric under Grace's nose. She had a strong Southern U.S. accent Grace couldn't place. "And is there a discount if I buy six of them?"

Caught off guard, Grace took the place mats and examined them. "There should be a tag. Yes, here. Five dollars each. And I don't think there's a discount. I mean, you're kind of expected to buy them in sets. What would you do with one place mat?"

The woman looked disgruntled. "It seems pretty expensive to me. I mean, that's $30!"

"These are hand-pieced and quilted by museum staff right here on-site," Grace told her. "They probably took a few hours each to make. The person who made them is only getting a small share of the cost, and the rest goes to the museum. So, really, they're probably only being paid about thirty cents an hour for their work."

The woman frowned but took her selection and joined the line at the counter. Grace looked up and caught Jane Persaud looking at her with wide eyes. Jane jerked her chin in a way that told Grace to linger and not leave yet. So she wandered through the aisles, looking at the merchandise, to kill time. She liked poking through the gift shop. Everything on the shelves had something to do with Canadian history or homesteading, and most was either handmade by staff or placed there on consignment by local artisans. Bottles of nonalcoholic apple cider that local farmers had made stood beside hand-thrown pottery, a basket held door hooks Toby forged out of iron, and there were rows of rag dolls dressed in period clothing. Jane's hand-dipped candles were slender tapers of creamy gold and white and smelled wonderfully of beeswax so sweet-smelling Grace wanted to bite into one.

Grace especially liked the books of old photographs, drawings, and daguerreotypes showing what Port Dover had looked like years ago. There were shots of the old town and lighthouse and paintings of what it had looked like before the War of 1812, when the town had been called

Dover Mills. There was an old flyer advertising the 1914 Port Dover Horticultural Society annual flower show. There was a portrait of the first settler, Peter Walker, who had come to the area in 1794, looking spiffy in his high collar, and a lovely black-and-white photo of Ethel Steele, a theater director who was said to still haunt the old town hall theater where she had directed so many productions.

A voice at her elbow said, "What a relief! I thought they'd never go."

Grace looked up from her musings.

Jane pulled a wry face. "I know. I'm supposed to be grateful so many people are visiting the museum. Don't tell anyone I just said that."

"Pretty busy today," Grace agreed. "I didn't want to distract you."

"Find anything to entertain you?" Jane peered at the cover of the book Grace had just replaced on the shelf. "Oh yes, that's one of my favorites. Did you see the picture of the women in their 1920s swimsuits on the beach? It's wonderful."

Michelle Dalby wiped her hands on her apron and came over to them.

"I heard what you said to that customer who was quibbling about the place mats, Grace," she said. "Thanks for putting a plug in for the poor underpaid handicrafters."

"I wasn't sure I should have said that," Grace told her.

"It doesn't hurt to remind them once in a while that someone actually *makes* all this stuff they're buying." Her eyes glinted. "Especially since I was the one who made those silly place mats!"

"You did? They were beautiful. You ought to sell them for more than five dollars," Grace said.

"Probably. But the museum seems to be more interested in selling quantity than quality."

"But they *are* quality," Grace protested. "You're very good. You could teach quilting."

"Now, there's an idea!" Jane said. "That would bring in money. Don't just sell the goods or do demonstrations—teach classes."

"Do you think people would be interested?" Michelle asked eagerly.

"Of course they would. People pay good money to take classes at community centers in everything from quilting to basketweaving," Grace said. "I've really enjoyed learning to spin wool from Laura. I bet other people would like to learn too. It might be another source of income for the museum. Think about it anyway."

"I will. I'll talk to my husband about it, and if he likes the idea, he can propose it to the board of directors. Goodness knows, they're always looking for ways to expand what the museum offers."

"There you go!" Jane said. "Turn it into an educational center and not just a tourist spot."

"There *is* a big interest right now in old pioneering skills," Michelle agreed. "My daughter says even the boys at the high school are getting into knitting. And there are all of those back-to-the-landers who want to know how to bottle fruit and dehydrate vegetables . . ."

"Maybe Martin would be willing to teach a workshop on basic home vegetable gardening," Grace suggested. "That would be popular."

"Let me grab a notebook, and we can write down our ideas," Jane said, going to grab one behind the counter.

They brainstormed for half an hour before business picked up again and Jane and Michelle were forced back to waiting on customers. Grace left for home, her head full of ideas about how to expand the museum's offerings and increase income. She found herself in a great mood striding along the gravel road. The creative juices were flowing, and it buoyed her spirit. But it was more than that; she discovered she was actually excited about the ideas they had discussed. For a fleeting moment, she let herself envision herself as director of a museum school—they could even hold classes in the authentic old schoolhouse—putting together workshops and courses for the community. The love of teaching, she realized, hadn't entirely left her system. How she wished she didn't have to go back to the States in September! She wanted—deeply, sincerely—to stay and help carry out the ideas she and the other women had thought up.

When the troops returned to the house that evening, sunburned and sandy, Declan came into the kitchen waving an interesting-looking stone he'd found. "Where's Grace?" he demanded. "I want to show her."

"I'm in here," Grace called from the living room, where she was looking through Martin's shelves for a book to read.

Declan hurried in to join her. "Look what I found."

Grace admired the stone, remarking on its unusual color and shape. "What are you going to do with it?"

Declan looked at it doubtfully. "What do you mean? It's just a rock."

"Are you going to use it as a paper weight or make something with it?" Grace prompted.

"Like what?"

She considered. "It looks a little like a blue sheep. See, it even has two points like legs."

"Yes. I think so too."

"So you could glue a little wool to its back and paint some eyes and a nose there, see? And if you prop it up against something, it could be a little sheep decoration."

Declan laughed. "Yeah, I want to do that. I have some craft paints in my room and a paintbrush."

"You go get them and a sheet of newspaper. And ask your grandma for some glue. I'll go get a handful of wool from the wool room and meet you back here in two minutes."

Declan ran from the room, and she heard his feet pounding up the stairs. Grace set down her book and went to the wool room. There was one more fleece in a bag in the cupboard, and she selected a fistful of the prettiest gray fibers for their project. She felt ridiculously excited by the idea. How long had it been since she had done a craft with a child? She grew still remembering fruity-smelling markers, Popsicle sticks, crêpe paper, and Elmer's glue. Buttons and bits of string, blunt-nosed scissors and poster paint. She and the children had made a piñata one year for Molly's birthday and stuffed it full of wrapped candies and gumballs. Somewhere in the storage unit in Salt Lake she still had the clay cup Mark had made her to hold pens one Mother's Day. She felt a squeeze in her stomach, the rise of anxiety. She had weathered through Mother's Day this year by ignoring it as much as possible. But now her loss threatened to rise up and engulf her once more. Would it never leave her? Most days lately, she felt fine, and then just when she thought the worst was over, back it would all come again like an avalanche to crush her.

Deliberately, Grace drew a deep, gulping breath, focused her thoughts on Declan, and closed the wool cupboard. Pushing the panic into the back of her mind, she let herself out of the room and went down the hall toward the living room. Declan wasn't back yet, but she could hear voices in the kitchen. Mason was talking to Laura. At the sound of her own name being spoken, Grace couldn't help pausing to listen.

"It was Grace this and Grace that. All he could say all day was 'I can't wait to tell Grace. I wish Grace could see this.'"

"Well, at least for once it wasn't Lark doing all the talking." Laura laughed.

"I hardly recognized him. He has never been that cheerful. He kept going on about how cool everything was. The way the water rippled the sand and pulled it from under his toes. The way the seagulls ate our sandwich crusts. The way the sunlight hit the water. And everything that caught his attention he wanted to share with Grace."

"I guess he's a little smitten."

"It's good to see him happy for a change," Mason admitted. "But it worries me a bit that he's become so attached to a woman who's going to be leaving again."

There was the sound of feet on the stairs, and Laura added in a low tone, "He's coming down now. We can talk later."

Declan clattered into the living room with his paints, brush, glue, and sheet of newspaper. Grace went to help him lay everything out on the table and pull up two chairs. As they worked together on his craft, she couldn't help watching him more closely than usual. He *did* seem happier overall. It wasn't just the chattering or the smile . . . It was deeper than that. He seemed less tense, certainly more at ease and natural than he usually was when Mason was visiting. And she realized he had been that way over the last little while. Was it just the joy of learning something new and enjoyable? Was it just the fun of discovering a passion for cooking? He seemed a bit more grounded now. Maybe he was beginning to come to terms with the changes in his life. Maybe it was just part of maturing. Or maybe what Laura had said was true, and Declan was a bit smitten with her. She wasn't sure. But Grace did know she felt a growing love for him. The idea gave her pause. The fact that she could find love in her heart again for another child was surely an important step in her healing, wasn't it? And perhaps being able to open himself to love was an important step for Declan too.

After supper, Mason set aside his cutlery and announced, "I haven't met this Matt person yet, and I probably should. I mean, just so I know who my kids are being exposed to."

There was a silence around the table, and then Martin set down his glass. "You know we wouldn't expose your children to danger or risk their coming to any harm," he said, a simmering undercurrent in his tone that surprised Grace. She'd never heard anything close to anger come from him before.

"That's not how I meant it," Mason said, holding up his hands.

"That's how I heard it," Martin replied.

"The children aren't ever alone with him," Laura added a bit tartly. "Give us some credit for some intelligence, Mason. We take the best care of them we can."

"Mom, I know—"

"I notice you didn't ask us to do a police background check on Grace, here, before she came," Martin said.

Grace felt her ears warm as Mason glanced at her, and she looked down at her plate and remained silent, wanting to stay out of it. Declan and Lark looked back and forth between the adults.

Mason spread his hands. "I trust your judgment. I'm not saying I don't. I only said I wanted to meet Matt. Is there something wrong with that? Don't I have the right to meet him?"

"It's the way you said it," Martin said.

Mason took a handful of his beard and pulled it. "I'm sorry. It came out wrong. I didn't mean to sound as if I didn't trust you. You know I think you're doing a great job with the kids, and I appreciate it so much. I just want to . . . I don't know . . . be more aware of what's going on on the farm. Be involved in it more. You didn't even tell me last week when the field got vandalized. You didn't mention that the person who did it was going to be living at Toby's. Don't you think I should know these things?"

Grace ventured to raise her eyes and saw Laura and Martin exchanging looks.

"We know you have a lot on your plate. We didn't want to worry you," Laura said finally.

"It worries me more when you don't include me," Mason said. His voice softened. "I know I'm not here very often, but when I am here and I volunteer to help with anything around the place, you shoo me away like it's none of my business and you don't need me around. You send me off to the beach and won't let me so much as help with the storm windows, for heaven's sake. I want to be part of this place. All I'm asking is that you let me be *home* when I'm here."

There was another deep silence around the table, and then Laura reached over to touch Mason's hand. "I'm sorry, Mason. I didn't realize that was how you were perceiving it. We were just trying to free up your time to spend with the kids. We didn't mean to make you feel left out."

"Of course not," Martin said.

"Maybe if you let me spend time working around the place *with* the kids, they won't see me as just a ticket to free ice cream and endless adventure," Mason told them, shooting Declan and Lark a look. "I want them to see that I care about you and this farm too. That I have a place here too."

"Of course, dear," Laura said. "We should have realized."

"If you want to muck out the barn any old time, you're welcome to," Martin added.

Mason's beard split with his grin. "Gee, thanks, Dad. That's swell."

Laura stood and started collecting plates. "Martin, why don't you take Mason over to Toby's right now to introduce him to Matt and then invite both of them back here for strawberry shortcake?"

Martin jumped to his feet. "Good idea."

"Grace, can you help Declan whip the cream? And, Lark, you get the bowls and spoons."

Everyone scattered from the table to busy themselves, and by the time all were seated again with the taste of strawberries and buttery cake in their mouths, Matt seated companionably between Toby and Mason, peace had been restored and hearts were lighter.

It helped, Grace thought, to air things instead of letting them fester. But it helped make the conversation even sweeter when it was accompanied by whipped cream.

CHAPTER SIXTEEN

SUNDAY MORNING, DECLAN AND GRACE were up early so the french toast was ready by the time the others came into the kitchen. Beaming with pride, Declan placed the plate of only slightly burnt toast ceremoniously in front of Mason.

"I made it myself."

"It's true," Grace said. "I only supervised."

Mason made a show of lavishly applying the butter and syrup, cutting a large bite, and rolling his eyes in pleasure while the others waited for his verdict. "That is the best french toast I've ever eaten," he pronounced in his deep voice.

The rest of them dished up their plates, and Declan sat and grinned through the whole meal. When they'd finished, Grace helped with the dishes and then hurried to her room to get ready for church. She looked forward to going now that she knew some of the other women. No one had pried further into her family or situation—she didn't know if Margaret and Annie had headed them off or if they'd just lost interest, but either way, she found it comfortable to attend now.

She was just getting into her car when Mason came around the side of the house. He saw her and came over, and she was struck once more by the sheer height and breadth of him. This was a man who could never slip unobtrusively into a room. The sunlight turned his hair the color of straw, and she thought about the miller's daughter spinning straw to gold. The thought made her smile.

"Heading somewhere?" he asked conversationally.

"Yes. Church is at ten."

"Oh." This seemed to catch him off guard. "I didn't know you attended."

"Yes. It's in Port Dover."

"I'll let you go, then, or you'll be late."

"Did you want to talk to me about something?" Grace asked. "I can take a few minutes; it's all right."

"Well, just about Declan," he said, shifting his feet and looking out over the fields toward the museum visitors' center, looking uncertain about how to begin.

"He's different lately, isn't he?" Grace said, smiling. "I know you were concerned about him, but he seems happier and calmer lately, to me."

"Yes, well, that's what—"

"He really is a good kid. You should be proud of him."

He looked at her. "I can tell you care about him."

"I do," she acknowledged. "I'm fond of both your children. I don't think you need to worry about Declan. He'll be okay eventually. He's taking all the changes in his life kind of hard, but just give him time. I—I know what loss feels like. And I know people heal and recover at their own rate. You can't do much to speed up the process."

He lifted a hand to scrub at his beard. "I—I worry that he's in for another loss when you leave in the fall."

She bit her lips together, nodding. "I understand that. I don't know what to say other than I'll try not to encourage it too much. I don't spend a lot of one-on-one time with him as it is. I don't know what else to do about it." She hesitated. "You know I would never purposely upset either of your children, don't you?"

"I know. I mean, I don't know you all that well, but I would like to believe you wouldn't."

"I wouldn't. And by the way, my police record is clean." She got into her car and drove away, leaving him chuckling and shaking his head in the driveway.

As she paused at the end of the driveway before turning onto the road, she glanced in her rearview mirror. Mason had pushed his hands into his pockets and was standing where she'd left him, watching her go. She got the feeling he hadn't said everything he had started to say, but he'd known she was in a hurry to get to church, and there hadn't been time to really speak in depth. But it was clear he was aware of Declan's growing attachment to her—and maybe hers to Declan—and it concerned him. It concerned her too. She felt she was gaining so much more from Mason's family than she could ever contribute in return, and the thought that she might in any way hurt one of them sobered her. She didn't want to add even a fraction to Declan's sense of loss. She was too intimate with loss herself.

She felt that old, familiar sorrow descend like a suffocating gray blanket on her as she drove to town.

The hardest part had been going through the cedar chest where she'd stockpiled the heirlooms, things she'd wanted to pass on to her children. So much stuff—Grandma's smocked baby dress, the handful of old silver dollars, Greg's father's watch, children's books she'd enjoyed in her own childhood, a china tea set Molly hadn't been quite old enough to inherit yet, the photo albums, a carving of a horse her uncle had made for her from poplar. She'd knelt by the chest, running her hands lightly over the treasures, and experienced a sharp, sickening pain at the realization that there was no one in the end to pass these things on to. Who would value them as she had? No one else would care about most of it. Yet she couldn't bring herself to discard anything. She'd finally stuck the trunk in the storage unit, along with the few bits of furniture she was keeping, and locked the door. She understood loss, all right. It was as the poem said: "*A past that was. a future that could have been.*"

* * *

At church, the Relief Society president, Sister Pierce, announced that there would be a fall fair on Labor Day weekend. It seemed awfully early to be planning it—it was the first week of June, after all—but apparently it was a big affair that would need lots of advance planning. Volunteers raised their hands if they wanted to serve on the food committee, promotion and advertising committee, decoration committee, or events-and-program committee. Margaret and Annie both volunteered for the events-and-program committee.

Margaret nudged Grace in the ribs. "Join us," she whispered. "You know all about staging performances."

Grace stared at her. "How did you know that?"

"Toby told me."

"When was this?" To her knowledge, Margaret had come to lunch with Toby only three times this past month, and Grace had been present all three times.

"When we were out last week. We ran up to Elora for a sheep auction."

"You did? How come I didn't know about this?"

Margaret shot her a little grin and wiggled her eyebrows. "You don't need to know *everything*."

"Have you been out with Toby other times too?" Grace was astounded.

Margaret gave a distinctly girlish giggle. "None of your business, sweetheart."

"But I'm your official chaperone!" Grace cried in mock dismay.

"Yes, well, I release you from your obligation," Margaret said, waving a hand dismissively. "Upon further reflection, I don't think your services are now required in that capacity."

"Is that a polite way to say 'Three's a crowd'?"

Margaret merely grinned again. "Now, say you'll join the committee with us. You'll have all kinds of good ideas to input."

"Yes," Annie Fisher joined in. "Come on, the only program I've ever organized was a family-night skit. Raise your hand."

"I'm only here until September 6," Grace said.

"Then you'll still be here for Labor Day. No excuses," Annie replied.

So Grace raised her hand and volunteered as well.

When she got back to the house after church, Mason had already left for the city.

* * *

Matt, against all Martin's expectations, had turned out to be a diligent worker. He arrived for duty promptly every morning wearing the new work boots and gloves he'd purchased just for this purpose. He took only brief breaks during the day and wordlessly did whatever he was told. What he lacked in muscle he made up for in brains, following directions precisely and carefully. He even came up with suggestions for reconfiguring the water hoses to improve the pressure of the watering drip system in the greenhouse. When he shyly suggested the improvement to Martin one morning, Martin considered the idea, clapped Matt on the back, and told him to make it happen. And Matt did.

Martin couldn't get the boy to speak up much, and asking him questions about school and home brought only sullen, one-syllable grunts in response. After awhile Martin gave up trying to carry on conversations, accepted things as they were, and let the boy work in peace and quiet, and Matt seemed to respond well to that approach. If he had a question about how to do something, he asked, but other than that, he kept to himself.

After he'd been at the farm a few weeks, Martin invited Matt to eat dinner with the family on Friday evenings, bringing Toby over as well. He thought perhaps it would be good for Matt to be at a table of friendly people once in a while instead of always being at Toby's solitary table. The boy seemed taken aback by the invitation. He looked uncomfortable at first, sitting formally at the family table with his elbows tight to his sides so as not to touch anyone, looking overwhelmed by the children's noise and chatter. He ate whatever was placed before him without, Martin thought, quite tasting it, though he always thanked Laura politely for the meal. Martin wondered if he was in the practice of eating at a table with his family at home but thought probably not. He suspected he more likely normally ate holding his lonely plate in front of a computer or TV.

But after a couple of meals with the family, Matt thawed to the point of joining in the general conversation and even asking for seconds at dinner. He let his elbows rest on the table and helped Lark butter her mashed potato. But Martin noticed that when everyone laughed at something funny, Matt rarely did more than smile. There was a suspicious look in his eyes, a tightness in his mouth, as if he couldn't quite understand the easy comradery surrounding him and didn't know how to participate in it.

* * *

Watching Matt's discomfort at dinner, Grace understood that feeling of being a fish out of water. She had felt it herself when she'd first arrived. However, she realized that now, as she exchanged jokes with Declan or good-natured ribbing with Toby, she felt as if she was in her own home, comfortable as part of the family; furthermore, the idea of family no longer haunted or hurt her. She wondered when the change within her had happened. And she thought perhaps the biggest difference in herself was that she had finally recovered something she'd lost long ago: she'd found hope. Maybe, just maybe, in spite of the occasional setbacks, she would be all right again. Since the accident, she had always told others she'd be okay, but now perhaps she really believed it herself. And watching Matt's face from across the table, she thought—if he stayed long enough—he might be all right again too.

Declan and Lark's spring festival was set for the coming Friday, and the children were in a pleasant tizzy getting ready for it. Both were to be in the school choir. Lark was also going to recite a poem for the program, and Declan was playing a piano piece he had been practicing for weeks. Everyone in the house was getting tired of hearing "Clowns Come to Town," but he insisted he had to get it just right.

"Dad's never heard me play it," he pointed out whenever someone suggested he play something else for a change.

Even though it wasn't his usual weekend to come, Mason had promised to take Friday off and drive up so he'd be there for the performance. Thursday evening, Lark laid out her best dress, blue with white ruffles, and Martin showed her how to polish her white leather shoes to go with it. Laura scrubbed both children thoroughly, even though it wasn't officially bath night, and not even Declan protested it. He selected his best Jacobs Sheep wool sweater to wear with his black dress pants and spent fifteen minutes wearing the outfit at the piano so he could "get the feel of it."

The children were heading up to bed when the phone rang. Laura went into the kitchen to answer it. Grace was in the living room, picking up scattered cushions and tidying newspapers, and couldn't help overhearing Laura say sharply, "What! Oh, Mason!" Grace froze, ears perked. She couldn't hear the rest of Laura's words, but she could tell from the woman's low, clipped tone that she was angry. Grace straightened and looked at Lark and Declan, who had come to a halt halfway up the stairs. Declan's face had grown pale, his eyes alert and wary. After a pause, Laura came to the kitchen door holding the receiver against her shirtfront.

"Declan, Lark, your father wants to speak to you."

Neither child moved. Declan thrust his chin upward. "He's not going to come tomorrow, is he?"

"I'm sorry. Something has come up. He wants to talk to you about it."

Declan turned and ran up the rest of the stairs. They heard his bedroom door slam above them. Lark came down and quietly took the phone from her grandmother.

"Hi, Daddy," she said. She listened briefly and then said, "But you promised you'd come. You were going to meet my teacher."

Grace could hear the muffled grumble from the phone. She closed her eyes and imagined Declan up on his bed, taking his disappointment out on his pillow. She felt a rush of anger toward Mason. How *could* he?

"I'm reciting a poem, and I'm singing in the choir," Lark said into the receiver. "Yes, Daddy . . . Okay . . . Okay, I'll recite it for you when you come next week . . . No, he went upstairs . . . I'll tell him."

Lark handed the phone back to her grandmother. "He's not coming, Grandma. He has to go to court tomorrow."

"I'm so sorry, honey. Maybe he can meet your teacher another day."

While Laura comforted Lark, Grace went upstairs and listened at Declan's door. She heard nothing. She tapped softly, and when he didn't reply, she opened the door and peeked in. The room was empty. The window stood open, the curtains blowing in the breeze. Grace closed the door and went back downstairs.

Laura, sitting on the bottom stair and holding Lark on her lap, raised an eyebrow. "How is he?"

"He's done a flit again. I'll get him." Grace went out and walked across the yard to the barn. The door was slightly open, and she let herself inside. The moonlight hardly penetrated into the aisle, and she stood for a moment, letting her eyes adjust to the gloom. She heard the horses stir and stomp, and then above her, a board squeaked. There was a shuffling sound in the loft. She went to the ladder and climbed partway up. "Declan? It's Grace."

There was no reply, but she heard the hay rustle. She climbed up the rest of the ladder and felt her way forward on her hands and knees, not standing upright for fear of hitting her head on the low beams in the dark. She thought of the ten-foot drop from the loft to the aisle below and patted the boards in front of her, searching for the edge. "Declan? I can't see, and I'm scared I'm going to fall. I don't know the loft as well as you do," she called. "Come here and help me, please. But be careful."

There was a pause, and then a figure darker than the gloom moved toward her, the boards creaking. She felt him stop beside her, and then a small hand touched her shoulder. "I'm here. You won't fall," he said.

"This is dangerous. Sit down." She sat cross-legged, found his hand, and pulled him down beside her, keeping hold of him. He didn't resist but leaned against her, and she put an arm around him in the dark. For a while, they were still, and then Grace said quietly, "I'm sorry he isn't coming, Declan."

She felt him straighten himself. "I didn't really think he'd come anyway."

"You were hoping though."

There was a slight pause. "Yeah."

"Maybe he didn't realize how important it was to you."

He shrugged.

"It isn't that he doesn't care about you and Lark. You know that, don't you?"

Another shrug.

"Your dad loves you very much. He's trying to show you he does by working very hard to earn a living so he can take care of you."

"Grandma and Granddad are taking care of us," he replied dully.

"Yes. That's the way things are right now. That doesn't mean it's how your dad wants it to be forever."

"He's not the same anymore," Declan said, wiping a hand across his nose. Grace was rather glad it was dark.

"And maybe you're not the same anymore either," Grace suggested.

Another shrug. "Maybe."

"Things happen in life that change us. That hurt us sometimes," Grace said. "But they don't change the love we have for each other. Your dad loves you as much as ever, maybe even more now. And he needs you to love him back and be patient with him while he gets on his feet. This has all been very hard for him too."

"I know. Grandma already told me that."

"Do you believe it? Do you know he loves you?"

He nodded. "I guess so."

"And do you think you can keep loving him and forgive him even when you're disappointed?"

"Yeah."

She gave him a small squeeze.

They were silent, listening to the movements of the horses below them, and then Declan said in a small voice, "I miss my mom."

Grace tightened her hold on him. "I know, honey. I'm so sorry you had to go through that."

"It just happened so fast. I didn't get to tell her good-bye. So Dad had us write her a letter so she'd know we love her."

Grace felt her throat constrict and swallowed back her tears. That had been a wise and sensitive thing for Mason to do, to give his children some sort of closure in the midst of their grief. She had heard of that sort of therapeutic intervention, and she was somewhat surprised Mason had thought of it. She hesitated, and then she said softly, "I believe you'll see her again, Declan. It may be a very long time from now, and you'll miss her in the meantime, but someday, you'll be with her again. She's all right where she is. And so are you. You have people to care for you and make sure you're all right. You're not alone."

Declan had leaned farther against her as she'd murmured the words, and by the time she'd finished talking, he was in her lap, his arms around her neck, his face pressed wetly into her shoulder. Grace held him and rocked gently back and forth, letting her own tears spill. It was dark, and no one would see. She let herself weep for Mark, Sam, and Molly, imagining she was holding their small, warm bodies, rocking them one last time. Letting her heart pour itself out and down her cheeks, emptying out the sorrow she had held in for so many months. And then she wiped her tears and was in the loft again, holding Declan, this child who needed comfort so badly. She felt a wave of love for him wash over her and knew she loved him for *him* and not just because he reminded her of her own sons. She sat and rocked and held him. And it was enough.

CHAPTER SEVENTEEN

THEY GOT UP EARLY FRIDAY morning to finish filling the CSA bins and set them in the shed for their customers to pick up. As Martin said, the whole thing was run largely on the honor system anyway, and surely people could find their own numbered bins by themselves this time. He tacked a sign on the shed door, giving his cell phone number in case anyone encountered a problem, and then they were off to the spring festival.

Grace rode in the backseat with the children while Martin drove with Toby and Laura crammed into the front seat beside him. She could have taken her own car, but somehow, it felt nicer to all be jammed in with the family. Lark was beautiful in her best dress, her dark hair captured in a thick bun that had taken Laura fifteen minutes to pin up. Her knee socks hadn't wanted to stay up until finally, in desperation, Laura had pasted them to her calves with dabs of corn syrup. Declan sat up tall in his wool sweater, his hair slicked down, a faraway look in his eye as he practiced the piano on his lap, running his fingers back and forth unconsciously across his thighs.

The school gym had been decorated with poster-paper tulips and daffodils taped to the cinder-block walls, and the families all filed into the rows of folding metal chairs while the performers scurried backstage to get ready. The gymnasium was already filling up with proud parents. Grace caught sight of Annie and Newton sitting near the back, and she waved when she caught their eye. Annie waved back, peering around the toddler on her lap, who didn't look too pleased to be surrounded by the crush of people. Grace saw Newton reach over and put his arm comfortably along the back of Annie's chair.

Grace felt a sudden jolt of pain; Greg wasn't here to put his arm around her. It wasn't *her* children who were going to be up on that stage. She was slightly disoriented, all at once stuck alone in this sea of couples, this gathering of proud parents. She fought to keep the threatening tears from reaching her eyes. They had been gone nearly two years. Why was she thinking of this now? It would do no good. When would such thoughts stop leaping out at her at unexpected moments?

She followed the Whelans to a row of chairs near the front, dead center, where, Martin said, he could get the best shot with his video camera.

"If Mason can't come, at least he can see his children perform," he said grimly.

Toby folded his long form onto one of the uncomfortable chairs, propped his cane against the seat in front of him, and crossed his legs. He surveyed the room. "I feel like I should know all these people. They've probably all come through the museum at one time or another."

"Probably," Laura agreed. "Though they may not recognize you in jeans and a sweater. They're more used to seeing you in your blacksmith apron."

Grace sat on the metal chair next to Toby's, reminding herself that he too was partnerless. A trickle of gratitude that he was here beside her started in her chest, easing the pain. She drew a deep breath and deliberately relaxed her hands on her knees. As the room filled, Grace tried not to bump into the woman sitting on her other side in the close space and distracted herself wondering how many elementary school concerts and recitals she'd been to for her own kids. Her boys had been involved in band and choir at their school. It wasn't as many as Annie had been to with her eight children, surely, but there had still been plenty.

The room echoed with metal chairs scraping the floor, people chatting, the last-minute sound checks of the microphones. The old, familiar energy shot through Grace, reminding her of all the performances she had organized and supervised from backstage. There had always been the last-minute dramas, the missing sheet music, the smell of resin and chalk. The exciting sound of the curtains being pulled open.

Then she thought inevitably about the last time *she'd* sung onstage before an audience. It had been at the Park City Egyptian Theater. But before her breath could get tight or her chest start to hurt again, the school principal mercifully tapped the microphone. The audience grew hushed, the program began, and the tense moment passed.

It wasn't that bad, really, compared to many of the school programs she'd attended. At least the little orchestra's instruments were tuned, and since everything was in French, it all sounded wonderful to her because she couldn't tell if there were mistakes or not. The choir sang, filing onto the stage to perform in neat rows, Lark in the front where they could see her stockings staying up beautifully and Declan in the middle row, sorted by height. Halfway through the program, Lark recited her poem in a clear, unhesitating voice, and many in the audience chuckled, obviously understanding more French than Grace. Laura applauded more loudly than anyone else and poked Martin several times to make sure he was capturing it all with the camera.

There were a few more numbers, and various parents popped up to take pictures, thus alerting everyone that these were their children. Grace amused herself trying to match which parent went with which child. And then it was Declan's turn to do his piano number.

Grace found herself sitting forward on the edge of her chair, her hands gripped into fists, offering a silent prayer that he wouldn't make any mistakes. He had worked so hard for this moment.

He sat at the beat-up school piano, adjusted his seat, and looked over the audience until he caught sight of his family sitting in their row. He gave a flash of a smile and then bent to his work, and it was the best he had ever played it. When he finished the simple tune, he stood and flashed another triumphant smile for the camera and headed offstage to the sound of applause.

Grace let her breath out with a whoosh and grinned at Toby. "Flawless!" she mouthed as the next child began to perform.

"Of course he was flawless." Toby bent down to mutter in her ear. "He had to show Mason he couldn't be beaten down, didn't he?"

There were no classes after the festival, and the children were free to come home with them. Grace couldn't tell if they were more excited about their great performances or the fact that they didn't have to go to class. Martin took them all out for ice cream to celebrate, even though it was only eleven o'clock in the morning. Snuggled in the backseat with the chattering children and her cup of mint chocolate chip, Grace rode back to the farmhouse with a feeling of quiet contentment.

The phone was ringing when they entered, and Declan dashed to answer it. They all heard the drop in his voice as he said, "Oh, hello, Dad."

Grace helped Lark sit at the table to finish her ice cream and tried not to eavesdrop. But to her surprise, Declan's voice became cheerful, and he told Mason animatedly about the festival and how well he and Lark had both done. He paused, and then said, "Yeah, I know, Dad . . . I know . . . It's okay. I understand." He shot a look across the kitchen at Grace and gave a lopsided smile. "It's all right. You can come to the next one . . . Yeah, see you, Dad." He handed the receiver to Lark. "He wants to talk to you next. But hurry, 'cause court's just on break."

As Lark began to describe the concert all over again for her father, Laura gave Declan a kiss on the cheek. "You were very nice on the phone with your father," she remarked.

"Yeah, well, he's just doing the best he can," Declan said and shrugged. "I'm going to go change. This sweater is too hot."

He went upstairs, humming "Clowns Come to Town."

Laura watched him go and shook her head. "Well, I'll be," was all she said.

* * *

When Grace emerged from her room early Monday morning, the sun was just rising clear and cool in the peach-colored east. The light breeze smelled of mown grass and last night's drizzling rain. Matt was sitting on the back-porch steps of the house, his elbows on his knees, fiddling with a strand of long grass.

Grace walked down her stairs and across the lawn to join him. "Hi," she greeted him. "Waiting for Martin?"

Matt nodded but said nothing, twisting the blade of grass absently around his thumb.

Grace sat on the step next to him and noticed his haircut, the back of his tanned neck showing a white band of skin where the sun hadn't touched. The businessman's cut made him look older. "What are you working on today?" she asked.

"Martin said something about some leaning fence posts to fix," Matt said. His voice was always low and gruff, but today it sounded as if he had a bit of a cold.

Grace leaned over to look him in the face. "Are you feeling all right? Your voice sounds funny."

"I'm okay."

"No, you're not," Grace said simply, observing his red-rimmed eyes. "What's the matter?"

Matt shrugged in embarrassment. "I guess I'm . . . I'm just missing Sylvie a bit."

"Your girlfriend?" Grace asked gently.

"Yeah. We were together for two years. I always knew she wasn't the type to settle on one guy forever. I'm surprised she stayed around as long as she did, really. But the longer she stayed, the more I—I imagined her staying for keeps, you know?"

"I know."

"I can't seem to get my head around the fact that she's gone." He shot her a sideways look. "Like I hear some music on the radio that I know she'd like, and I want to text her about it, or I hear something funny I want to tell her about, and then I remember . . ."

"Oh. Yes."

"This morning it was just seeing the sunrise and wishing I could share something so beautiful with her. I guess that sounds pretty corny. I'm pathetic." Matt tossed the grass away and wiped his palms on his jeaned thighs.

"Not at all," Grace told him. "I felt the same way after my husband died."

He stared at her. "He did? I didn't know you were a widow." Matt flinched at the word, as if regretting its use, but Grace only nodded.

"Yes. I don't tell a lot of people. But, Matt, I was just the same as you—wanting to share things with him, tell him things, and not being able to do it. I couldn't grasp the idea that I'd never be able to do those things with him again. I would hear a car in the driveway and think for just a second that he was home. That any minute he'd walk in the door and say it had all been a stupid mistake."

Matt shook his head. "That must have been bad."

"It was. It still is a lot of the time. But everyone goes through some kind of loss. It's part of life."

"Well, yeah, I know that," Matt said. "And losing your girlfriend isn't as hard as losing a husband."

"I don't know. Maybe it is, for you," Grace told him. "It may be incredibly difficult for you now, but you will emerge stronger from it at some point. You'll find in time the pain of it eases a little."

"Has it for you?" He searched her eyes, shy to ask but needing to know.

Grace thought about her reaction at the school concert, but then she nodded. "Lately, yes. It still comes and goes, I won't lie. But I think the last couple of months I've spent here on the farm have helped me a lot, more than I'd expected. More than I could have hoped for. It's helped me come back to myself, you know?"

Matt rubbed his thighs again, looking out over the grounds toward the distant buildings of the pioneer village. "Until that . . . happens, how do you get through it?" he asked.

"Well, you remind yourself to keep breathing in and out. And it helps to remember that there are other people around you who care about you, and if you'll open yourself up to them, they'll help you through it," Grace said. "I really think that's our main purpose here in life: to just be here for each other, to pick up the pieces for each other."

Matt frowned down at his work boots. "There's nobody around me," he muttered. And before Grace could protest or say anything further, he stood and strode toward the barn without looking back. She watched him go, her mouth open, her heart clenching.

Behind her, the screen door opened, and Martin came out onto the porch. He stood on the step beside her, watching Matt's retreating figure. "I overheard," he said quietly. "I didn't mean to eavesdrop."

Grace shook her head, unable to form words. She felt like crying. She couldn't imagine feeling so alone in the world. And yet, what would she have said to Matt if she'd had the chance? That *she* was there for him? She was going back to Utah in the fall.

"I didn't know you lost your husband," Martin said. "I'm sorry. It must be difficult to be reminded."

Grace shook her head and brushed her sleeve across her eyes. "It's not that. Did you hear what Matt said? He doesn't feel there's anyone in the world who cares about him, who will help him through tough times."

"He told me his mother left when he was a teenager, and I gather his father doesn't have much to do with him. And now he's lost the girl he cared about." Martin gave a sigh and sat down on the step Matt had vacated so abruptly.

"Then it's true. He doesn't have a family to help him through anything," Grace said. "No wonder he's gotten into trouble."

Martin nudged her with his shoulder, and his Irish accent thickened as he said lightly, "Now, I wouldn't be saying that, exactly. He has all of us, doesn't he? We're his family. He just doesn't realize it yet."

Grace smiled. "He's lucky to have you and Laura and Toby."

"And you. You care about him too."

"Of course I do. But I have to leave in a couple of months."

"And what does your location have to do with it?"

She blinked at him. "What do you mean?"

"You're family too, no matter where you are," Martin said simply. He stood and dusted the seat of his jeans with his hands. As he headed toward the barn, he grinned back at her over his shoulder. "You just haven't realized it yet," he said.

Grace tried to watch for opportunities that week to have another conversation with Matt, but it was as if he was avoiding her. He seemed embarrassed at having opened himself up too much to her, and now he kept busy and engineered things so they were never alone. So Grace contented herself with nodding and smiling when she saw him, offering him a warm hello each morning and trying to look somehow *available* in case he wanted to talk. It hurt her to think that he felt so alone and lost. It gave her an unexpected feeling of empathy that she doubted she would have been capable of if she hadn't gone through the struggles she had. She would never be able to say she was glad she had gone through it in the first place—and she knew she wasn't entirely *through* it yet—but at least something good and nourishing had come out of it. If she could use that new empathy to help and reach out to others, it hadn't been for nothing.

It also surprised her to realize how much she cared about Matt's happiness. She watched him working, his scrawny shoulders rounded, his face expressionless, his eyes clouded and unhappy, and she told herself, *This is someone's son.* Her own sons could have ended up like him; who was to say they wouldn't have? But no, she assured herself; they would have had two loving parents who were involved and who cared about their lives. Matt didn't seem to have that. Would it have made a difference to him if he had? She felt sure of it.

It wasn't fair. A kid who was obviously sweet and well-intentioned deep down got off to a rocky start in life with no strong parental figures to guide him. A woman who deep down so wanted to be a good parent was deprived of her children. And the children who could have grown up to be strong, wonderful, contributing adults did not grow up at all.

* * *

Martin kept a watch on Matt. Like Grace, he felt all Matt really needed was some parental attention and a second chance to get back on the right path. He believed the boy was inherently good and had a lot of potential.

But he wasn't content to sit back and just look available. He sought Matt out one day where he was mucking out stalls in the barn.

Matt looked up as he entered, and Martin waved a hand to show he didn't intend to stop him. Matt returned to his work, and Martin leaned against the half wall and watched a moment. He propped one boot on top of the other and studied the dirt caught in the creases of his hands. "Going okay so far?" he asked shortly.

"Yeah. Almost done here."

"I meant in general. Do you like it here?"

"On the farm?" Matt shrugged and heaved a scoop of what Martin referred to as organic fertilizer into the wheelbarrow. "It's okay. I like it okay."

"I wanted to ask you . . . when you are done here this fall, when your hours are up, what are your plans?"

Matt shrugged again. He finished the pitchforking and began to spread clean sawdust over the stall floor. The rich scent of fresh-cut wood filled the barn, and as Martin breathed it in appreciatively, he saw Matt do the same.

"Are you planning to go back to community college? Finish your apprenticeship?"

Matt hesitated, then straightened and looked Martin in the eye. "No. I mean, I want to go back to school, but not to be an electrician."

"What do you want to do?"

The young man set his rake aside, took off his gloves, and stuck them in the hip pocket of his jeans.

When he didn't answer, Martin tipped his head to force Matt to look him in the eye. "What do you want to do?" he repeated.

"You'll laugh."

"Try me."

Matt took a deep breath and then said in a tone meant to convey that he didn't really take any of this seriously, "I was looking online. There's a horticulture program at the University of Guelph that looks pretty interesting."

"You want to do horticulture." It was a statement, not a question.

"Yeah. I think so."

"Why would I laugh at that?" Martin asked. "I think it sounds like a great idea. I think you have an aptitude for it and a real interest in it. I've noticed that about you just in this short amount of time."

"I do? I mean, you think I'd be good at it?"

"Yes. I don't have a single complaint with the work you're doing here. I think you have a good brain in your head and can learn quickly. You sense the importance of the work we do here. You have the patience and gentleness it takes to work with plants."

The corner of Matt's mouth twitched, and he rubbed self-consciously at the colorful, scrawled tattoos on his forearms. "No one's ever called me gentle before."

"They didn't look close enough, then. Gentle is a good thing to be."

Matt kicked at the deep sawdust, stirring up a cloud with his boots. "It doesn't matter anyway."

"What do you mean?"

"I mean I can't afford to go to an actual university, so it doesn't make any difference what I'd be good at or what I'm interested in."

Martin rubbed the back of his neck. "Well now, if you don't go back to school, what will you do this fall?"

"Go back home. Try to find a job. Maybe the fish 'n' chip shop will take me back," Matt said gloomily.

"Is that what you want?"

Matt snapped his head back and met Martin's gaze with an angry look. "No. I just said I didn't, didn't I?"

"Don't give up on the school idea. If you want to study horticulture, do it."

Matt threw out his arms. "Didn't you hear me?"

"Yes, but I don't accept that as an argument. If you want to go to university, you'll find a way to do it."

"Even if I had the money, I don't have the grades to get in."

"Did you finish high school?"

"Yeah."

"What was your grade point average?"

"3.0."

"That isn't so bad. You could take a few make-up courses at the community college and bring your grades up. I'd give you a recommendation."

"You would?"

"Sure." Martin straightened and headed toward the barn door. "Don't let anything stop you from helping yourself. You're worth the effort." He paused at the door and looked back toward Matt, who stood watching him with narrow eyes. "I'll make you a deal, son. You work hard, bring the grades up, and if you get accepted to the horticulture program, I'll make sure you have the money to go."

"Wait! What? You'd do that?" Matt gasped, astounded.

"Like I said, you're worth the effort."

"But . . ." Matt struggled to comprehend. "I'm not even your kid."

Martin smiled. "Says who?" He left the barn, leaving Matt standing with his hands dangling and his mouth open.

CHAPTER EIGHTEEN

As Grace was walking past the general store the next afternoon on her way back from a visit with Michelle and Jane to further discuss plans for the Copper Creek Educational Center, she saw Caleb Fisher leaning bored in the doorway, and an idea struck her. She waved and walked over, and he straightened.

"Hi! Working today?" she asked.

"Yeah, Sarah had a dentist appointment, so I came over after school to cover for her."

Grace gazed out over the sun-drenched fields toward the distant greenhouse.

"You know, if you want, when your shift is over, you could come over to the farm and Matt could introduce you to the big horses. He's working at the farm for the summer."

The boredom dropped from Caleb's face, and he said eagerly, "Yeah? Sure, I'd like that."

"He's a bit older than you, but I think you'd get along with him," Grace said. "Just drop by the greenhouse and find me, and I'll show you where to find him."

"Thanks! I'll be over at six o'clock," he said as she waved and continued on her way.

Caleb seemed like a good kid, Grace thought as she walked along the road toward the farm. Friendly, not in any trouble. Caleb would enjoy seeing the horses, but that hadn't been her motive. It would be good if Matt could make a friend closer to his own age while he was here.

When Mason came the next weekend, Martin thought he seemed a bit cautious around Declan at first, as if waiting to see what his son's reaction toward him would be after his absence from the school concert. But Declan actually greeted him at the breakfast table instead of going out to the barn, and both he and Lark vied to be the first to tell him all the latest news. Mason visibly relaxed as he watched his son, his expression one of relief and gratification. Declan was a far cry from his usual sullen self, and with mute astonishment, Laura and Martin watched him yammer away.

After breakfast, when the children ran off to dress for the day and Grace had gone to meet Matt at the greenhouse, Laura turned to Mason and Martin.

"I never! Did you hear Declan talk? He hasn't been this animated since Christmas vacation."

Mason shook his head. "I was all braced for two days of the silent treatment."

"Yes, well, you still might get that from me for missing the concert," Laura said, taking the dishes to the sink and starting to wash them. "I know, I know, you had court. You couldn't control it. But, Mason, you need to keep your promises to the children. It was so important to them. Especially to Declan. You should have seen the disappointment on his face when you called."

Mason bristled. "I know that, Mom. You don't have to remind me."

"If this was the first time it had happened, I'd agree with you," Laura replied, turning to face him with suds on her hands. "But it isn't the first time you've let them down, is it? You can't do that to children."

"Declan seems to have gotten over it," Mason responded. "You saw him. He was fine toward me this morning."

"Which is just short of a miracle," Laura answered. "Those children aren't going to stay little for long. You can't keep missing important things in their lives."

"What do you want me to do, Mom? Tell my client he has to go to court alone, without representation? I can't control court-date changes. I'm sorry things didn't go as planned. I feel bad enough, and you harping on me isn't helping."

Martin stepped between the two, holding up his hands placatingly. "We understand, Mason. Really, we do. But you also need to understand that the kids need to know they can rely on you."

"They know they can."

Laura wiped her hands on a towel and then stood gripping it, looking down at the floor. "I don't know, Mason. Sometimes I wonder if this whole thing is right. If maybe they would be better off living in Toronto with you."

Martin blinked at her. He knew having the kids here was hard on her, but he had never heard her come so close to admitting it.

Mason spread his hands. "We've gone through all that already, Mom. Do you really think they'd be better off in a daycare somewhere instead of here with their grandparents? Or are you really saying you two just don't want to keep them anymore?"

Laura slapped the towel down on the counter. "You know full well we love having those kids stay with us. It would rip me apart to send them back to the city with you. But it's just so hard on them to be apart from you. I'm trying to think what would be best for them."

"A babysitter in the big city isn't better for them than their grandparents!"

"I agree, and that's why they're here. I'm just—I'm just second-guessing everything. Lark is all right, but Declan really feels it when you're not here. He's getting into trouble at school. His grades are suffering. He keeps getting kept after class in detention."

Mason scowled. "Why didn't you tell me this before?"

"Because I felt, like you, that staying with us was for the best, and I thought he'd settle down eventually. But he hasn't. It's getting worse. Well, at least until Grace came to stay with us. That seems to have had a calming effect on him lately."

"Yes. I've seen that myself." Mason cleared his throat. "I don't think it's a good idea to let him get too attached to her."

"Why not? She's good for him."

"She's only here until fall."

"I don't know how you can prevent him from liking her," Laura said.

"He shouldn't spend so much time with her."

"He doesn't, really. Just the occasional cooking session. Most of the time, he's at school and she's out working in the fields."

"Still, it worries me that Declan's gotten so wrapped up in her in such a short time," Mason said. "He'll only be hurt when it's time for her to go. He needs to learn he can't depend on her."

There was a pause.

"Are you talking about Declan now or yourself, Mason?" Martin asked quietly.

Mason scowled and looked away out the window. "What do you mean? Declan, of course. I'm just trying to keep him from being hurt."

"But you could also see it the other way around," Laura added. "You could want him to soak up all the happiness he can while he has the chance. Before she goes."

"But it will just hurt him worse!"

"Maybe so, at the time. But think of all the happy memories he'll have after she's gone. You wouldn't want him to cut himself off from the chance to have those, would you?"

"Grace happens to agree with me. She said she would try not to spend so much one-on-one time with him."

"Oh, Mason, you didn't say anything to her, did you? If you only knew how much both she and Declan have blossomed in the last little while!" Laura said. "It isn't fair of you. If you aren't going to spend time with him yourself, you can't begrudge him the time he spends with someone else. And, frankly, son, you could use a few happy moments yourself."

Mason struggled a moment, his hands flexing in frustration, and then he growled. "What do you mean, if I'm not going to spend time with him myself? I do, every moment I can! I feel guilty as sin every time I have to go back to Toronto. I know it's important to spend every minute I can with my son."

Laura put her hands on the edge of the sink and leaned on them, her head bowed. "I know, I know. I'm sorry I said it that way. I know you're doing your best." She straightened and looked at him. "Maybe I'm just impatient and haven't given it enough time. Maybe it will all work out all right anyway. But I have to say, Mason, those children need you to be involved in their lives, and I don't think seeing you twice a month is cutting it."

Mason dragged his fingers through his hair, making it stand on end in gold feathers. "What more can I do?"

"I think it would help if you came every weekend instead of every other one. It might help everybody."

"Then I will rearrange things so I can," he said. But even as Mason spoke, Martin knew from the sag in his son's shoulders that he didn't know how he could pull it off. He knew Mason's partners were already carrying the bulk of the load on weekends. If he told them he couldn't take his turn at *all* . . .

He watched Mason draw himself up. "I'll figure out a way," he said firmly.

Laura let out a long sigh. "Good. Let's try that. I think it would help give Declan the message."

"What message is that?"

She tipped her head back to look her towering son in the eye. "That you value him as much as he values you."

After the conversation, Laura went into her wool room and Mason went outside. After giving Mason a little time alone, Martin quietly followed his son. He found Mason stomping back and forth inside the barn, his fists in his pockets. When Martin approached, Mason stopped and faced him squarely, and the scowl on his face reminded Martin of when his son had been a teenager sulking over some blowup with his mother. Some things didn't change with age, he mused. Back when Mason had been a teenager, they had lived in a two-story house in Port Dover. Mason's favorite place to sulk had been the dilapidated shed in the backyard. He supposed the barn was as good a substitute as any.

"I swear, Dad, sometimes talking to Mom makes me feel just rotten," Mason said.

Martin shook his head and sat on a bale of straw, leaning back against the wall.

"I mean, does she think I *like* being separated from them? That I *wanted* to miss the dad-blamed concert?" He spread his hands wide. "She practically said Declan has glommed onto Grace because I'm not here for him."

"Well, now, Grace is pretty likeable in and of herself whether you're here or not," Martin remarked. "I don't think your mother meant to hurt you."

"I know she's just thinking of the kids. But, Dad, you know I'm already torn apart."

"I know," Martin replied evenly. "You feel you need to make a decent living to keep this whole show going, you need to pull your fair share of the weight at work, but you need to be with your children too."

"Exactly," Mason said, resuming his pacing. "I feel bad enough already that I've dumped them on you. I'm not blind as to how hard this has been on both of you. You didn't plan to raise two little kids at the age when most people are retiring."

"We like having them here; you know that. We're happy to help you however we can."

"I don't know. Maybe she's right. Maybe I should take them back to Toronto." Before Martin's heart could stop cold at the thought, Mason went on. "But I don't want them to grow up there. I never did. I don't like the city. Living there in the first place was Janet's idea, not mine." Martin opened his mouth to remark on this surprising comment, but Mason rounded on him before he could speak. "And just what did you mean by that crack about whether I was referring to Declan or myself? Is that what you really think? That I'm not worried about my son's feelings; I'm just still wrapped up in my own pain?"

"Now, Mason—"

"What father wouldn't spare his son pain if he could?"

Martin stood. He was a full foot shorter than his son and couldn't look him straight in the eye, so he stepped up on a bale of straw to bring them to the same level. His voice was thunderous when he answered. "None! A father will do whatever he can to promote his son's happiness. But no matter how much he loves his child—*because* he loves his child—he can't protect him from pain in this life. I can't, and neither can you. And it wouldn't be doing our children any favors if we did."

For a moment, they stood frozen, glaring at each other eye to eye.

Then Mason's lips twitched in his beard. "Don't fall, Dad. Your bones aren't what they used to be."

They both began to laugh at once.

Martin gripped Mason's shoulder to steady himself as he climbed down from the bale. "You can say that again," he muttered. "But don't tell your mother I admitted it. She still thinks I'm invincible." Safely on the ground once more, he looked up at Mason. "Do you hear what I'm saying though, son?"

"Yes, Dad. I love you too."

Martin nodded sharply. "Pain is part of life, Mason. You can let it strengthen you or break you; it's your choice."

"I know."

"And it will be Declan's choice. You can't spare him from it. He has a *right* to that choice."

Mason looked away, out the open door of the barn, to the sun on the fields. "Yes, Dad. I've got it."

"Now go walk it off, and when you're ready, go back in the house and talk to your mother like an adult."

Mason's lips twitched again. "Yes, Dad."

He left the barn. Martin watched him go, then sat slowly on the bale of straw, rested his elbows on his knees, and put his head in his hands. He suddenly felt impossibly old and unbearably sad. He knew what he had said to Mason was true; life constantly presented opportunities to learn and grow, and that was how it should be. But knowing that didn't make it any easier to watch his child go through it. It didn't prevent the helplessness and weariness he was feeling now.

Briefly, just for a moment, Martin allowed himself to wish he had someone or something bigger and stronger and wiser than himself to lean on. He wished the strife in his family and Laura's over religion hadn't trampled his own belief in God. It would be a tremendous relief, he thought wistfully, if that whole matter of God turned out to be true. Then he wouldn't have to be so alone through his struggles. But until that happened, he couldn't rely on it. He had only himself and Laura. Well, and he had the comfort he drew from the earth and the plants he worked with. As he'd said to Grace, it was enough to be getting on with.

After a few minutes, Martin stood, consciously straightened his spine, lifted his chin, and walked back to the house.

* * *

A herd of schoolchildren was swarming in and out of the museum schoolhouse, noisy as crows, with sticky candy in their hands and backpacks strapped to their shoulders. They jostled against Grace, laughing, not noticing her. Their teachers barked orders and called admonishments, trying to keep them all in order. Overwhelmed with the noise and motion, Grace pushed through, rounded the corner of the building, and bashed into someone coming in the opposite direction.

"Oh!" Grace gasped as the basket she was carrying went flying. Woolen skeins flew into the dirt and bounced into the grass.

"I'm so sorry," Mason stuttered, scrambling to retrieve her load. "Did I hurt you? I didn't see you."

"I'm fine. It was my fault for not watching where I was going," Grace said quickly, ignoring the throbbing toe he'd stepped on. She bent to help him refill the basket, dusting off the balls of yarn and trying to disentangle bits of twig from one of the skeins.

"Did I ruin them?" Mason asked morosely.

"I think they're fine. Nothing they haven't handled before. I mean, it's not like sheep wear plastic wrap, do they?" She replaced the full basket on her hip and gave a laugh. "A little dirt will give them authenticity. The tourists will gobble that up."

"I'm sorry again. I was going too fast, trying to get past the crowd. I know these tour groups are important to my parents' income, but sometimes I get claustrophobic."

"I know what you mean. I feel completely the same way. It's great the kids are coming to the museum, but I wish they *wouldn't*, you know?"

He smiled. "Where are you headed? I'll carry it for you."

"I'm taking them to the gift shop for them to sell. But that's okay; I can carry it."

Mason lifted the basket from her. "I'll take it. It's the least I can do after nearly knocking you down."

"Thank you." Grace fell in step beside him as they turned toward the gift shop. He seemed in a dark mood as he strode briskly along, so she didn't say anything, just walked beside him and left him to his own thoughts.

After a little while, he seemed to come back to himself and shook his head, giving her a small rueful smile. "Sorry, I'm not good company today, I'm afraid."

"Is everything all right?"

He started to give the pat answer "Everything's fine," but something in her direct blue gaze made him hesitate. "Not really," he admitted. "Just had a squabble with my mom."

"Oh, I know how those go. My sympathies." Grace laughed. "Though I actually can't imagine Laura fighting with anyone."

"Don't let her small stature fool you. She could take on a grown wolf with her bare hands," Mason said glumly.

"I'd pity the wolf. Is there anything I can help with?" Grace offered.

He frowned. "It's nothing we haven't fought over before, and no doubt we'll go a few more rounds again."

They went into the visitors' center and found Jane Persaud alone at the gift shop counter going over a pile of receipts.

She laid aside her pencil, perched her glasses on the top of her graying head, and greeted Grace and Mason warmly. "Lovely! We just sold our last ball of yarn last night. Tell Laura thank you. And it's good to see you again, Mason. In town for the weekend?"

"Yes."

"We don't see enough of you these days," she said. "Come by sometime when Robert's working; he's missed you."

"I'll do that. And you can tell him I'll be around a bit more in the future. I'm going to start coming up every weekend," Mason told her.

Grace glanced at him in surprise but said nothing, though she could surmise what his fight with Laura had been about. Grace hid a smile as they exited the gift shop and stepped from the visitors' center into the bright sunlight once more. "You know, I'm glad to have the chance to talk to you, Mason. I have the feeling we didn't really get to finish our conversation the other day because I had to leave for church," Grace said as they walked slowly toward home. "Was there something else you wanted to say?"

"Oh." Mason shook his head. "It doesn't matter. We covered the basics of it."

She could see he didn't want to pursue it further, so she dropped it and fished for something else to talk about. "Do you know I was from Port Dover originally?" she asked. "I lived here as a child."

"You did?"

"My family moved to the States when I was twelve."

"I grew up here too. Maybe we went to the same school. We're about the same age. Thirty-five?"

"Just younger. Maybe we did. Isn't that a weird thought?"

"I think I would have remembered you if you were in my class," Mason said thoughtfully. "Did you go to Doverwood?"

She shrugged. "I don't recall the name of my grade school. I only vaguely remember being here. I don't think I remember the museum at all."

"I think it's been here since the 1940s."

"Oh. Maybe I never visited. I didn't recognize it, anyway, when I was looking up farms I could apply to. I was just looking for something far away, and when I saw this was near Port Dover, it felt like the right place. Like returning to myself."

"Why did your family move?"

"My father got a job in Utah. I'm a dual citizen now. That's why I'm able to work here."

"Oh. I never even thought of that."

She laughed. "And you an immigration lawyer."

"I figured you had a work permit or something. It's not like it's a paying job anyway."

"It's definitely paying, just not financially." She paused, but he didn't follow up on the opening, so she left it. She couldn't think of another topic, and he showed no signs of offering one, so she lapsed into silence. They left the noise of the schoolchildren behind and soon were alone on the winding road home.

A few minutes later, as Toby's house came into view, a question occurred to her. "Toby told me he was a sheepherder even when he was young, but when did he become a blacksmith? Did he move here at the same time as your parents?"

"Actually, he was here first. He was the main caretaker and grounds-keeper of the museum for many years until he got too old to work full-time. So now he's semiretired and just does the smithing and leatherworking demonstrations and whatnot. The museum let him stay on in the house; I think they have an agreement that he can stay there until he dies. If he ever does. Somehow I can't picture it."

Grace didn't want to think about Toby dying. "And your parents?"

"My folks were hired here shortly after Toby retired fifteen years ago while I was away at university. Dad ran a small fruit market in town before that."

"I'm trying to figure out how someone who grew up in such a beautiful countryside could stand living in Toronto. I would think you'd hate the city. But—"

"I do hate the city," Mason said.

Grace blinked at him. "Then why do you live there?"

"It's where the work is. An immigration lawyer has to work where there is an immigrant population. Toronto has that in abundance. I think about half the city is from somewhere else."

"And do you like being an immigration lawyer?"

He was silent a moment, head down, watching his feet on the gravel. Then he glanced sideways at her. "You know, I don't think anyone has ever asked me that before."

"Haven't they?"

"The answer is no. I don't particularly like it. I don't hate it, but it isn't really me."

"But then—"

"It provided the things Janet wanted—the children's mother," he said. "A nice home and the right social circles were important to her. She came from a much wealthier family than mine, and it was what she was used to. I didn't have the same goals, but I was twenty-four and desperately in love with a girl I didn't really understand. So I let myself get talked into a career I wasn't sure I wanted. I resisted becoming a corporate lawyer though. At least I held my ground on that. It would have paid better, but I know I wouldn't have liked that environment."

"Well, it's not too late to change careers," Grace said, gazing out over the fields toward the greenhouse. The sunlight glinted off the roof like a spotlight, almost blinding, and she had to look away. "I loved my work as a music teacher. I immersed myself in it. But I don't think I really want to go back to it. It's time to try something different."

In truth, if she was honest with herself, she didn't want to try to go back to the same life she'd had before at all. She couldn't recapture it, and anything approximating it would end up hollow and unfulfilling. She wanted to create an entirely new life. How, she wasn't quite sure yet.

"Do you know what you'll do instead?" he asked.

"Still working on it," she answered. "I'm open to ideas. What about you? If you weren't a lawyer, what would you like to do? Take up farming like your dad?"

"Definitely not. But I think maybe I'd enjoy working in the not-for-profit sector. Some charitable organization where I could still use my legal training. Or even . . ."

"What?"

"Don't laugh. I think it sounds fun to teach English as a second language. It's all the work I do with immigrants, you see. Knowing English is such a pivotal thing for them. It can be the vital difference between a satisfying life or deep poverty in a new country. I know men with PhDs in physics and engineering who have had to give up good careers in order to come to Canada. Now they work delivering pizza because they don't know English well enough to do anything in their field. One woman I know used to be a biochemistry professor in China, but here in Toronto, she's working as a cashier in a grocery store to support her kids. If her language skills were better, she could change her whole life. As a teacher, it would be great to be able to have such a huge effect on someone's happiness."

Grace saw the color rise in his cheeks above his beard, the light brighten his eyes as he spoke, his whole being suddenly engaged and energetic. She had never seen him look so animated. "I think you've found your passion," she told him. "Why don't you do that?"

"It would mean going to teacher's college."

"It's only a year or two, isn't it?"

"How would it be, giving up years of schooling and a solid legal career to go teach ESL for fifteen bucks an hour?"

"The immigrants you spoke of gave up good careers to pursue something they thought was worthwhile. Is it the drop in income that worries you or the drop in prestige?" Grace tried to lighten the comment with a smile, but he looked thoughtful as he considered her words.

"I'm pretty sure it's just the loss of income. I never cared about prestige or social position the way Janet did. But I do have financial obligations I have to meet."

"Well, maybe if you can't afford to do it full-time, you could do it on the side and pursue your legal career part-time. Find a balance. Life is all about balance, as I've finally figured out. A bit late, but better late than never."

They paused at the back door of the house, and Mason turned to Grace. "I'm sorry again that I bumped into you," he said, smiling, "but I'm also glad I bumped into you. I enjoyed talking to you."

"Me too."

"See you at lunch."

"Good luck with your mother," Grace said.

"Oh. Yeah." Mason took a deep breath, squared his shoulders, and, giving Grace a wink, went into the house.

CHAPTER NINETEEN

THAT SUNDAY, GRACE AND MARGARET both arrived at the church's front door at the same time.

"Good morning," Grace greeted her friend, holding the door for her.

"Thanks," Margaret said, but something in her face and tone made Grace look at her more closely.

"Are you okay? You look sort of down."

"I'm fine." Margaret waited while Grace hung her sweater in the cloak room, then they walked into the chapel together, running the usual gauntlet of young, suited missionaries eager to shake their hands. But when Grace went to sit in what had become her usual seat, she saw Margaret had hung back and taken a seat near the back of the room. Puzzled, Grace went to sit beside her.

"Okay, what's up? I can tell something's bothering you."

"It's nothing you can do anything about," Margaret said. "I'm just out of sorts today. I don't mean to be rude, but I'd rather not chat today."

"Okay, we'll sit here in silence and listen to the prelude music," Grace replied.

They sat in stony silence for about thirty seconds, and then Margaret burst out, "I had a fight with Toby."

That surprised Grace. "I can't imagine Toby fighting with anyone."

"Well, to tell the truth, I had the fight and he just stood there and listened," Margaret admitted. "The man won't argue back. It's very frustrating."

"What was the fight about, can I ask?"

"I'd rather not talk about it. What's done is done."

"But surely you're still friends."

"I don't know. I really don't." Margaret shot her a miserable look and then looked away. "Oh, look, Marjorie Dawson has had her baby. And she has it out in public already. How can a woman bear seven children and still look that good?"

Grace followed her gaze to where a woman surrounded by well-wishers was showing off a blue-wrapped bundle. "You're just changing the subject," she began, but just then Annie Fisher approached.

"There's another woman who still looks good after having a jillion children," Margaret said morosely.

Grace choked on her laughter and turned it into a cough.

Annie greeted them both, oblivious to Margaret's remark. "Hi, Margaret! Hi, Grace! I was hoping to see you today," she said. "I wanted to thank you, Grace, for arranging for Caleb to see the horses at the farm. He's been on cloud nine ever since. Driving all of us nuts talking about them nonstop."

"I'm glad he enjoyed it," Grace said.

"And he's been talking about the cool tattooed kid who showed them to him. He asked me to find out his cell phone number if you know it."

"His name is Matt. But I'm sorry. I don't know if he has a cell phone or what the number would be."

"Caleb just wants to invite Matt to a movie. A group of kids is going to see some car-chase-smash'em-up-testosterone-filled action thing this Friday."

"I'm sure Matt would like to come. I'll give him your number and have him call Caleb tonight to get the details."

"Good idea. Thanks!"

As Annie moved away, Grace turned back to Margaret, but just then the bishop stood to start the meeting, and further conversation wasn't possible.

When Grace got home that evening, she went over to Toby's house. He didn't answer her knock, but she found him a little later walking back from the sheep pasture with his cane. She walked down the lane to meet him.

"This mud can't be good for your shoes," he observed, noting her Sunday pumps.

"I saw Margaret at church today," she said without acknowledging what he'd said.

Toby nodded, continuing toward his house.

Grace fell in step beside him. "She seemed very sad," Grace told him. "What happened between you two?"

"What did she say?"

"Just that you had an argument. She didn't give me details. You two seemed to be getting along so well, Toby. What would you have to fight about?"

"A disagreement in viewpoints," he replied shortly.

"I know it isn't any of my business—"

"No."

"And I don't want to pry—"

"Yes, you do."

"All right, I do. Can't you iron things out with her? She feels really bad about it."

"Facts can't be changed, Grace. You can't iron out facts."

"What facts?"

He didn't reply. They reached his house, and he moved to open the door. Grace put a hand on his, stopping him. He turned to look at her, and she read sorrow in his face. She sensed without any doubt that Toby felt as deeply as Margaret did about the disagreement.

"Whatever it is, Toby, I wish you'd talk to her about it. Or if you can't talk to her, talk to me. You were there for me when I was ready to talk, and I'll be here when you're ready to talk."

"There's nothing more to be said."

"There's one thing to say to Margaret, at least."

"What's that?"

"That you love her. Because you do, don't you? Maybe she needs to hear that."

He grew still, his eyes on hers, but he didn't reply.

"Have you told her so?" Grace asked.

"No. It wouldn't be appropriate."

"Why not?"

"Because I'm eighty-four; that's why not!" he suddenly barked. "She's only seventy-five. She doesn't need to be saddled with a gimp-legged old geezer who smells of sheep."

"Isn't that for her to decide?"

"That's just what she said."

"Is that what you fought about?"

"She won't listen to reason. She's got it in her head what she wants, and she won't budge."

"And what is it she wants, Toby?"

He shook his head. "Me," he said glumly.

"Exactly. She wants *you.* As you are. It's the eighty-four-year-old geezer she has fallen in love with, and it's the eighty-four-year-old geezer she wants. Sheep and gimp leg and all."

"She just thinks that's what she wants," Toby replied.

"I think at her age she's probably pretty good at knowing her own mind," Grace said.

"What's that quip supposed to mean? Are you calling her old?"

"You know I didn't m—"

"Because she isn't old, Grace. She's young at heart, as young as you. She's young and beautiful and sweet and funny . . ." His voice trailed off, and he put one hand up and drew it down his face. Against his calloused hand, his whiskers sounded like sandpaper.

Grace leaned her forehead briefly against his shoulder, then looked up into his face.

"Talk to her, Toby. You don't really want to lose her, do you?"

He shook his head. "I want her to be happy."

"And I want *you* to be happy. Which would make you happier: being with her or without her?"

"With her, of course."

"Then there really isn't anything to argue about, is there?"

Toby drew in a deep breath. "But could she really be happy with someone like me?"

"I know she could," Grace said firmly. "After all, you're a fine specimen of a man. You told me so yourself."

When he began to laugh, she knew it would be all right.

Grace and Laura were in the wool room. Grace was telling Laura all about the plans for the educational center, which the board of directors was considering, and Laura was teaching Grace to knit. The children were at school, and Grace was grateful they weren't around to witness her humiliation. It turned out she had no coordination whatsoever, something she had never suspected before.

Laura laughed and undid the row of uneven stitches for the third time, then handed her back the needles. "Try not to be quite so tense," she suggested. "Hold them lightly. Not like you're trying to impale someone with them. They aren't switchblades."

Grace sighed. "You make it look so easy."

"I've been doing it since I was five," Laura said offhandedly. "You just started. Be patient with yourself."

"Yes, well, that isn't my strong point." Grace sighed.

"Really?" Laura grinned. "I wouldn't have known."

"I know. It's like when I was learning to spin. It takes practice."

"You also can't judge something until it's finished. Not spinning, not plowing, not knitting, not the cake in the oven . . . and not raising children. Martin reminds me of that from time to time. The kids aren't done yet, and I can't panic about how they're turning out yet. But if Declan is still hiding naked in the lilac bushes when he's forty, we'll know we have a problem."

Grace laughed and took up the yarn again. She held it as she had been shown and tried to keep it from slipping the wrong way on the slick needles. Laura sat at her spinning wheel, her foot and hands working rhythmically. The soft hush of the spinning wheel filled the room, and Grace tried to relax her shoulders and neck.

And then Laura stopped working and looked at Grace determinedly. "Speaking of raising children, I've been wanting to ask you something."

"Oh? Is it about Declan?"

"No, not really. It's just . . . You seem to have such a way with children, Grace," Laura said. "I suppose it's because you used to run a music school."

"Actually, most of my students were adults," Grace told her. She paused, then lowered her knitting needles, wondering if Toby had told Laura her story. But from the probing look on Laura's face, she could see he hadn't. She added quietly, "But I did have three children myself."

Laura's hands dropped into her lap. "Oh, Grace. I wondered if maybe you had, but I didn't know how to ask . . ."

"Two boys and a girl." Grace told her simply what had happened. And once again, as with Annie and Toby, she found she could talk about it without the usual searing pain. She wondered again if it was because she was finally healing at last. Or maybe because she knew she was speaking with someone who cared. She knew Laura and Toby loved her, and she had known instantly upon meeting Annie Fisher that she was a friend just waiting to be met. That made the difference, perhaps. Whatever it was, she could breathe again.

When Grace finished, Laura's eyes were bright with unshed tears. "I'm so sorry," she said. "I didn't know, or I wouldn't have brought it up."

"It's all right. I'm able to talk about it now. I couldn't right at first. When I first came here, I mean." Grace bent over her needles again. "But being here has helped me a lot, Laura. Your accepting family, your kindness. The work itself. I think working in the earth has helped to . . . well, *ground* me. No pun intended."

Laura smiled. "Martin always says there's nothing that nature can't heal."

"After this summer, I agree." Grace held her hands still a moment, looking fondly at her friend and employer. "I think my religious beliefs have also helped me heal. We Mormons believe that families can go on forever, not just in this life but in the afterlife too. I believe I'll see my husband again one day and be with my children. I'm still their mother, even if I can't be with them right now."

Laura looked at her a moment, then nodded vigorously. "That's a lovely thought. I like that. It sounds *right*."

"Yes. I've always liked that concept."

"I've never liked that phrase 'till death do you part.' I've always felt that something you experience so strongly here shouldn't be lost just because you die."

"There are things you have to do in order for that family bond to be perpetuated," Grace said. "I can explain it to you if you want."

"Yes," Laura said, her voice sure. "I'd like that. Do you mind telling me?"

"You teach me; I teach you. After all, Copper Creek is going to be an educational center, isn't it?" Grace said with a grin and lobbed the tangled ball of yarn and the needles into the basket.

The next Saturday, Grace drove to Port Dover. She parked her car just down the road from the schoolteacher's house—she really must learn his name, she told herself—and stepped onto the sidewalk. She didn't bother locking the car doors. It was Port Dover, after all, not Toronto, and she wasn't going to be gone that long. She strode toward his house, gripping the small basket of fresh-picked blueberries she'd brought. But the closer to the house she got, the slower her steps became. When she reached his gate, she kept right on walking, eyes straight ahead as if her destination were farther down the road. At the corner, she turned and stopped, resting her back against a maple tree on the boulevard.

"It's just a friendly gesture," she muttered. "I was just in town. Thought I'd drop by. To thank you for the lemonade the other day." She snorted, hearing herself. She sounded like one of his high school students, justifying being somewhere she had no business being. "Yeah, I spent half an hour picking blueberries and then drove twenty minutes just to thank you for a glass of lemonade you gave me two weeks ago. You probably don't even remember it. You probably haven't thought of it since."

But I have.

This was ridiculous. She straightened and walked back toward the house, and this time as she passed it, she glanced to her left. There was no car in the driveway. No sign of life. Grace hesitated, then darted through the gate, up the walk, and onto the porch. She set the basket of berries in front of the door and hurried back to the sidewalk and continued back to her car without looking back.

Safely in the car with the engine running, she put her face in her hands and didn't know if she felt like laughing or crying. She raised her head and eyed herself with amusement in the rearview mirror. Her face was flushed pink, and her hair was straggling from its braid.

"Maybe," she said kindly to the pathetic image, "you're not quite ready yet."

She turned the car for home.

CHAPTER TWENTY

As summer deepened, the produce going into the CSA bins altered. Matt enjoyed seeing how the green onions were replaced with fat white onions, the beets with chubby eggplants. Each customer got a pound of Roma beans, a bunch of kale, a handful of fresh basil, a bunch of celery, a head of pungent garlic, green beans, chard, spinach, two fat zucchini, a few green peppers, a pound of new potatoes, and, as a finishing touch, a bouquet of small sunflowers. Sometimes he noted Laura would also slip in a jar of crabapple jelly or a small bottle of maple syrup made on-site at the museum sugar shack.

The work of the farm turned more to harvesting and less to weeding. Matt had never worked so hard in his life, but he liked it. It seemed every moment was spent digging or picking or washing. Grace worked alongside him most of the time in easy companionship. He had noticed his thin figure had started to fill out and his skin was turning as dark as Grace's and Martin's. As if the work in the sun had branded him as *belonging* in this place the way they did. It seemed easier to talk to them these days too, easier than when he'd first arrived. He had to admit he didn't even think about Sylvie every minute anymore. His head was too taken up with the things he was learning, the people he'd met around the museum, his new friends, his new awareness of the weather, the work itself. He even told Grace a little bit about his father and was embarrassed when he heard the yearning affection creep into his voice, but Grace hadn't seemed to notice it.

"Maybe," she suggested, "when your service hours are up and he comes to pick you up, he could spend a couple of days on the farm with everyone and you could show him what you've been doing."

Matt was excited about this idea. "I think he'd like to meet you all," he said.

"We could have a picnic lunch and take him on a tour of the museum. Maybe go for a ride on the wagon behind the horses. I always love doing that."

"Yeah, that never gets old," Matt agreed. He sighed in contentment. "I'll ask Laura and Martin about it. I don't think Dad's ever been on a farm before. He might find he likes it."

"The way you do," Grace said.

"Yeah."

"Did you go to that movie with Caleb and his friends the other night?"

"Yeah, that was fun. They seem okay." He didn't want to let on how much he had enjoyed hanging out with a bunch of teenagers, but they had been okay. Friendly and nonjudgmental.

"Caleb's a nice guy," Grace said. "It's good to see you hang out together."

"I don't have much time for it though," Matt said doubtfully. "Martin always has something else for me to do. When I finish one thing, it's another."

"You're still entitled to time off once in a while," Grace said. "It's okay to ask. As long as you get your service hours in, it doesn't really matter *when* you do them, does it? I mean, knocking off for the day one time at four instead of five won't really make much difference."

"I guess not," Matt said. This hadn't occurred to him before. They worked in silence awhile longer, and then Matt straightened and looked at the buckets of new potatoes they had been rubbing free of dirt with their gloves. "Why don't we just put them on the lawn and spray them with the hose?" he asked, stretching the small of his back. "Wouldn't that be quicker?"

"Because you don't want to get them wet if you're going to be storing them for any period of time," Grace explained. "If you just knock the excess dirt off a little, keep them dry, and then let them cure for a few days, they'll keep longer without going bad."

"Is that why we don't wash the carrots either?"

"Yes. But you take the green tops off so the fronds don't continue to respire."

"What do you mean, 'respire'?"

"Carrots are still alive when you take them out of the ground. The fronds still breathe, and they can draw the moisture out of the carrot root unless you remove them. If you leave them on, the carrots will go soft and bendy faster."

"Oh yeah, is that why the carrots you see at the grocery store don't have the green tops on them?"

"Yes. At least, that's what Martin says."

"It's weird to think they stay alive after you pull them out of the ground," Matt said.

"I know. I helped Martin thin them when they were just tiny sprouts. We tossed them on the compost heap, but they didn't get covered up, and when I looked a few weeks later, there were a bunch of full-size carrots lying on the heap. They'd kept growing in the open air after we'd picked them."

"Weird. Vegetables are weird, you know?"

"Well, they're certainly more interesting than I'd ever thought."

"I know. Like kohlrabi."

"What about kohlrabi?"

"It looks like an alien ship from outer space," Matt said. "That stuff is trippy."

"I guess." She shrugged.

"You're a good teacher, like Martin," Matt told her and returned to his work.

Grace stood a moment, blinking down at the potato she held in her gloved hand with a bemused expression. "I didn't even have to think about the answers I just gave you," she said. "That means I'm not just retaining what Martin has taught me; I'm *understanding* it." A smile blossomed across Grace's pretty face as she stretched her arms wide and said, "I guess maybe I am still a teacher after all, deep down. Music or vegetables—there isn't much difference."

* * *

Regarding service hours, Martin was not even keeping track of what time Matt arrived each morning or left each day, though he supposed he probably should. He trusted Matt to keep track of the hours himself. As Matt's and Grace's proficiency grew, Martin left more and more of the work in their hands, allowing himself to spend his days doing repairs around the house, exercising the horses, and catching up on all the little tasks he'd been unable to get to before. A couple of times, he'd even slept in past sunrise.

"I want Matt to finish his schooling," Laura confessed to Martin one night as they readied for bed. Martin had told her of his conversation with Matt in the barn. "But I have to say, I'd also like to see him come work for us full-time. He makes your life much easier."

"Yes, he does," Martin said. "And Grace does too. It's been a long time since I let myself sit and have a lemonade on the porch in the middle of a workday."

"You need to do that more often."

"So do you."

They eyed each other a moment, and then both started to laugh.

"This growing-old thing is for the birds." Laura sighed, reaching to snap off the lamp. "How long do you think we can keep up this type of life?"

"I have a few years left in me," Martin assured her, sliding into the bed beside her and tucking her against his chest. "Besides, as long as old Toby is still galloping around here, I can't very well slack off, now can I? Think of the shame."

"That's another thing that worries me. Toby will probably outlast both of us, but he's over eighty. He can't possibly keep up the pace forever. Who will look after him when we're too old and feeble? He needs someone around him."

Martin chuckled. "I don't think you need to worry about that."

"That Margaret woman, you mean?"

"He was out with her again last night. Going for fish and chips, he said. They've been seeing a lot of each other."

"You've noticed that too? Do you think it's serious?"

"Let's just say I don't think he'll be alone in his old age. You can take that worry off your list."

Laura nodded. "It's hard to imagine! Finally finding love at eighty-four! Now if we could just say the same about Mason, I'd feel at peace."

"I understand what you mean, but I don't know if he'll ever get to that point again, Laura. Will he ever let himself love again?"

"I don't know. But I'm praying so."

Martin couldn't help laughing. "You? Praying? After all your diatribes over the years about how religion only causes damage?"

"Yes, yes. But I might be changing my mind." Laura gave him a poke. "Don't laugh. I think Grace's belief in her religion hasn't damaged her. I think it's helped her heal." She had shared with him, with Grace's permission, the story Grace had told her. He'd been shaken to learn what Grace had gone through but somehow had not been surprised, and he felt he understood her a lot better.

"Are you sure that's what's doing it?" Martin asked now. "Not just having a loving family around her?"

"Well, sure, that too," Laura said. "But . . ."

"But what?"

She hesitated, then asked quickly. "Would you mind much if I decided to check out her church? Maybe go with her and Margaret on Sunday?"

Martin was surprised, but he tried not to let it show in his voice. This was obviously something she felt strongly about; he could tell by the nonchalance she forced into her voice. "Sure, I think that would be a good thing," he said.

"You're sure you don't mind?"

"Why would I mind? If it makes you happy, go. Goodness knows this family could use all the happiness it can get."

* * *

Laura accompanied Grace to church the next Sunday. Grace noted Laura was wearing her best print dress and heels and had trapped her unruly hair into a french braid. As she climbed into Grace's car, Laura admitted she didn't know if she was jittery out of nerves or out of simple eagerness. "I'm really looking forward to going," she said. "But I don't know what to expect."

"It's pretty low-key," Grace assured her, easing the car down the bumpy lane. "You don't have to worry about when to stand or kneel or any of that. You sit the whole time. And there are no responses or written prayers that you have to know."

"That's a relief," Laura told her.

"Margaret will be there too, and my friend Annie. You'll like the other women too. It'll be fine." Grace explained the format of the three-hour block of meetings, and by the time they arrived at the church, Laura had stopped fidgeting and looked more confident.

It all went as Grace had hoped it would. The swarm of missionaries at the door was welcoming but not overwhelming. The bishop, Annie, and Sister Pierce made a point of coming to greet Laura and shake hands. And, of course, Margaret put an arm around her and drew her in without a break in her animated chatter. By the time they got to Relief Society for the third hour, Laura was chattering back as if she'd always been part of the group.

The lesson in Relief Society was on how to gain a testimony for one's self. Grace was ecstatic; she couldn't have asked for a better topic if she'd arranged it. The teacher, a woman Grace didn't really know named Sister Lyle, started off with the story of Joseph Smith's First Vision. But she soon perceived that Laura wasn't familiar with some of the basic doctrine, so she slowed the lesson right down and made sure to explain the background of the topic simply and in a straight-forward way so Laura could follow along but without singling her out or drawing attention to her unfamiliarity with the lesson. Laura participated with unabashed questions and comments of her own and seemed to accept the idea of personal revelation without a qualm. As they left afterward, several of the women shook Laura's hand and invited her to come again the following week.

"I will, thank you," Laura responded. "I certainly will."

Once they were in the car headed home, Laura said, "That was nice. Thanks for bringing me."

"I'm glad you liked it. They're a pretty nice bunch of people." Grace hesitated, then asked offhandedly, "Do you have any questions about what they talked about today?"

"No, I think they explained things pretty well. And everything I heard seemed to fit with what I feel already."

"Oh?"

Laura fiddled with the end of her belt and seemed to gather her thoughts a moment before speaking. "What with the way I grew up and the troubles in our families that religion caused, I got turned off the idea of formal churchgoing a long time ago. But I always sort of had my own beliefs about things, about God and such, in the back of my mind. I've always felt people should be able to talk to God directly and get an answer back. I mean, we're His children; we call Him our father. Why wouldn't He talk to us?"

"Exactly."

"My father used to say humans were too sinful to approach God and that's why they needed ministers to speak on their behalf. But that never sat well with me. I mean, when Mason was younger and misbehaved, I certainly talked to *him*!"

This made Grace giggle. "That's a good parallel," she agreed. "And I suppose you would expect him to talk to you no matter what."

"Of course. Why would God be any different with His children? So anyway, I didn't go to church," Laura went on, "but I tried to live a good, ethical life the best I could."

"Sure," Grace said. "I could tell that about you right away when I met you."

"Thanks." Laura looked out the window as the fields zipped past. They had left the boundary of Port Dover and were out in open countryside. "It's just that lately, 'the best I can' doesn't seem to be enough. Things have been hard, what with Mason and the kids and everything. I don't know if I'm doing the right things. I don't know if I'm up to the task in front of me. It's all been a trial of my faith, to be honest. And I feel like I need a little . . . I don't know . . . a little extra *something* to guide my decision-making, you know?" She laughed self-consciously. "I need all the help I can get."

"I certainly understand that," Grace said. "I felt the same thing after I lost my family. I'd always gotten along just fine—I'd thought—on my own. But when my feet got knocked out from under me, I realized I needed more than just myself to get me through. I'd never felt so alone or helpless. I'd always believed in God all my life. I grew up knowing about Christ's sacrifice for mankind, but it was more of a theoretical concept. I really had to put it to the test after the accident. I had to sincerely ask for the first time in my life if He was really there and loved me personally. If the Atonement was for me specifically and not just for mankind as a whole."

"And did He answer?" Laura asked with a wry smile.

Grace nodded. "Yep. He did."

"And how did He answer?"

"He led me to you and Martin," Grace said. "He knew it was just what I needed to feel loved and whole again."

Laura considered this a moment, then nudged Grace with her elbow. "I think that's the first time mucking out stalls has been called an answer to prayer." She laughed. "Martin would get a kick out of that."

That evening, Grace decided to take a walk along the river before the sun set and the mosquitoes came out. The light was golden in the trees, and she could smell that happy, dusty scent that indicated dry grass and good weather. She was thinking ahead to tomorrow's tasks and marveling over the fact that she was actually looking forward to getting up at five in the morning when she heard voices and the shrieking laughter of children. She found Mason, Lark, and Declan coming up from the riverbank, and all three were dripping with water. Mason's shoes and khaki trousers were slick with mud, and there were weeds caught in Lark's pigtails. The grin on

Declan's grimy face was triumphant. In his arms, he held a soggy, squirming bundle.

"Oh my! What happened?"

Mason ruefully wiped at the water dripping from his beard, then bent to rub his hands off on the grass. It didn't help much. He looked like a man who'd been living wild in the woods for months.

"We went for an unexpected swim," he told her. His face was grim, but she caught the spark of mischief in his eye.

"I see that."

"Look what *we* rescued!" Declan shouted and pushed the wet, muddy bundle into her arms.

Grace did her best not to squeal. The cold, quivering mess turned out to be a bedraggled golden retriever puppy, which twisted in her arms in an attempt to lick her face. Grace gave up trying to hold it away from her blouse and cuddled it close. She could feel its heart beating, and its tail was going a mile a minute against her rib cage.

"The poor little thing! Was it in the river?"

"We were walking along with Daddy," Lark told her excitedly. "And a car went across the bridge."

"And the driver threw the puppy out the window into the river!" Declan exclaimed indignantly. "He just tossed him out like a sack of garbage."

"You're kidding!" Grace was shocked.

"So Daddy jumped into the river to save him. And *we* jumped into the river to save Daddy," Lark said.

Mason shook his head. "I don't know who would do something like that. It was horrible. I wish I could have gotten the license plate number."

"This poor puppy's certainly lucky you were there to see him and save him," Grace said. "I'm glad none of you drowned."

"Nah, we swim there all the time," Declan assured her. "The river's pretty wide and slow there." He laughed. "Actually, Dad didn't need saving. We just wanted to jump in too."

"Still, that's quite a drop for the puppy. That bridge must be twenty feet high."

Grace knelt on the ground and set the puppy on the grass, keeping a protective arm around him. The children sat beside her and rubbed the dog with their hands, cooing and exclaiming over him and smearing the mud farther into his fur. He was indeed a boy, and he looked none the worse for his adventures. He squirmed from child to child, happily trying to lick all the faces at once.

"I figure he's about ten weeks old, maybe," Mason said, dropping to his knees on the grass and giving Lark a one-armed squeeze. "He doesn't look injured anyway. Just overexcited. We'll take him to the vet tomorrow to make sure he's okay, just to be safe."

"Tomorrow's Monday. You'll be back in Toronto," Grace said.

But Mason shook his head. "I don't have court. I'll cancel my appointments. I mean, it's not every day a dog literally falls into your life."

She beamed at Mason. "He's certainly in need of a bath."

"He's beautiful!" Lark declared. "He's perfect."

"I wonder why they threw him away?" Declan said, fondling the dog's ears affectionately. "Who could throw away such a perfect puppy?"

"Maybe they sold the rest of the litter but didn't have any luck selling this one," Mason said. He looked at his children. "What shall we name him?"

The joy on the children's faces was stunning. Grace felt her breath catch in her throat. She could have hugged Mason for giving them such joy.

"We get to *keep* him?" Declan cried.

"It seems to me he's been delivered to our family," Mason said. "Not just *anyone* was walking along the river right when he landed."

"We should name him Dumbo," Lark exclaimed.

"What? That's a stupid name," Declan said.

"But he flew, just like Dumbo! And he has big ears."

Mason coughed to hide his laughter. "I don't know if we want to remember his flying through the air," he said. "I'm sure that was a pretty traumatic thing for him, and he might not want to be reminded of it."

"How about Lucky?" Grace suggested. "That seems logical."

"I know two people at school who already have dogs named Lucky," Declan said. "I want him to have an unusual name. A—a *unique* name. Because he's special."

"We should name him Chance," Mason said, "because he's been given a second one."

Declan considered this and nodded. "That's good. I don't know any other dogs named Chance."

"I like it too," Lark said. "Wait till I tell Jenny!"

"Chance it is." Mason stood and picked up the puppy. "Let's get him home and cleaned up and dry. Maybe Grandma has a basket we can make into a bed for him."

As the children scampered excitedly ahead along the road, Grace fell in step beside Mason. She couldn't stop reaching out to rub the puppy's floppy ears and get a little lick in return from his pink tongue. "He's so sweet. But what's Laura going to say?"

"This isn't the first time I've brought a dog home unexpectedly, and it probably won't be the last." Mason chuckled. "I was always bringing home strays as a kid. Sometimes I got to keep them, and sometimes Dad found homes for them. Mom's pretty good about going with the flow."

Grace thought Laura had probably just learned to put herself on a back burner and adapt, but she wasn't sure how she would feel this time. She had just admitted to Grace that she was feeling overwhelmed. How would she feel about taking on the care of yet another living being dumped on her again?

She needn't have worried. Laura took one look at the shivering, tail-wagging armful and melted like meringue. Making kissy sounds and talking as if to an infant, she gathered the puppy in her arms and bore him off to the bathtub, taking the children with her.

Mason wiggled his eyebrows at Grace. "What did I tell you? She's a softie." He pried his wet shoes off and headed upstairs to the shower. Laughing, Grace went to change clothes and see if her paw-printed blouse could be salvaged.

They all spent the evening lounging on the family room floor, playing with the puppy. Now that he was dry and clean, he proved to be a beautiful animal, and Grace felt sure the vet would give him a clean bill of health. Chance's coat was caramel gold, fading to white on his chest, and his long tail whirled with joy as he scampered clumsily from person to person. Even Toby sat on the rug and batted a tennis ball around for the puppy to pounce on. Grace thought Matt was especially captivated by the animal. His eyes followed the dog around the room, his face caught in a permanent, delighted smile. For the first time, in that moment, he seemed completely at ease and happy, and his laughter came spontaneously as he played. It made him seem more his true age instead of a burdened man.

Lying on her stomach on the couch, her chin on her folded arms, Grace looked around at the bright faces surrounding her and decided

Chance was the perfect name for a pet in this household. It was all about second chances here.

CHAPTER TWENTY-ONE

On July first, everyone had a day off for Canada Day. Mason drove from Toronto, and they all took a picnic down to Powell Park. A pipe band stood in a circle at the center of the grounds and wheezed out a succession of spirited tunes, and there was a face-painting booth and cupcake-decorating table for the children. A lot of the people in Port Dover had had the same idea as the Whelans, and every picnic table was crowded, so Laura spread out a tartan blanket under a tree for them to eat on instead. Grace helped her set out cold chicken, potato salad, carrot sticks, donuts, and cans of grape Crush. She could think of no greater pleasure than lying about on a blanket in the middle of a weekday drinking cold pop and watching Mason, Martin, and the children play Frisbee.

Chance wanted to join in, but Matt, who had quietly taken over much of the puppy's care, kept him on a long leash so he wouldn't run off. The dog looked very smart in his new black collar.

Margaret had come along for the day, and she and Toby took a walk around the park, openly holding hands while chatting with people they met and admiring the handicrafts on display at the vendors' booths. After awhile, Laura went to join them.

Full from lunch, Grace was about to doze off in the shade of the maple tree when she heard her name being called. She sat up and saw Annie waving to her some distance away. She climbed to her feet and went over.

"We're just taking a quick break, and I wanted to say hi," Annie said.

It took Grace a second to register the fact that Annie was wearing a green-and-blue kilt and a heavy black vest over a long-sleeved white shirt. She took in the long knitted stockings and high-laced shoes, the jaunty Glengarry hat. "Why are you dressed like that, Annie? Aren't you roasting in this heat?"

"We're piping today. That's our band over there."

"Piping?"

"Newton and I and most of the kids play the bagpipes. I thought you knew."

Grace shook her head. "No one told me, or else I've forgotten. Do you really all play?"

"Except for the two youngest ones. And Caleb. He plays the snare drum instead."

Grace looked around and saw various other uniformed pipers milling in the crowd. She didn't know why she hadn't recognized them before, especially Newton, who stood several inches taller than most other people. The Glengarry on his head made him look even taller. He was deeply engaged in a conversation with a group of admirers who had stopped to talk to him about fifty feet away. The group included a spike-haired young man with a nose ring and black leather jacket covered in buckles, two elderly blue-haired women in prim shirtwaist dresses, and a young bespectacled father in a golfing shirt with his toddler riding on his shoulders.

"The pipes speak to everyone," Annie murmured in Grace's ear.

"So I see."

"We have to start again in a few minutes. We have two more sets to play, and then the Paris-Port Dover Pipe Band is going to perform. You don't want to miss them."

"How many bands can one small town support?" Grace laughed.

"You forget you're in Canada now. You can't have any civic function, wedding, funeral, parade, or bar mitzvah without bagpipes. I've even played for a Hindu wedding. Say, is Laura here with you today?"

"Over there somewhere, with Toby and Margaret."

"I want to be sure to say hello to her too," Annie said. "Will she be coming back to church with you on Sunday?"

"Yes, she says so."

"Excellent! By the way, Grace, if it's all right with you, I'd still like to introduce you to that friend of mine, Angus. He's here today, somewhere," Annie said, waving a hand vaguely to encompass the entire bustling park.

Grace cocked her head to one side. "Is this the Angus you wanted me to meet at your house on Victoria Day but couldn't find?"

"That's the one."

"Newton said he'd been kidnapped twice."

"A year ago, yes. But he's none the worse for the wear. I'll tell you about it sometime . . . or better yet, I'll let him tell you about it. It would be a good conversation starter. He's very nice, and I get the feeling you two would hit it off."

"Annie, you aren't setting me up, are you?" Grace asked, wondering if the idea took her aback or amused her.

"Why not? A girl can never have too many friends."

"I'm not ready to meet anyone."

"I'm not asking you to marry the man tomorrow," Annie said. "Just say hi to him." She started to move away, adding cheerfully over her shoulder, "The wedding can wait at least a month or two." She strode off, the tassels on her laces swinging with each step. Grace shook her head and headed back to her blanket. She supposed it wouldn't hurt to say hi to the fellow, whoever he was, but she was promising nothing more than that. She certainly wasn't interested in dating anyone yet.

But even as she thought this, the image came to mind of the lean, smiling schoolteacher sitting with his foot up on the swing, a sparkle in his eyes.

When she returned to the picnic blanket, Laura, Martin, and Matt were lounging there, nibbling on more lunch. She told them the Fishers were the pipers they'd been hearing across the park. "Except for Caleb," she said. "He's a drummer."

"He is? Cool! He didn't tell me that," Matt said.

"Trust Annie to be a piper," Laura mused. "Well, I guess someone has to do it."

Her Irish husband nudged her and laughed.

"They're about to play again, if you want to go over to listen," Grace said.

Matt jumped to his feet and headed across the park, Chance dancing along beside him. Grace dropped to the blanket beside Laura and reached for a carrot stick, congratulating herself on limiting her intake of donuts to only one.

Laura ran her hands through her wild curls and sighed happily. "This sure beats wearing a long dress and leather shoes," she remarked, wiggling her toes in her sandals. She nodded in the direction in which Matt had just disappeared. "Does he seem different to you?"

"Matt? A little. More relaxed, maybe, and he talks more now than he did when he first came."

"I think it's helped him to make some friends near his own age in town," Laura said. "We all need friends, and Matt does especially."

"Yes," Grace agreed, thinking about the elusive and potential new friend Angus. "I suppose so."

Laura looked away over the grass, where Declan and Mason were wrestling good-naturedly over the Frisbee. "Did Matt tell you? He's going back to school this fall."

"Is he? That's good."

"He's going to take some classes at the community college to bring up his grades and then apply to the horticulture program at the U of Guelph."

"You're kidding!" Grace stopped with her carrot stick halfway in her mouth. "Really? That's wonderful!"

"I guess something has rubbed off on him on the farm," Laura said, then laughed. "And I don't mean dirt."

"That's great for him."

"I hope he does well. I hope he turns out okay. But I'll miss him when he goes."

Grace couldn't help laughing. "Do you remember when you first heard he was coming to the farm? You didn't like the idea, as I recall. Now you don't want to let him go."

Laura rolled her eyes. "I have a confession to make. When you first came, I wasn't too excited about you either."

"Me?" Grace was stunned.

"You looked so fragile and skinny," Laura admitted. "I thought you'd last a week at the most. But Martin seemed to take a shine to you, so I figured I'd give you a chance. And you ended up surprising both of us."

"I did?"

Martin nodded. "You didn't let the hard work beat you; you rose to the challenge and became stronger."

"You could match any man we've had work for us, stride for stride," Laura said. "And you don't look so pale and breakable now."

Grace wasn't sure what to think of this. She reached for another donut and chewed it pensively. "I'm not so thin now either," she muttered.

Laura leaned over to put a hand on Grace's arm. "I don't want you to leave in September, Grace. You've become one of us now. I don't want to let go of you."

Grace felt tears start in her eyes, and she squeezed Laura's hand in hers. "Thank you," she said. "I don't want to let go of you either, any of you. I wish I didn't have to."

"You know you're always welcome back here," Martin told her. "Anytime you want to come, the door is always open."

"Thank you. But I don't know when I'll be able to come back. If there's some way . . ."

"There's always a way to come back," Laura said firmly.

* * *

July was hotter than anything Grace had experienced in Utah. The humidity sat over everything like a thick, stifling blanket, and the merciless sun sapped the energy from every living thing. The horses sagged in the paddock, blowing heavily through their nostrils. Cicadas sounded like static in the trees. Chance took to lying in the shade all day under the porch. Even the very grass looked dispirited and tired, fading to brown like a sepia photograph.

"I don't want anyone risking heatstroke," Martin told Grace and Matt one morning. "Everyone knock off work by three in the afternoon, and drink plenty of water. Don't overexert yourselves."

Grace was glad to have the excuse to avoid the worst heat of the afternoon. Her little room above the coach house wasn't air conditioned, so she spent most of her time in the main house, where Laura had set up a series of floor fans to channel air through the house so the humidity wouldn't make the wool stick to her skin as she worked.

Declan and Lark were irritable because they were unable to go out to play. Grace tried to give Laura a break by entertaining the kids with board games and crafts, but more often than not they ended up sprawled on the couch in front of a fan, watching DVDs. There just wasn't the energy to do much else.

The vegetables still marched on, however, coaxed by Martin's diligent irrigation. They tried to do most of the field work in the evening after the worst of the heat. Grace considered how natural it felt to walk home in the dark and wash carrots by lamplight, and it struck her again how very different her life had become. She wasn't the same person anymore, and she was glad of it.

The heat lasted several weeks, and then autumn arrived in a hurry. Grace first noticed it when she was walking over to the house one morning for breakfast and saw Chance and Matt playing fetch with a ball in the yard.

"Hey! You have energy again!" she said, greeting the puppy as he ran to entwine himself around her knees. He wagged his tail so hard it made his whole body shimmy side to side.

"Yeah, the humidity has broken," Matt said, tossing the ball from hand to hand. "You can feel the difference overnight."

And it was true. The evenings grew steadily cooler after that, and Grace found she could walk outdoors without her clothes going soggy. There was a new, refreshing tang to the air, and the smell of the earth underfoot made Grace start to think of pumpkin pie and baked apples.

With the cooler temperatures, Grace's own energy returned, and the horses began to lift their heads and trot to the fence when Martin went to feed them. The children began to talk eagerly about the friends they would see when school started up again, and Laura began making lists of the school supplies and clothes they would need.

"I swear Declan has grown four inches over the summer," she told Grace. "I dug out his good gym shoes from last year, and they're about two sizes too small already."

"I remember," Grace said. "My boys were the same. They never wore anything out because they grew out of it so fast, and they were both about the same size so I couldn't even reuse their things as hand-me-downs. I had to donate everything."

"I think this calls for a shopping day in Cambridge. You can get some good deals at the Southworks Outlet Mall. Want to come?"

"I'd love to!" It had been ages since Grace had gone shopping, and a day on the town with Laura and the kids sounded fun. She realized she spent most of her time in jeans and old T-shirts, and it had been months since she'd had her hair cut. Somehow, she hadn't really noticed this before, but now that she became aware of it, she knew she was itching to wear something nice, to get pampered in a salon, to wander through bookstores and music shops and eat in a restaurant.

The work on the farm had slowed somewhat, and the main thrust of the harvest was yet to come, so Martin could spare Grace for a day. The drive to Cambridge was cheery, with the car windows rolled down and the kids bouncing to the music on the radio in the backseat. Grace knew a trip to town was exciting for them, even if only to Cambridge. It was scarcely bigger than Port Dover, but a change of scene, she knew, was important now and then. She self-consciously felt as excited as the kids.

They got the school shopping out of the way first, filling the trunk of the car with stiff new jeans and tennis shoes; chemical-smelling three-ring binders; bright, new backpacks, whose brightness would last about three days, Grace knew from experience; and packets of colored pencils and markers that smelled like bananas. It was fun to help the kids pick out clothes and the other supplies they would need, and part of her had to admit it was especially fun since she wasn't paying for any of it. She hadn't been back-to-school shopping in two years, and she enjoyed the children's happy chatter.

She knew there were commercials on TV showing children groaning and moaning about school starting up each fall, but in her personal experience, kids liked going back to school, at least right at first. They got to see old friends they hadn't seen all summer, and there was something invigorating about the smell of new paper and the squeaky cleanliness of school hallways that had sat empty all summer. It brought back memories of her music school in Salt Lake City reopening after summer break, the flurry of organizing classes and training newly hired teachers, putting together newsletters and curricula, running staff meetings, figuring out finances, ordering new sheet music, getting chairs out of storage, decorating bulletin boards, getting the pianos tuned.

Did she miss all of that?

Maybe a little.

Did she want to go back to it?

She thought about the work involved in putting together the winter concert—endless rehearsals with the chamber orchestra and pianists. Singing her warm-ups in the dressing room while Mike, her tech guy, tested the lighting onstage. The audience's noise falling to a hush as the opening bars sounded. The click of her heels on the wood floor as she took center stage. The really nice burgundy gown she wore for special performances. The glow she always felt in her chest as she began to sing.

Grace looked down at her stained tennis shoes, then her work-ruined hands and smiled at herself in genuine amusement. She was a long way from the stage now, almost unrecognizable to herself, and the burgundy gown had gone to Goodwill along with the high heels. Did she want all of that back? Did she miss it? No, she honestly didn't. But her voice . . . yes. *That* she wanted. The feeling of sending her voice soaring clear and high, like releasing a bird into the air. She didn't need an audience for that; singing itself, just for herself, had given her immense pleasure back then. She wondered if perhaps it could again.

They took the kids to a semiformal restaurant for lunch and then split up while Grace went to the hair salon for a bit of pampering and Laura took the kids to get new winter coats and boots. Then they met up again at Baskin Robbins for ice cream—pralines and cream for Grace, tutti frutti sherbet for the kids, and rocky road for Laura.

"Feels good to sit down." Laura sighed as they perched on the pink stools at the tiny tables in the shop. "These bags are heavy."

Grace peeked into one of them, her eyebrows raised. "That jacket looks too big for Declan. Is it for Martin?"

Laura twirled her cone expertly, catching the drips with her tongue. "It's for Matt," she said nonchalantly. "I figured he might need one for fall."

"Grandma got him a backpack too," Lark added, her mouth ringed with sherbet. "It's not got Spider-Man on it like Declan's though. It's just plain blue."

Grace hid her smile behind her ice cream. She knew Matt must be done with his service hours by now, but no one had mentioned anything about his leaving. School started after Labor Day. Time enough yet.

When they finished their treat, Grace nipped into a store to replenish some of her disastrous wardrobe while Laura indulged in a once-a-year manicure. Grace didn't bother; what was the point when she was usually up to her elbows in dirt? The kids lounged on plastic chairs and looked bored while they waited, and then they were back in the car and heading home.

"Thanks. I needed a day like this," Grace told Laura. The air from the windows was sending her new haircut flying, but she didn't care. It was a good cut; it would be fixable. She could still taste the pralines and cream on her tongue.

"Me too. I've never had another girl to go out with me," Laura said. "Martin and Mason are no fun to shop with. They just stand around looking like trapped deer in the headlights." She glanced in the rearview mirror; the kids had fallen into sticky dozes in the warmth of the backseat. "Janet—Mason's wife—never was one for hanging out either," she said, lowering her voice a little.

"You didn't do things with her?"

"She almost never came to visit. She didn't like to leave the city. Said the countryside was too full of 'nature' for her taste. Mason would bring the kids to visit, or we'd drive into Toronto to see them."

Grace shook her head. "If I lived here, I'd never leave the countryside." She hesitated. "Well, except for the occasional trip to the salon and Baskin Robbins, of course."

"Yes, the city has its merits," Laura said peacefully. She tapped her new pink nails on the steering wheel. "I know nineteenth-century women didn't have nails like these . . . but authenticity is only worth so much, don't you think? They aren't flashy, and I don't think anyone will notice."

"My lips are sealed," Grace said.

Laura smiled. "*I'll* notice though," she said with satisfaction.

CHAPTER TWENTY-TWO

"It's approved!" Michelle Darby greeted Grace without preamble as she entered the museum gift shop one day.

"What is?"

"The Copper Creek Educational Center! The board met yesterday, and they said we have the green light to do whatever we like so long as it fits the mandate of the museum and pays for itself."

"Which means no budget," Jane added. "But we have rooms to meet in already, and we're already paying staff anyhow, and we can do all our advertising on the website and by word of mouth. So the initial outlay will be minimal, and if we get people to sign up for the courses, they will pay for themselves, plus some."

"That's excellent news!" Grace said. "Have the staff you've talked to agreed to teach the workshops?"

"No one has said no yet," Michelle told her. "They all seem pretty enthusiastic about it. It gives them some variety. But it's still in the early planning stages, of course. We still have to coordinate it all and decide what to focus on first."

"That's where the real work will come in," Jane said, nodding. "We have to find the time to pull it all together. What we really need is a director to spearhead it."

"I wish I could help you," Grace said regretfully. "It sounds like something I'd really enjoy."

"Well, to be honest, even if you could stay past September, we couldn't offer you the job," Jane pointed out. "We have no budget to pay you."

As Grace walked back to the farm, she thought about this, and it occurred to her that she wasn't being paid right now anyway. She was working in exchange for room and board. Couldn't the directorship of the educational programming be the same sort of position? No one else would want that sort of position, probably . . . but *she* would.

* * *

One Saturday in early August, Grace was working in the greenhouse alone while Matt and Martin were elsewhere. The glass panels in the ceiling were raised to regulate the temperature, but the mugginess within had plastered her hair and clothing to her skin. She turned on the hose to wash the brick floor, and the cold water sent a fine spray into the air, dampening her further.

She was almost finished when she heard the door at the end of the room swing open.

"Can I speak with you?"

Grace looked up to see Mason standing in the doorway of the greenhouse. The look in his eyes made a funny feeling start in the pit of her stomach. His eyebrows were lowered, and he didn't look pleased. Somehow when he frowned, he looked larger. She turned off the hose and let it drop into a puddle. "Certainly."

Mason toed off his shoes, put on clogs, and came inside, closing the door behind him. In spite of whatever was bothering him, he didn't forget Martin's injunction about outdoor shoes. His hair was curling over his collar in the humidity, making him look even more like a wild mountain man and less like a lawyer than usual. She wondered how he could stand to wear a thick beard during the summer, though she supposed it would be a welcome insulator when winter came.

"What is it?" she asked. "Is everything okay?"

"No, actually, everything's not okay. I was with Declan a minute ago."

"Is he all right?" Grace felt a frisson of fear.

"He told me that a long time ago, when he was upset, you told him he would see his mother again one day. That maybe it wouldn't happen for a long time, but someday he'd be with her again."

"Yes?" Grace said, confused by his angry expression.

"Why would you tell an eight-year-old boy that? Don't you think he's been hurt enough already?"

"I—I was trying to comfort him."

"Telling lies is not comforting. It's just cruel." Mason's voice rose to a roar, and he cut himself off with effort. In a lower tone, he demanded, "Have you said the same thing to Lark?"

Grace took a step back. "No, I haven't. But—"

"Thank goodness for that. Don't ever tell her she'll see her mother again. Janet's not coming back."

"I'm sorry," Grace stammered. "I was just sharing my beliefs with Declan. I thought it would comfort him when he was missing her. They've certainly helped me. Maybe they would comfort you too, Mason. I truly believe the dead aren't lost to us forever."

Mason stopped short, stunned, and then he scowled. "Their mother isn't dead! Why would you think that?"

Grace felt as if he had slapped her. "Oh! I—But Martin said—"

"Janet's living in Florida with a twenty-six-year-old financial planner."

"I—I didn't know," she said. "Your father just told me she was gone. And the way everybody spoke, I just assumed . . ."

"She isn't coming back. I don't want her to come back. And I don't want you getting Lark's and Declan's hopes up that she will. She left them without even saying good-bye. She hasn't phoned them once since she left."

"I understand. I'm so sorry."

"You can't keep meddling or promising them things that aren't going to happen," he said. "And while we're at it, they're both getting too attached to you. I told you I could see it coming. I know you said you'd try not to let it happen, but it's not good enough."

"But I can't entirely prevent—"

"Look, just stay away from them."

Grace put her hands on her cheeks, feeling the heat of them. She must be bright pink. "I'm sorry. I haven't meant—I was just trying to help. I—I love your children."

"Well, don't! There's no point to it." Mason was yelling again. "It will only hurt them. Why don't you have your own children and leave mine alone?"

Grace stood thunderstruck, feeling the blood rush from her face. She was unable to speak, to think. The fury and frustration on his face was like a fist to her stomach. She brushed by him and ran from the greenhouse.

Grace was careful to avoid Mason the rest of the weekend. She kept to her work in the fields and spent any free hours in her room instead of going to the main house. When Sunday night came and she saw Mason's car pull away, she felt an intense sense of relief. It would be another week before she had to face him again.

She felt absolutely stupid. What a horrible mistake to have made! But how could she have known the children's mother had left instead of died? How could she have surmised anything else from the way people had phrased it? Grace spent fruitless hours vacillating between scolding herself and defending herself, having heated exchanges in her head, composing her defense and marshaling her arguments, even while she knew deep down she would never say any of them to Mason. He was right to be angry. She was an interfering idiot. She had meant well, but she had acted without possessing full information. She had no excuse. But she had had the best of intentions in comforting a mourning child.

If she was honest with herself, half of her anger—maybe more than half—was directed toward the unknown Janet in Florida. How could she hurt her little children that way? How could she hurt *Mason* that way? Didn't the stupid woman realize how precious each moment she had with her children was? She had *chosen* to lose her children. And Grace, whose arms still ached to hold her own babies, couldn't fathom it. It wasn't fair. How must it be affecting Declan to know his mother had *chosen* to leave him behind? Would he ever recover from it, or would he bear the scars the rest of his life? Would Mason?

Somehow, this last question seemed the most important of all.

"I didn't mean to speak out of turn," Grace muttered to herself as she hosed out the CSA bins one morning. She was having the umpteenth argument in her head, which had begun upon waking and followed her through breakfast and out to the barn. "Mason has to understand my motives were good. How dare he judge me."

Her own words brought her up short, and she stood staring at the bubbling hose in her fist. The water fell and splashed in the mud around her feet, soaking her tennis shoes, but she hardly noticed. Her own words echoed in her head.

How dare *he* judge *her*? How dare *she* judge *Janet*? What did Grace know about her, after all? Not a thing. She didn't know what personal demons the woman was dealing with. She didn't know what depth of unhappiness must have existed to cause a mother to leave her family. She didn't know Janet's history or hopes or dreams for herself.

Quietly Grace set down the hose and turned off the spigot. She felt chastened, her own glaring misbehavior loud in her mind. Maybe, just maybe, Mason's ex-wife deserved compassion, not judgment. After all, whatever the reason, she had to live with being separated from Declan and Lark. Nothing could make up for that. Such a loss would be unthinkable.

And yet Grace was going to have to lose them too.

The breath went out of her. Without meaning to, Grace found herself on her knees in the mud, her hands over her face, rocking back and forth and weeping—for herself, for the children, for Mason, for the whole unfair mess.

CHAPTER TWENTY-THREE

Already the cooling temperatures at night were starting to bring out brilliant colors in the maple trees. Everywhere Grace looked, the dull green and brown of August were changing to bright crimson and salmon. Then one night it was too cold to leave her window open. The next morning, there was a thin skim of ice on the horses' water trough. The mud hardened to putty-colored rock, jagged with tracks and ruts, and the leaves of the vegetable plants in the field started to yellow and go brown at the edges.

"It seems like autumn is early," Grace remarked to Martin on Friday morning as they filled the CSA bins. "It's like we've skipped right from summer straight to frost."

"It's not a hard frost yet," Martin said. "We still have at least a few weeks of harvest left. But, yes, I think it will be a difficult winter. The horses' coats are thickening already. Have you noticed? Chance is shedding out his summer coat too. And the geese are leaving already. It feels early. But nowadays, you can't predict the weather or seasons very well."

Even though autumn was Grace's favorite season, it still saddened her to see the trees changing and the potatoes being dug. It meant September was right around the corner.

With the change in seasons, the CSA bins' contents had evolved again. Grace worked with Matt and Martin to load each bin with butternut squash, half a dozen ears of corn, green beans, cherry tomatoes, leaf lettuce, parsley, plums, lemon cucumbers, savory, baby russet potatoes, cantaloupe, apples, red and green cabbages, and onions. Laura also gave each customer a small jar of honey gleaned from a neighbor who kept bees, along with a recipe for honey-glazed ham.

As they worked, Chance bounded gleefully around them, twining between their legs and tripping them up and generally getting underfoot.

The puppy was growing at an alarming rate and had settled comfortably into the routine of the family now, and he seemed unscarred from his unfortunate start in life. He loved Lark and Declan and was always overjoyed to greet CSA customers coming to pick up their bins. But Matt appeared to be his special favorite, and he followed the young man faithfully around the farm wherever he went. Watching the dog, Grace was struck by how cheerful the little animal could be and how trusting he was of people despite how he had been treated. He'd been thrown from a moving vehicle into a river, but he still loved people and didn't allow the actions of one to taint his love of the rest.

Grace welcomed the work as the harvest entered full throttle, keeping her body and mind busy, forcing herself to the point of exhaustion so she would have the excuse on weekends to retire to her own room over the coach house, pleading herself too tired to join the family for evening DVDs or other activities. She missed their company, the bright smiles of the children, and she tried not to notice Laura's questioning looks. She told herself it was better this way. She had to honor Mason's wishes. And it was better to begin the withdrawal process now before September came. Better not to let her heart get any more entangled than it already was.

* * *

One evening, Martin and Mason were sitting on the couch with Lark between them as Martin read aloud from *Farmer Boy*, Lark's favorite. They all looked up as Laura marched into the room.

"I need to talk to you, Mason," she said without preamble. "Lark, honey, run and get ready for bed."

"We're in the middle of the chapter," Lark protested.

Martin took in the steely look in Laura's eye and quickly told Lark, "You can finish it when you're in your pajamas. No arguments, now."

Lark slid reluctantly from Mason's lap and went up the stairs.

Mason looked at Martin, who shrugged, then eyed his mother warily. "What's up?"

"That's what I want to know. One minute everything seems fine, and the next minute Grace is walking around looking like a waif without a friend in the world. She's spent the last two weekends hiding in her room. What did you do?"

Mason held up his hands. "It's nothing to do with you, Mom. I'm sorry, but—"

"That girl's happiness is everything to do with me," Laura interrupted. "So if you've done something to ruin it, I have the right to know about it."

Mason stood. "It was a misunderstanding, Mom. She thought Janet was dead—"

"What? Oh."

"No one explained to her that she was . . ."

"So? What does that have to do with anything that's been going on?"

"I—I might have gotten angry with her." Before Laura could speak, Mason hurried to defend himself. "She told Declan he would see Janet again one day. It upset me to have her say that to him."

"Oh. Oh, Mason, she misunderstood. She was just trying to explain her beliefs. If she thought Janet was dead—Well, she told me the same thing about her beliefs, that families can go on after death. She must have meant to comfort him. She didn't mean—How could she have known?"

"I know. I've thought about it since." Mason spread his hands. "I was angry. I spoke without thinking."

Martin stood, a sick feeling creeping into his stomach. "What did you say to that girl?"

A flush crawled up Mason's cheeks that his beard couldn't entirely hide. "I might have . . . well, I told her she was meddling and I wanted her to stay away from the kids. That she should have her own children and leave mine alone. I know it wasn't polite. You don't have to tell me."

Laura shook her head. "Oh, Mason. You have *no idea* how cruel that was. Grace did have her own children. Two boys and a girl. They died in a car accident, along with her husband, almost two years ago."

Mason stared at his mother with horror on his face. "I—I didn't know! Why didn't you tell me?"

"I'm sorry, but she told me in confidence, and I didn't feel it was my place to share it without permission," Laura said. "It's beside the point. That poor girl is our guest. She came here looking for healing and hope. And you just stomped all over her heart."

"Mom—"

"You have to make it right, Mason," Laura said fiercely. "She reached out to your son with nothing but love, and you slapped her down."

"She'll never listen to me now."

"Whatever it takes, Mason, fix it." Laura spun on her heel and marched from the room. Chance, who had been dozing on the carpet, got up and slunk to his bed in the corner, ears back.

Mason spread his hands. "It was a mistake, okay?" He turned to his father. "Just chalk it up to one more stupid thing I've done in a long line of stupid mistakes! One more thing to regret to throw on the pile!"

Martin looked at his son in silence a moment, then sat back down and asked quietly, "What are you talking about, Mason? What regrets?"

"How can you ask that, Dad? My whole life is one flub-up after another."

"How so? Janet leaving—that wasn't your flub-up," Martin said. "She chose to leave."

"Yes, but I drove her to that choice. I didn't see how desperate and unhappy she was. I didn't see how disappointed she was—or maybe I did, but it was just easier not to notice. I didn't know what else I could do to make her happy."

"That's right. There was no making her happy. You bent over backward trying to please her, Mason. You worked like a horse—"

"At a career I didn't like. That was another mistake—to go into law just to please her."

Martin felt his mouth fall open and floundered in his mind for a proper response, but he could come up with nothing. "You don't like being a lawyer?" he finally asked.

"Not really. But I fought through law school and racked up school loans and clawed my way into a firm. And now Janet's gone anyway, so it was all for nothing."

"You did the best you knew how at the time," Martin said. "It wasn't a mistake to try to please someone you cared about. You shouldn't regret that."

"But I didn't make her happy in the end."

"People have to make themselves happy. Other people can't do it for them."

"The platitudes aren't really working for me here, Dad."

"But it's true; Janet was determined to be miserable no matter what you did. And if she decided she could find happiness with someone else, you couldn't prevent that. But I bet she hasn't found it with him either. She never will if she expects someone else to provide it. Happiness can only come from within."

"There's still so much else I regret, Dad. I've been so wrapped up in my own loss that I haven't been able to deal with Declan's and Lark's sorrow on top of my own. So I've dumped them on you and Mom even though I know you're exhausted and overworked, but frankly, I'm too tired trying to maintain this career I don't want and too—too *dispirited* to try to change anything!"

Martin shook his head. "Why haven't you said anything before this?" he asked.

"And now, on top of all that," Mason went on, throwing his arms wide and endangering the candles on the mantel, "I've gone and squashed a woman who was only trying to show kindness to Declan. And I can't defend myself by saying I did it out of a sense of protection or even self-righteousness; I did it because I'm frustrated that *I* can't have those kinds of conversations with my son. I can't reach him. He blames me for Janet leaving. And then here comes along this total stranger who *can* talk to him. Go ahead and say it: I'm a jealous idiot."

"At least you're honest with yourself," Martin said. "Sure, maybe things haven't always gone right. But this is one mistake you *can* make right. You can talk to Grace. But if you don't do it quick, you'll cost your son the friendship of one of the nicest women he's ever known."

"What's the point? She's leaving in a week or two anyway."

"But you can't let her go feeling like this," Martin said. He stood and put his hand on Mason's arm. "It's important that you try, not just for her sake or Declan's but for yours too. It doesn't matter what mistakes you may or may not have made in the past. You can start over again right now. With this."

Grace was in the barn, sitting on one of the straw bales with Death and Taxes looming over their half walls above her whuffling their breath in the quiet of the evening. Through the window, Grace could see the half-moon and the stars just coming out. Bats flitted past, dipping crazily after mosquitoes, looking too ungainly and flappy to be aerodynamic. A breeze high up moved the tops of the trees, though the air in the barn was still and redolent with the steadying smell of horse and hay. She thought it ironic that she now found the horses' presence comforting, like two giant, gentle protectors watching over her, and the barn had become her favorite place to go to think.

She held one of the barn cats in her lap, a black, foul beast with a heart blacker than its fur, but he was tolerating her attention for the moment, curled up with his amber eyes half closed. It wasn't often one of the cats let her touch it, especially if Chance was around. The energetic pup kept the cats high in the rafters whenever he was about the barn.

She'd been sitting and stroking the cat's dusty hair for twenty minutes, making it warm and staticky, but when the barn door creaked and opened, the cat instantly rose to its feet, its claws puncturing her jeans and embedding themselves in her thigh. Grace gave a small cry of pain and clapped her hand to her leg.

"Sorry, I didn't mean to frighten you," Mason said quickly, stepping into the aisle and leaving the door open behind him. "I'm not here to fight again."

"It's not—the cat scratched me."

"Oh. Are you okay?"

"It's fine," she said shortly.

"Am I interrupting anything? Do you have time to talk?"

"I was just sitting. I come here to sit sometimes. It's quiet."

He hesitated, then sat beside her on the bale. Grace moved aside slightly, making room. His long legs stretched out across the aisle, and he folded his arms, making him seem even wider. The cat gave a hiss, and Grace folded it in her arms against her chest like a shield.

"Mom says you leave on September 6," he said, his deep voice low.

"Yes. Two weeks away."

Mason's beard dipped to his chest as he looked down, avoiding her gaze. "I couldn't let you go without telling you how sorry I am for biting your head off a couple of weeks ago. It's taken me this long to get up my courage to apologize. Well, and Mom and Dad let me have it for upsetting you."

She smiled at this and buried her mouth in the cat's fur, then pulled back again and sneezed from the dust caught in its hair. The cat jumped down from her lap and disappeared into a dark corner, and Grace folded her arms, suddenly empty, not knowing what else to do with them.

Mason cleared his throat. "I was way out of line. I have no defense, except to say this hasn't been easy for me, being on my own and trying to deal with Declan. I get touchy sometimes."

"It hasn't been easy for your children either."

He nodded. "I know. You're right. I'm sorry for how I spoke to you earlier. I shouldn't have said that. It was unkind of me, and unfair."

"I shouldn't have explained my religious beliefs to an eight-year-old without his father's permission," Grace said quickly. "I was out of line too."

"I've thought about it, and I don't think a bit of religion will kill my son. You've noticed we aren't exactly a religious family."

"Your mother has been coming to church with me the last few weeks."

"She has?" He gaped in astonishment. "*My* mother?"

"She didn't tell you? She seems to be enjoying it. She says she's learning a lot."

"Sheesh. My mother's found religion. My ancient uncle has a girlfriend. Apparently I've wandered into a parallel universe, where there's a lot going on I don't know about. Including . . ." He hesitated. "My mom told me about your husband and children. I'm sorry. I didn't know, or I never would have said what I did. I hope you don't mind that she told me. I kind of pulled it out of her."

"No, I'm glad she did. It isn't easy for me to tell people." Grace took a shaky breath. "But now that you know, you can understand me better and why I tried to comfort Declan. I thought his mother had died."

"Well, I guess we should have clarified that up front," Mason muttered.

"Regardless of whether she's in heaven or Florida, it's still a loss for Declan," Grace said sadly. "I know what loss is, Mason. For months, I couldn't shake the guilty feeling that I should have been in that car with my family when they died. I was just trying to ease Declan's pain."

"I know. I'm sorry I didn't know what you were going through yourself."

She shook her head. "It's taken me a long time to realize I can go on living. That I need to. That I *want* to. And that I can let go of old dreams and find new ones."

She could see him consider this. "And have you? Found new ones?"

Grace closed her eyes briefly, thinking again about the poem stuck to her mirror in her room.

Softened by the dreams, strengthened
by the hope, sparkling dewdrops shone through the

tragedy. In that twilight zone between 'was' and 'is,'
at the crossroads of existing and living, she took her
first steps . . .

She opened her eyes. "I'm finding out there's the possibility of new ones," she said, smiling. "Your dad especially has shown me that. Even out of torn and trampled ground, you can grow something new and useful and beautiful. I won't let the ruins of my past destroy my hopes for what's left of my future. But the plans aren't concrete yet, no. I assumed when I first came here that I'd go back to Salt Lake City when it was over, but I'm not sure now what's there for me." She shrugged. "The world is a blank canvas. I'm trying to see that as an exciting thing, not a scary one."

"I think I'm just starting to get to that point myself," Mason said slowly. "Of seeing there are possibilities and the chance of a different future. I've been as stuck in my grief as you have been in yours."

"I know. But maybe now we're both getting ready to move forward."

"I guess so." He smiled at her. "My plans are maybe a bit more concrete than yours though. I haven't told my folks yet, but I'm moving my practice to Port Dover."

"What? You are?"

"I decided this morning. I'll have to find some other specialty because there's not enough work for an immigration lawyer. But I'll manage. I'll be close enough to help my dad here on the farm more often, and my mom will still watch the kids after school. But they'll live with me."

"That's wonderful, Mason!" Grace said sincerely. "That sounds perfect. And maybe someday you'll make it to teacher's college after all."

"Maybe." He chuckled. "Probably. But one step at a time."

"I'm glad."

"It's taken me long enough to figure it out," he said ruefully, rubbing the back of his neck with his hand in a way that reminded her of Martin. "But the decision feels right, to be near the farm and my folks and to have the kids with me. I love the feeling when I'm here, and I hate going back to Toronto every week."

"I know. I dread having to leave this place." Grace sighed. "I've really come to love it here. I love your parents as if they're my own."

"Why don't you stay, then?"

"What, you mean with your parents?"

"Why not? They love you too, and they'll always be glad of the help. Mom and Dad won't admit it, but it's becoming too much work for them, and I know Mom especially would be glad if you stayed. Dad says Matt will be going away to school this fall. But I could see you becoming a permanent part of this place."

Grace considered this. Laura *had* said she didn't want Grace to leave, and she felt she had meant it. Was there a way to continue working for the Whelans under the same arrangement and help with the educational center at the same time? Why not? Wintertime was sure to bring a slowdown of the farm work, and there would be time to focus on the center, at least until spring. After that, they would have to see. Would the museum let her become a part of it, as Toby and the Whelans had? She felt a quickening of her pulse. "If I wanted to stay, how would I go about it?"

"You told me yourself you're already a citizen. You can legally stay in Canada. Just don't go home."

Grace began to laugh. "Is it really that simple?"

"Yes. Think about it. I know Mom and Dad would be happy to have you stay on. Even if it's just while you're deciding what to do next."

"I'll think about it," Grace said, knowing in her heart that she had already decided. She knew what she wanted to do next. Suddenly the gray fog had lifted from her heart and the future lay bright and exciting before her. She imagined Laura's face when Grace told her she wanted to stay on. And wait until she told Michelle and Jane that she would be here—no salary required—to help get the new program underway! Her mind was already spinning with more ideas, ways to advertise and get the word out about the new venture, other classes they could offer, changes they could make to the website. She impulsively reached over to touch Mason on the arm. "Thank you."

"For what?"

"For the invitation. For saying your folks love me. It means a lot to me."

He shrugged and sobered, leaning forward to rest his elbows on his knees. "I guess everybody needs someone to love them," he said.

"Even you?"

He turned his head and eyed her a moment, then smiled. "Even me. I guess. Maybe. But . . . not quite yet, you know? I'm not ready to move *that* far forward yet. Maybe one day, but not now." He hesitated, then asked, "Are you?"

"Ready? I don't know. When the accident first happened, I thought for sure I'd never love anyone again the way I loved Greg."

"And now?"

Grace looked up at the rafters, where pigeons nestled for the evening. She could hear the soft wispy sounds of their settling, the soft swish of the horses' tails. "Like I said, it's a blank canvas. I don't know what I'll paint on it yet. Maybe someday . . ." She swallowed hard. "Maybe someday," she finished lamely.

"There's the possibility, but you're not looking that far forward yet."

"No. One thing at a time," she agreed.

"I'm the same. For now, I'm just focusing on the next immediate steps that I *can* see. Deciding where to live, what to do."

"When will you tell your folks you're moving to Port Dover?"

"In a day or two. I want to get everything settled first, tell my partners at the firm." He hesitated, then straightened and put his arms around Grace in a comfortable hug. His beard tickled the top of her ear. "Thank you for being a friend to my children. And thank you for helping me see what's important. I won't forget again."

* * *

Martin, standing thunderstruck in the doorway of the barn, backed carefully away. He had come to bed the horses down for the night, but it would wait. He wouldn't interrupt the scene in the barn for the world.

Slowly he walked back to the house, pondering what he had heard. He felt a sense of lightness and relief. Mason was coming home. He would help with the farm when he could, and Laura wouldn't have the full-time care of the kids. And Grace said she'd consider staying. Things were definitely looking up.

Laura was folding clothes on the living room couch, with Chance chewing on a stray sock under the coffee table. She looked up with a fond smile as Martin came in. "All done?"

"Well, no. I'll go back down later to look after the horses."

"What? Why? I thought you went out—"

"I did. I'm back again." Martin tried to keep his face straight. "Mason and Grace were in the barn, and I didn't want to disturb them."

"Mason and—Oh!" Laura's dark eyes widened. "Is everything all right? Do you think he's apologized?"

"Yes, it's all right."

"Did she accept his apology? Could you tell?"

"Oh yes, she did. Not only that—she's willing to consider staying on here for a while longer."

"She is? Did he ask her?" Laura's face lit up. She dropped the shirt she held and came to hug her husband. "I've asked her before, but I don't think she seriously considered it. I'd be glad if we could keep Grace. I like her a lot."

"There's more. Mason is moving his practice to Port Dover."

Laura's mouth dropped open, and she gave a little breathless "*Oh*!" "Did he say that?"

"Yes. He's getting details squared away, and then he's going to tell us, so when he says something, act surprised. He hasn't told his partners yet. But the plan is to keep the kids with him in Port Dover, and you can watch them just after school. It will be a lot easier on you."

"Yippee!" Laura did a little dance, and Martin laughed. "That's such a relief. I'm a terrible woman for saying so, but I did need a break; I truly did. And it would be so much better for the kids to be with their father."

"I figured that would make you happy."

She stilled and looked up at him. "You know what would make me *really* happy, Martin, is if Mason had someone to grow old with. Grace too. It saddens me to see such nice people be alone."

"It's early days for both of them, I think."

"I didn't mean them ending up together."

"No, I know you didn't."

"I mean, it would be great if that happened, don't get me wrong, because then we'd get to have Grace for keeps. But I don't get the sense that things are headed that way."

"No," he said. "But at least I think they're both finally healing a little. We need to just keep loving them both and see what happens." Martin bent and retrieved the soggy sock from Chance, draping it on the back of the couch, away from his reach.

"You know what, Martin Whelan?" Laura said. "I'm glad I have *you* to grow old with."

"And I you," Martin replied, taking her in his arms again.

"Though when I get really decrepit, you have my permission to set me adrift on an ice floe. I won't blame you a bit."

"I'm not letting go of you ever," Martin said. "I think it sounds beautiful growing old with you, Laura. We can have wheelchair races and hide each other's teeth. It will be a riot. Think of the fun we'll have."

Laura grinned up at him. "You know what else, Martin? You don't have to let go of me when we die either."

"What are you talking about?"

"You know how when we married, the vow said 'till death do you part'? Well, families can continue beyond death. It's something I learned at church with Grace. You don't ever have to let go."

"That's a wonderful thought," Martin said.

"Come into the kitchen for some mint tea," Laura said, "and I'll tell you all about it."

That Sunday at church, Grace noticed that when it came time for the opening hymn, her throat didn't feel quite so tight, and while she still didn't sing aloud, she was able to just sit and enjoy the sound of the others singing. Her heart didn't race, and even though she waited for it, the old familiar sorrow didn't swamp her. Intrigued, hopeful, she tried humming along for the final hymn, a little louder than her usual whisper. And it was nice. The sound felt good in her throat.

At home after church, she parked her car and went directly out to the barn in her good dress and shoes, carefully closing the door behind her. She checked every stall and the tack room to make sure no one was around. She felt ridiculous but nervous and eager at the same time.

When she was sure she was alone, she cleared her throat and glanced up at the rafters. A pigeon fluttered above her and then grew still. She thought a brief, heartfelt prayer, and then she hummed her way up the scale and down again. Cautiously she tried it again with her mouth open a little. She wasn't warmed up, her voice cracking on the high *A*, but she tried it again, a little louder now, and this time her voice held true.

Gaining confidence, she stepped up on a bale of hay, hugged herself with her arms, and tipped her head back. After a few more warm-up exercises, she softly began to sing the first song that came to mind. It was a children's song she remembered her mother singing to her and that she had sung to Molly at bedtime. As her voice rose to the rafters, filling the air, she felt the constriction in her chest ease. It felt as if she were breathing deeply for the first time in a long while. She completed the song and began it again, her voice rising fully now, tears of gratitude washing down her cheeks.

Sing your way home
at the close of the day.
Sing your way home;
drive the shadows away.
Smile every mile,
for wherever you roam

It will brighten your road,
It will lighten your load
If you sing your way home.

CHAPTER TWENTY-FOUR

THE CULTURAL HALL AT THE church had been festooned with fat pumpkins and vases of crisp autumn leaves. Strings of little orange and white lights outlined the doorways. Rows of folding chairs had been placed before the raised stage at one end of the gym, and someone had hauled in a piano.

As the members of the congregation greeted each other and found seats, Annie, as chair of the events committee, bustled around making sure everyone was ready for their performances. Sister Macey, the elderly organist, took a seat at the piano and played some prelude music with the usual vibrato, but no one really listened as conversations rose in volume. Grace, standing with Mason, saw Margaret chatting with some other women, and she and Mason went over to say hello.

Margaret turned, and her face lit up when she saw them. "Hi there! I'm glad this was on a weekend so you could come, Mason."

"Yes, well, I'll be around a lot more now, not just on weekends," Mason told her. "And apparently you will be too! I was thrilled when Uncle Toby told me the news this afternoon."

"Yes, keep October 1 free. That's the date we've chosen. I wonder if Annie would be willing to play the pipes for the wedding."

"I'm sure she'd be happy to," Grace said.

"Will you two come sit by me and Toby? He was leery about coming to the church tonight, but he was willing to give it a try, and the roof didn't collapse when he came in, so things are going great so far."

"Mason can sit with you if he likes, thanks, but I have to go warm up," Grace said, laughing.

"Sure. I'll just go get my folks and the kids, Mrs. Hanmer," Mason said, then added with a mischievous grin, "Or I guess I can call you Auntie Margaret now?"

"Just don't call me Antediluvian," Margaret said with a spark in her eye.

As Mason left to find his family, Grace went to find a quiet room to do her vocal exercises in.

But Annie, who had come looking for her, stopped her with a hand on her arm. "Wait. Before you disappear, there's someone I want you to meet. I've been trying all summer to introduce you, and it's never worked out. But I finally have you both in the same place at the same time." Annie turned and caught the attention of a man standing farther down and waved him over. He was very tall, built—to Grace's mind—like a stork. He wore a tweed jacket frayed at the cuffs, a skewed brown tie, and brown corduroy trousers. But he was familiar and beautiful, and she couldn't help exclaiming with delight. It was *him*, the history teacher.

His handsome face registered astonishment and then relaxed into a broad, friendly, and slightly conspiratorial grin. His grip as he shook her hand was firm and warm. "You," he said.

"You," she echoed.

"You already know each other? But that's brilliant!" Annie said, pleased.

"No, not really," Grace tried to explain. "I mean, we've met a few times."

"We've seen each other," the man agreed. "We shared lemonade once."

He remembered. Grace found herself nodding like an idiot. "The blueberries were from me," she said.

"They were? I wondered. Thank you." He still had hold of Grace's hand. "I'm Angus Puddicombe."

"You're the elusive Angus! I'm so glad. I mean, I'm Grace Whittaker."

"Annie and Newton Fisher are old friends of mine."

"Watch the word *old*," Annie interjected.

Grace could hardly think what to say. This was the man Annie had wanted her to meet. It had been Angus all along.

"Grace, Angus has been meeting with the missionaries and has been making noises about coming to hang out with us at church, so I invited him and Kenneth along tonight to meet everyone before Sunday. That way when he comes, he'll already see some familiar faces."

"Oh. Well, welcome! And who is Kenneth?" Grace asked.

Angus released her hand and stepped slightly aside, and for the first time, Grace noticed the little boy peering from behind his slim legs. He looked to be about eight years old, with short, spiky hair and a shy smile. His tie was a miniature version of Angus's, and he had the same jacket and corduroy pants.

"Oh. Hello, Kenneth. Hey, you look like your dad."

Kenneth glanced up at Angus, and they both wrinkled their noses at each other, grinning.

"Actually, Kenneth is my foster son. He's staying with me for a while."

"Angus isn't married," Annie said cheerfully. Pointedly.

"Oh."

"Subtly done," Angus said, nudging Annie with his elbow. He shot another grin at Grace. "No, not married. An aging bachelor."

"Aging is suitable for a teacher of history," Annie said. "And you're aging well, Angus. Like fine cheese."

"Oh, even better. Give the girl a mental image of something smelly molding away in a cave. That's the ticket."

Grace couldn't help laughing. "Well, it's nice to finally and formally meet both you and Kenneth," she said.

"Kenneth was also kidnapped with Angus last year," Annie said brightly. "That's how they met, and it led to Kenneth coming to live with Angus."

Angus glanced at Annie. "Have you told the poor thing my whole life history?"

"Just the interesting bits."

"I can't wait to hear the rest of the story," Grace told him.

"Certainly. I'm happy to fill in any details Annie left out." He laughed.

"Another time though," Annie said. "The show's starting in a few minutes. I've got to go find Newton. He and some of the kids are playing the pipes tonight."

"Just some of them?" Angus asked.

"We didn't want to have all of us play, or we'd shatter the windows. They're probably warming up out in the parking lot. If you'll excuse me . . ."

She slipped away, and Grace smiled at Angus. "I need to warm up too. I'm singing tonight."

"I look forward to it."

"Don't get your hopes up too high. It's been awhile since I've sung in public," Grace admitted.

"I'm sure you'll be fine." Angus reached to shake her hand again, holding it for just a moment with his palm warm against hers. "I'll see you after the program . . . ?"

"Sure." Grace paused, thinking again what a nice smile this man had. "I'd like that," she heard herself say. And realized she meant it.

"In fact, if it isn't too bold, can I ask if I can take you home with me afterward?"

Kenneth glanced up at him, eyebrows lifted. Angus turned pink.

"I mean to Annie and Newton's house," he added hastily. He ran his hand through his shaggy brown hair, mussing it. "That didn't come out right, did it? What I meant was, the Fishers are inviting people to their house after the show for apple pie and ice cream. If you'd like to come, I could take you, I mean." He fumbled to a stop, and Grace couldn't help laughing. She touched him lightly on the arm. It was as if they both had to keep reaching out to touch the other, to assure themselves the other was real.

"I'd love to come, thank you."

He nodded vigorously. "Super. I'll see you after the program, then. Come on, Kenneth, we've detained the lady long enough. Let's find seats."

Grace turned once again to go find a room to warm up in, but Margaret was at her elbow, smiling gently.

"Any friend of the Fishers is bound to be a nice person," she said reassuringly.

"Er . . . yes."

"I didn't want to say it in front of anyone else, but I'm so glad you're going to be singing for us tonight," Margaret said. "I know what it means. Don't think I don't."

Grace gave Margaret a one-armed squeeze around the shoulders and hurried out. She still wasn't entirely sure her voice was going to cooperate this evening. She wasn't sure she was ready for this step. But it was here, ready or not, and she wouldn't let Margaret and the others down. Over the past couple of weeks she had practiced several more times in the barn, and she knew her soprano was as good as ever. But it had been two years since she'd sung in front of people, and she was annoyed with the jittery feeling in her hands and stomach. She never used to suffer from stage fright. She felt like one of her own beginning students.

When all was ready and everyone was quiet, the Primary children opened the program by singing "It's Autumn Time," followed by a poem by the bishop and then a short recitation by an elderly man named Alfred Green. A teenage girl named Penny did a short lyrical dance meant to represent autumn leaves twirling in a breeze, though Martin leaned over and whispered to Grace that it looked more like egg beaters in a bowl. There were a few other items on the program, including a juggling act, a stand-up comedy routine, and a piano duet (Joplin) an elderly couple dressed in 1920s garb performed. Assorted Fishers marched into the gym wearing kilts and playing the pipes, with Caleb on the snare drum, which got everyone stirred up and sent a few of the older folks scrambling to turn off their hearing aids. They marched out again after a mercifully short piece. Then Sister Macey gave a trill on the piano as a signal, and the clapping audience fell into hushed expectation. Grace took a deep breath and stepped onto the stage. She was the last number on the program.

She wore the simple yellow dress she often wore to church, and her hair was pulled into a ponytail. She had thought of dressing up more, concocting a more impressive appearance, but instinctively she'd known it was best to feel comfortable and stick to the familiar. She was being anachronistic tonight and singing a Christmas song. When she had finally agreed to sing for the program, the song had been Margaret's instant request.

Sister Macey played the opening bars of "O Holy Night," and Grace looked up at the folded basketball standard above the audience, unconsciously curled her hands into fists, and began to sing.

At first it went fine. Her voice was strong, sailing up to the high ceiling, pure and clear on every note. It felt wonderful to raise her voice again and not just in the barn with its sound-dampening wood and hay. She knew it was going well when she saw tears on Laura's face and a beatific smile on Margaret's. A few rows behind them, Angus Puddicombe was watching, enrapt, his mouth slightly open, and Grace felt a funny little shiver go through her. It wasn't an unpleasant feeling, but it was unexpected.

But when she got to the line "Fall on your knees," something went wrong. Grace was horrified to feel her throat suddenly tighten and tears start down her own cheeks. Crying from relief and joy by herself in the barn was one thing, but to do it onstage in front of everyone? The air went out of her lungs in a whoosh. Her voice broke, and she abruptly cut off the sound. In all her years of performing, this had never happened to her before. Her heart began to pound heavily, and she gripped her shaking hands together tightly.

In humiliation, she looked at the pianist. Sister Macey was blinking back tears too. But bless her heart, she just kept repeating the same line over and over in the music, like a plane in a holding pattern, waiting. She nodded at Grace encouragingly. So Grace swallowed and began again to sing where she'd left off, and this time her voice didn't betray her. It returned full and confident, soaring on the high notes, rising over the audience, and she was able to finish.

Embarrassed, she turned to leave the stage, but she was astonished to hear the room behind her erupt in applause. And there were the Whelans and Matt waiting for her just offstage, Matt clapping enthusiastically and smiling. Behind him stood his father, who had come down for the past two days and who would be driving Matt to his new dorm room in Guelph later that night. School started Monday, but Matt had lingered to the last possible moment so he could come to the show. Grace gave him a tight hug, and he returned it, laughing.

The children danced up and down in excitement as they clung to Mason's arms, and Mason, unable to shake hands, gave Grace a nod of approval. Then Laura's arms opened, and Grace went into them gratefully. Others were flocking around her, hugging her, touching her shoulder, filling her with approval and acceptance. She saw Margaret at the fringe of the group, beaming at her, and Grace felt the tears start again. Margaret and Toby pushed through the crowd to reach her side.

"That was beautiful, my dear," Toby said, his work-roughened hand patting Grace's cheek lightly. "Exquisite."

"Angelic," Margaret pronounced. "Just like before."

"Just the word I would have used," Angus murmured, appearing beside her. His face shone as he gazed at Grace.

"Show's over," Annie announced, though the crowd had fallen into chaos and no one really heard her or cared. Everyone was talking and laughing, and the smaller children were starting to run up and down the aisles. Annie looked around the room and nodded with satisfaction. "A success," she pronounced. "Pie and ice cream at my house."

Angus held out his hand to extricate Grace from the crowd. "Ready?" he asked.

Grace looked up into the eyes of this man whose name she had only just learned and felt the warmth of his lopsided grin, his hand around hers, and she knew that funny little shiver she had felt was joy, pure and simple. She was filled with a peace and anticipation she hadn't known for a long time, the feeling of coming home.

"Ready," she said.

EMBER
BY RASHMI PLUSCEC

the landscape of her mind lay barren—bruised
by a steady downpour of acid rain. a past that
was. a future that could have been: in memoriam

the tears had fallen, groping for the lights that had
been brutally snuffed out, leaving behind a void.
not blackness. not emptiness. just a nothingness . . .

Into that void, the flood of bitter questions had
finally settled, the tide of helplessness had now
receded. tired of running down her cheeks, down

memory lane, the teardrops paused to consider a
new identity. softened by the dreams, strengthened
by the hope, sparkling dewdrops shone through the

tragedy. In that twilight zone between 'was' and 'is,'
at the crossroads of existing and living, she took her
first steps. Perhaps homage would be paid to the lost

pieces of her heart yet . . . perhaps some day
the phoenix would rise from the ashes again.

ABOUT THE AUTHOR

KRISTEN GARNER MCKENDRY BEGAN WRITING in her teens, and her work has been published in both Canada and the United States. She received a Mississauga Arts Council MARTY Award in established literary arts in 2012, and her book *Garden Plot* was nominated for a Whitney Award for excellence in LDS literature in 2011.

Kristen received a bachelor's degree in linguistics from Brigham Young University and has always been a voracious reader. She has a strong interest in urban agriculture and environmental issues. She enjoys playing the bagpipes, learning obscure languages, growing wheat in the backyard, and making cheese. Her latest adventure was joining the local handweavers and spinners guild.

A native of Utah and mother of three, she now resides with her family in Canada.

You can read more about Angus Puddicombe's double kidnapping in *Desperate Measures*. For more information on Kristen and her books, check out her website at www.kristenmckendry.webs.com, where you will also find a link to her blog, "My Daily Slog Blog."